C000177222

Sleeper Cell

A Secret War on the
Streets of London

Alan Porter

Eyelevel Books

First published 2015
by Eyelevel Books, Worcester, England

© Alan Porter/Eyelevel Books 2015

ISBN 978 1902528 793

First edition
r-b

Sleeper Cell is a work of fiction. Any resemblance between characters in
the book and real people is unintentional. Real organisations, events and
locations mentioned in the text have been fictionalised to protect individuals
and operations conducted by them. Where events are depicted as
occurring in real locations, those events are entirely fictional.

also available as an ebook

Typeset and Designed by Eyelevel Books
Cover image: Aleksander Mijatovic

For more about Alan Porter and a list of other works, visit
www.alancporter.com

For AM
1934-2014

Day One

1

Ruth Morgan was less than two hundred yards from the hotel when the bomb exploded.

The hot June morning was shattered by huge, sharp boom, followed a beat later by the deafening roar of falling rubble and the tinkle of breaking glass. Ruth saw only the leading edge of the fireball before she was hunched on the ground, hands over her head. The sound echoed off surrounding buildings and rippled the leaves on the trees in the park.

She looked up. Through the ringing in her ears she heard the screech of tyres out on Kensington High Street, the flap of hundreds of birds' wings and a sound like heavy rain as rubble cascaded from the sky. All around her people stood or crouched, stunned, silent.

Only Gavin was moving.

Her bodyguard was running across the park towards her. He always followed at a discrete distance, but this morning he had been slow stabling his horse and she had not waited. She had set off for Kensington Palace, along the back of the Serpentine, to pass the rear of the Park Hotel on her way to meet the royal couple at twelve.

She had been lucky. If she had taken the front way, past the hotel's main reception, she would have been killed.

She stood up. The bright sunlight was already becoming milky, the shadows losing their hard edges as the dust cloud spread out. She tried to run. Her legs felt weak, her movements stiff and disjointed.

She could have been killed. One different decision and she'd be dead.

Maybe that had been the idea. They'd targetted her father five years ago; maybe now they were coming after her.

Gavin caught up with her. He dropped his phone into his pocket and took her arm. He led her to the shelter of a tree, all the time scanning the park and the road beyond, checking, watchful.

'Are you alright?' he said. His voice was distant, muted by the ringing in her ears and the constant hiss of falling debris.

'I'm fine.' She cleared her throat. 'You need to get to the hotel. They'll need someone who knows what they're doing. Shit, Gavin, was that…?'

'It was a bomb. I need to get you somewhere safe.'

'I'm going to the Palace! How much safer do you want?'

'We don't know the Palace wasn't the main target. I've seen this before, remember? The first one's a distraction. Foot soldiers make the most of the chaos that follows.'

'Then stop making me a sitting duck out here!' She looked him in the face. The man who bore a three-inch scar across his face where an Iraqi bullet had come within a whisker of blowing his head off… she'd never seen him so edgy before.

'Let me go,' she said. 'The longer you keep me out in the open, the worse it gets for both of us. And *them*.' She nodded towards the hotel. A couple staggered around the corner: a man holding a woman upright, both of them grey with dust and glistening with blood. The man waved an arm in their direction and Gavin held his hand up.

'OK, go,' he said. 'I'll call Palace security, tell them you're on your way. Check in with Downing Street as soon as you're safe.'

'Of course. I'll speak to you later.'

Someone screamed inside the hotel, a long, animal howl. Others were shouting now, calling for help. A police motorcyclist weaved through the stopped traffic and leaned his bike on the stand. He ran into the dust cloud. All around people were on the move. Some ran towards the building, cameras in hand; most ran away through the ragged lines of cars. People were coming from the building too now, grey and dazed, some nursing horrific injuries. There were sirens in the distance.

Ruth stood for a moment as Gavin followed the lone police officer into the chaos, then forced her legs to move. There was a rumble as another part of the hotel collapsed. More screams. Car alarms in the underground car park. Someone behind her shouted. She turned and saw the car approaching, fast, along Broad Walk.

It passed her and swung hard left to block her path. The passenger door burst open.

'Miss Morgan. Come with us.'

The Specialist Protection Branch officer flashed his ID at

her and opened the rear door of the Jaguar. The clip on his gun holster was open, as if he was expecting trouble.

'I'm going to the Palace,' she said.

'No, you're coming with us. Prime Minister's orders. We need to get you out of here. Now.'

She looked towards the Palace gates where security officers were beginning to swarm, MP5 carbines across their chests. There was another loud explosion from the hotel: a car's fuel tank maybe.

Or a second bomb.

'Please,' he said.

'OK, OK.'

Gavin Byers worked for her – he did what he was told. Specialist Protection worked for the government, and she was as much a subject of their authority as anyone else, whoever her father might be. She opened the rear door and slipped in. The SO1 man rounded the back of the vehicle and got in beside her.

They sped off north and turned right onto Bayswater Road, into a stream of emergency vehicles heading towards the hotel.

2

'Raha,' the nurse said from the doorway, 'you've got a visitor.'

She glanced at him. 'Who is it?'

'No idea. Governor phoned through to say a man's on his way to see you. Come on.'

'Here? Not in the interview suite?'

'Why, you thinking of making a run for it?' He smiled. 'We'll get you a room in the treatment annex. You don't want to go where they have to screw the furniture down.'

Golzar wiped her hands on the towel draped across her knees and stood up. Her cell, like all the cells on F Wing, had its own tiny wash room and she went through and ran a glass of water. Her midday pills were still in the little paper cup that the orderly had brought half an hour earlier and she quickly swallowed them. Her face in the steel mirror was shiny with fluocinonide cream and a pulse beat in her neck.

'Miss Golzar?' the nurse said.

She stepped out of the cell. 'One man?' she said.

'Why don't we go and find out?' He motioned for a guard.

'Don't cuff me,' Golzar said. The nurse gave her a sympathetic look. 'Please.'

'It's standard procedure,' the nurse said. 'Got to be done. Put your hands out in front of you.'

She did and the rigid handcuffs were snapped around her wrists. Her only means of defence was lost. If someone had been sent to kill her, this time they were going to succeed. The nurse consulted his clipboard.

'The activities room's empty,' he said. 'I'll send your visitor down when he arrives.'

The guard took her by the elbow and walked her towards the treatment annex.

Raha Golzar had been in Low Newton Prison for fifteen months now, a paranoid schizophrenic with an IQ of 180 but living in a world of unstable and dangerous fantasy. At least, that was what her file said. There had been no arrest, no trial, no legal process. They had lured her into a trap. Someone had decided she was a liability and they needed her off the streets. Even in liberal Britain, they had ways of making their enemies disappear. For a while at least.

Between pointless meetings with her psychiatrist she participated in their structured activities, learned to cook, meditated or played chess. She even sang 'Yellow Submarine' once. But all she really did was wait. She rarely spoke to any of the other women on the wing, and only to the guards and nurses when it was in her interest to do so. They'd tricked her once; they wouldn't do it again.

The guard unlocked the door to the activities room and led her in.

She sat in one of the dark green Chesterfield sofas and flexed her wrists in the cuffs. Sun streamed in through the window and the room was uncomfortably hot. She hated the English summer. Her immune system was shot from years of abuse and she found the damp, humid climate unbearable.

Her visitor was brought into the pale green room five minutes later. Tall, athletic and wearing an immaculate wool suit even on this hottest of days, he had the bearing of a high-ranking official.

'Raha Golzar?' he said.

She nodded.

'My name is Donald Aquila,' he said. 'I've been retained as your legal counsel.' He took a file of notes from his case and opened it on the table between them.

'Could you leave us?' he said to the guard.

'Patients are not allowed to be out of sight,' the guard said.

'Then stand outside and watch through the door. This is a legal representation.'

The guard shrugged and stepped out. He left the door an inch or so ajar and leaned against the wall, watching through the narrow window.

'Legal counsel?' Golzar said. 'Who are you really? MI5? 6? Mossad?'

'I'm your lawyer,' Aquila said.

'And why would I need a lawyer?'

'You're being moved to Holloway. Your trial will start on Monday.'

'Trial? On what charge?'

'Section 5 Terrorism. I can't be any more specific than that right now.' He smiled. 'Blame the new Security Act.'

'Do you know who I am?' Golzar said.

'Of course I do. My employers just need to make sure we're all on the same page with this.' He looked down at the papers on the table.

'Let's begin,' he said. 'You are an Iranian national, seconded to the Occupied Palestinian Territory as a nurse. You were arrested in West Jerusalem in a case of mistaken identity…'

Golzar looked at the guard. He was staring at the floor now, satisfied that this meeting was not about to turn ugly. He would be unable to hear much of their conversation amongst the low-level chatter on the wing and the noise from the Programme's kitchen next door. Music drifted along the corridor from the room at the end where five inmates were making leaden progress through the Beatles' 'Yesterday'.

'Miss Golzar?' Aquila said.

'Arrested?' Golzar said quietly. 'I was shot when I got off the bus at Tsvi Krokh Square. If I'm going on trial I will defend myself.'

'Is that a threat?'

'Make of it what you want. If you know who I am, you know what I've done. If I go down, I take a lot of people with me.'

Donald Aquila closed her file and leaned forwards, his elbows on his knees.

'You know how this has to go,' he said. 'By your own admission, you're a danger to them. For fifteen months you've been safely out of sight. All the people who mattered thought you were dead.'

Golzar gave him a non-committal shrug.

'If they've already trumped up charges against me,' she said, 'it won't make any difference what I say.'

'No it won't, which is why it's my job to make sure this never gets to trial. Anything you might have told your doctors here was either coerced or said in confusion as a result of your arrest. They won't believe you of course, but it'll smooth the first stages of the process.'

'You know about my first interview?'

'Enough.'

'Do you know who was behind it?'

'British Secret Intelligence. That's why they were so convincing. It was never a debrief. It was a trap to make sure you could be detained here with no awkward questions. Penhalligan swallowed the lot and fortunately you've been smart enough never to retract it. It was the one thing that, ironically, kept you safe.'

Golzar studied him for several seconds. She leaned back. 'And who do you work for, Mr Aquila?' she said.

'You.'

'But who sent you? I've seen enough Legal Aid lawyers in here to know you're not doing pro bono. Someone's paying you and by the look of you, you charge well.'

'The few people on the outside who knew you were still alive needed you contained. Now they want to change your containment. It's my job to minimise the damage. Believe me, there are people on the outside working in your best interests.'

'As long as I stick to the script.'

'For now, yes.' Aquila looked at her for a moment. 'We've got a very narrow window of opportunity. British officials have spoken to Penhalligan and he's happy that you meet the criteria for transfer. He just needs to tick some boxes, fill some forms, and you'll be on your way.'

'And if I don't want to be on my way? What assurance have I got that you can keep me alive once I'm out?'

'None. The problem is, you've got very little choice. You've seen what they can do. Even if you stay here, do you really think they can't get to you? Miss Golzar, things are going to move. The process has already started. They will play this out however you choose: trust me and you might survive it; try to do it alone, and you have very little chance.' He stood up. 'Are we agreed?'

'I tell them what they want to hear, you minimise the damage. It doesn't sound like much of a deal to me.'

'It's the best you're going to get. Do what you've got to do. I'll see you in Holloway.'

He picked up his file and left. The meeting had lasted barely four minutes.

Golzar was taken back to F wing and uncuffed. She sat at a table in the central association area and massaged the burning itchy rings left on her wrists by the cuffs.

This was only the second time in fifteen months that she had spoken to anyone from the outside. British Intelligence had always known who she was and where she was being held, yet they had sat on her for all this time.

So what had changed? Why did they want her back in play now?

Jean Gerber shuffled over and took a seat across the table. Without a word she laid out the chess pieces and moved queen's pawn forward two spaces. Gerber was the only person Golzar had allowed anywhere near her during these months of incarceration, and that was largely because this skinny waif of a woman had never uttered a single word to her. Their regular chess games started spontaneously and ended as soon as one of them was defeated. Always the same, win or lose, Gerber would gather up the pieces and shuffle away again. Golzar liked that – the result was irrelevant; only the process mattered.

Golzar sat for several seconds with her finger on her king's pawn.

This was what she had been waiting for. But were they offering her a new beginning, or a final end? Would they really dare to put her on trial with all she could expose in the process?

She moved the pawn out. Gerber replied with queen's bishop. Same aggressive opening as always.

Over the years, Raha Golzar had killed somewhere approaching six hundred people... that she knew of. Even by the standards of the inmates on the Primrose Programme that was an extraordinary total. But unlike most of her eleven fellow pilgrims on the road to redemption, she was not a monster. She could count on the fingers of one hand the people she had killed close up. The rest had just been her job, experiments in the laboratories in Russia and Kazakhstan, and always willing victims. Prisoners in Russian jails often found the idea of a quick death and a few roubles for their families preferable to the hell of the ex-Soviet prison system. Golzar certainly did not consider herself insane.

Jean Gerber had killed only twice, but her methods amused Golzar and drew her to this odd, silent inmate. F Wing's grapevine had it that eleven months earlier she had murdered her ex-husband and his new wife with a nail gun. She had then nailed her own feet to the floor and laughed while the police tried to arrest her.

Golzar liked that too: such creativity.

3

Twelve minutes after the bomb had brought chaos to the western end of Hyde Park, Prime Minister's Questions had been suspended in the House of Commons.

Richard Morgan was driven back to Downing Street for the emergency COBR meeting in the Cabinet Room. By the time he arrived, forty-five minutes had elapsed since the bombing and cars were bringing the major players into the heart of government. Morgan's own vehicle was followed by another carrying Sarah Forsythe, his Deputy Prime Minister, and Emma Whitehouse, the newly-installed Home Secretary.

Richard put his head around the usually-locked door of the diplomatic knights' rooms by the front door. Lord Silverton, Parliamentary Under Secretary for Security and Counter-Terrorism, was in hushed conversation with the former ambassador to Israel. Richard left without interrupting and walked along the corridor to the rear of the building.

He paused. He had five minutes. Time to make a call, put his mind at rest.

He ran up the main stairs, past the stern portraits of his predecessors, and into the private flat at the top of the building. Mary, his wife of twenty-seven years, was in Brussels for a conference and the flat was exactly as he had left it. He dialled the cordless phone as he walked to the bedroom for a change of jacket. It rang until the voicemail message took over. He disconnected the call and dialled again. Gavin answered his phone after three rings.

'Gavin, it's Richard. I'm trying to get in touch with Ruth. Could you pass the phone to her?'

'I'm sorry sir, she's not with me. I'm at the bomb site.'

'Then where is she?'

'I left her at the palace.'

'How long ago?'

'About two minutes after the bomb.'

'She's all right?'

'She's fine. Good ride this morning, nothing out of the ordinary. No one paying any undue attention. She was a long way from the bomb when it went off.'

'You're certain she's safe now?'

'She's in probably the safest place outside of where you are right now. The royal couple were expecting her, so she's under their protection now.'

'Good. Thank you. Tell her to call me when you see her. Her phone's off.'

'Probably Palace security being over-cautious. I'll let her know.'

Richard dropped his jacket onto the bed and, without replacing it, jogged back down to the Cabinet Room on the ground floor. He had used this light and airy room at the back of the building as the COBR committee room throughout his term as PM. He hated the stuffy underground chamber that the media loved to call COBRA, a place and a name that embodied far too much menace for Richard's liking.

Already at the table were Sarah Forsythe, Lord Silverton and Emma Whitehouse. The Foreign Secretary, Oliver Grant, was in Washington and was being briefed separately on any implications for the Foreign Office. As Richard took his place at the table the door opened again and an aide ushered in the head of the Metropolitan Police's Counter-Terrorism Command. James Thorne was the only person in the room in uniform, and it struck Richard that during his two years as PM, he was the only one who ever had been. It had, to date, been a very peaceful tenure.

Two large computer monitors stood at the end of the table, onto which were patched feeds from John Nash at the government's listening facility GCHQ, and David Bates, Chief of the Secret Intelligence Service.

'So what do we know?' Richard said. 'Let's start at the beginning so we're all on the same page.'

All eyes turned to the man in black uniform at the end of the table. Thorne glanced at his file then began.

'At twelve noon an explosion destroyed part of the Park Hotel on Kensington Road and caused some superficial damage to the Embassy of Israel in Palace Green. We are awaiting reports from the Ambassador. Significant damage was also caused to shops and residential flats opposite the hotel. Search and Rescue are going through the area and the buildings will be made safe and screened so Kensington High Street to the west and Kensington Road to the east can be reopened by the end of the day. A number seventy bus, eastbound, has been destroyed along with six private vehicles in the vicinity at the time. Again, these have been evacuated and screened and will be removed as soon as we can get heavy equipment into the area. Kensington Palace is undamaged.'

'Do we have and reason to believe this was accidental?' Richard said.

'It's too early to say, but the explosion being in the hotel's car park strongly suggests a bomb. We've cordoned off the area and have bomb squad technicians on the way.'

'Casualty figures?' Richard said.

'Unknown within the building,' Thorne said. 'Eight are confirmed dead on the main road, with multiple injuries. We are liaising with the Embassy as we speak, but they are unlikely to be very forthcoming. Unless you can pull some strings, PM?' Richard did not have chance to reply before Sir Malcolm Stevens, MI5's Director General, arrived.

'Sorry,' he said. 'Traffic's a nightmare. Where are we?'

'CTC are filling us in on casualty figures,' Lord Silverton said. 'So far, not as bad as it might have been.' Richard caught the hint of a smile in his voice. He'd tried to rid his government of the old networks of Eton and Sandhurst, but there was little he could do about the outside agencies.

'Mortality within the parking garage and the west side of the hotel could push the figures far higher,' Thorne said. 'It'll be several hours before Search and Rescue get through it. There may be more survivors trapped. Hospitals are on a major incident footing and blood is being helicoptered in from surrounding facilities.'

'Assuming this is a bomb, do we have any idea who was behind it?' Richard said.

Those assembled in the meeting room turned to the screen where David Bates was talking to one of his staff over at SIS HQ at Vauxhall Cross. He turned to face the camera.

'No one has claimed responsibility yet,' he said, 'but that would not be unusual at such an early stage. We should have credible attribution soon. All live agents in the field have been updated. We've got moles in a number of the major players.'

'Was this designed to derail the peace talks?' Richard said.

'We can't rule it out, but right now it's perhaps not the most likely scenario. Any of the groups with the motive to sabotage the talks would likely lack the means. Hassan Nasrallah has his devotees, and Hezbollah make plenty of noise on the internet, especially when it comes to Israel. But there's no significant support in Britain. Same for the al-Aqsa Martyrs' Brigade. They've been more active in Israel since the leaking of the peace talks and they've got support from extremist wings of both Fatah and Hamas, but no credible overseas operatives. Likewise Islamic Jihad: no activity outside the area and no meaningful links to anyone in the UK. To get anywhere near a group the politics and contacts to do what we saw this morning, we'd have to go right the way out to Palestinian fedayeen...'

'Who had links with the IRA...'

'And that's one hell of a stretch. The IRA splinters are so well infiltrated that it seems impossible that we wouldn't have known about a plan like this.'

'Which I fear may leave us with the Armageddon scenario,'

Commander Thorne said.

'Which is?'

'ISIS have sleeper cells in Europe,' Bates said. 'It's a natural progression from near-enemy insurgency to far-enemy terrorist organisation. We've expected it for months, and with Britain's recent support for air strikes on northern Iraq, that looks like the most probable source for today's events.'

'Do we have any evidence?' Richard said. 'The last thing we want to do is give credit to ISIS unless we're certain. The boost it would give to home-grown sympathisers could be disastrous.'

'I agree,' Bates said. 'However, only two groups exist that are capable of an attack like this: completely undetected, right in the heart of the city, with what appears to be a sophisticated bomb.'

'ISIS and al-Qa'ida.'

'Yes. We can rule AQ out – the proximity to the Embassy just doesn't fit their ideology right now. But it could fit Islamic State. Any allegiance that existed between Israel and ISIS back in 2013 is long dead, and the Embassy would be a good symbolic target if they are stepping up operations.'

John Nash, over at GCHQ in Cheltenham, cleared his throat and leaned slightly towards the camera.

'We have been monitoring a new organisation,' he said. 'We gave them no real credibility as they seemed to have come out of nowhere, but in light of today's attack we are revisiting what we know of them.'

'And they are?'

'Harakat al Sahm – The Movement of The Arrow. They

first appeared on the social media feeds of third-tier ISIS fighters three months ago. They appeared to be nothing more than a sub-sect who shared ISIS ideology. Their Twitter and Facebook accounts attracted a few curious sympathisers, but posts were infrequent, non-specific and clearly not written by anyone on the front line. It was as if they were just populating extremist feeds with links that went nowhere.'

'And that's changed recently?' Richard said.

'Chatter has increased in the last twenty-four hours. Again, non-specific. There were symbolic indications of a significant event coming, but nothing – I have to stress that, *nothing* – that indicated what it might be or that it was aimed at Britain. The reference to 'the arrow' would also seem apt. They're striking out of established IS territory.'

Richard sat staring out of the window for a moment, his fingers tapping on the desk.

'OK,' he said. 'So IS have got the means to do this and the motive to hit London, but we can't categorically say that their target was the peace talks.'

'Not categorically,' Commander Thorne said.

'Then that's our line: we distance this from the talks. We can not afford to make any link between the two. I think we agree that this has all the hallmarks of a militant Islamist operation but we need a credible attribution. The media are not going to be interested in the subtleties. Call in the best people you have, stop at nothing to get a name. Get a clear motive. We must be in a position to close this down, for it to be a past tense event before the delegates arrive. Something reassuring in time for the morning papers would be good.'

'We're going to need to make an announcement to the media much sooner than that,' Sarah Forsyth said. 'What do we tell them?'

'I'll make a broadcast later in the day. Fix something for the six o'clock news. For now, we appear to be in full control of the situation and our joint forces dedicated to upholding the rule of law and democracy. I think it's important that for now we don't raise the threat level from Severe to Critical either. That risks setting off panic. This must not turn into an excuse for sectarian anarchy.'

'Prime Minister,' Lord Silverton said. 'With respect, I think that is a mistake. You need to address the country now. An information vacuum will attract hysteria if it is not confidently filled.'

'Sarah,' Richard said, 'get an interim statement drawn up, and circulate it to the news agencies. Frame it as an unexplained explosion; don't use the word bomb. And make sure the press office toe the line: this is an isolated incident. I will make a statement, but not until we've shored up our defences and got on top of this thing.'

Lord Silverton removed his glasses and placed them on the desk in front of him. 'And if there's another attack?' he said.

'I am relying on you all to make sure there isn't. Find the culprits. Now, if you will excuse me, I must speak to the Israeli Ambassador. God knows what capital they'll get out of this.'

4

Leila Reid's landline rang at 1.25pm, almost an hour and a half after the bombing. She listened to it cut off mid-way through the third ring and the answering machine click in. Her voice on the recorder was followed by a man's, but she could not hear what he said. It would be nothing she wanted to hear.

She kicked the light summer duvet off and lay staring at the ceiling. The bedroom was filled with muted sunlight and stale moveless air. A vague sensation in her stomach told her it was breakfast time.

The mobile on her bedside cabinet rang, a perfect mimic of an old-fashioned dial phone. Awake now, she reached out and peered at the screen. No name and not a mobile number she recognised. She pressed Answer. She could do with telling someone to go fuck themselves.

'DS Reid? Hello?'

'Hello? Who's this?'

'It's DCI Lawrence.'

'Good morning,' she said.

'Afternoon, and it's not a good one. Where are you?'

'In bed.'

'Well get up; we need you here.'

'At CTC? Didn't you fire me six months ago?'

'You weren't fired, Reid. You're on suspension.'

'We both know it's coming. You just haven't found a legal way to do it yet.'

'Think of it as you wish. Anyway, we're suspending your suspension. We've got a situation.'

'What's happened?'

'You haven't heard? Where have you been?'

'Asleep.'

'There's been an explosion near the Israeli Embassy.'

'Shit.' Leila sat up. 'And Counter-Terrorism's on it?'

'We're convening in anticipation. Commander Thorne's at Downing Street now. We're putting together the Executive Liaison Group.'

'I'm not cleared for ELG work.'

'No, but you are still cleared for investigations on the ground, and you're still the best this department's got.'

'Thorne'll never go for that.'

'He's already signed off on it. It's not an open door back to your old job, but it's a chance to show you're still an asset.'

'An asset.'

'Leila, we need you here. What did Moore say on 911? 'A good day to bury bad news'? Well this could be your good day to bury a bad reputation.'

'No, Michael. I'm sorry, but I'm just not playing politics any more. Not again. Goodbye.'

Before her old boss could reply she disconnected the call

and threw the phone back onto the cabinet. She planted her feet on the cool wooden floor and sat for a moment staring at the points of bright sunlight forcing their way through the curtains.

The phone rang again.

It would ring eight times before going to voice mail.

She stood and drew back one of the curtains. Hard, merciless sunlight streamed in through the dusty windows and formed a hot pool at her feet. In another half hour it would have moved far enough to start baking the front rooms of her small but adequate Victorian terrace in Upper Tooting. By nightfall the whole house would be an oven. She stepped back out of the sun, still unwilling to answer the phone.

The fifth ring. He was persistent.

Should she answer? Should she go back? Was there anything they could offer her to make things right again? She had already decided weeks ago that she would let her suspension run its course then resign, assuming they hadn't found a way to fire her in the meantime. It had crossed her mind that she could return for a while, knowing that she would be sidelined from any major investigations, then sue for constructive dismissal. But she had grown dull these last few weeks.

Six.

She wanted to move on, maybe go back to the Middle East. She needed an edge, grit in her shoe, something to make her *feel* again.

Seven. She picked the phone up, her thumb hovering over the screen.

Eight.

She hit Answer.

'Tell me one thing,' she said as soon as the phone connected. 'Why did you tell me Thorne's approved my coming in when he hasn't?'

Micheal Lawrence breathed heavily at the other end.

'I'm going to hang up now,' Reid said.

'OK, wait… He said he wants to assemble the best team we've got. He didn't mention you, and nor did I. I figured once you've proved your worth to the investigation, he's more likely to get you back here full time.'

'Don't lie to me again.'

'Again? That sounds hopeful.'

'If you don't lie to me again.'

'How did you know?'

'How did I know that the guy who hung me out to dry in an IPCC inquiry wouldn't want me back on the team? What do you think? Plus, you're calling from your own person cell, not the desk phone. My caller ID didn't recognise your number. It's a big clue you're not dealing straight.'

'Fine. You want the truth? I need you back here. Or rather, I need you out there, feeding back useful intel without getting bogged down in false trails. You understand this business better than anyone.'

'So what do you want me to do? Assuming I agree.'

'Just go to the site. Get a feel for it. You'll know within five minutes whether this fits with you. If it does, call me. If not, you can go back to bed.'

'I'll take a look. You'll have my answer within the hour.

And call whatever monkeys you've got manning the perimeter at the Embassy. Tell them I'm on my way.'

'Already done. I'll speak to you in an hour.'

This time Lawrence hung up first.

She ran down to the kitchen and threw a couple of slices of bread into the toaster. She dressed from whatever she could find in the basket of clothes waiting to be ironed and splashed cold water over her face. She resisted the usual urge to turn on the radio, preferring not to have her first impressions of the morning's event filtered by the news media. She had to get this fresh. An explosion (that was the word Lawrence used – not *bomb* but *explosion* – so it might yet prove to be nothing) near both the Israelis and the Palace would have the media in a frenzy of speculation. They had rolling news to fill, and they would fill it with whatever they could come up with on the spur of the moment. None of which helped her. Intuition was fragile in the face of innuendo.

With a slice of dry toast in her mouth, she quickly assembled the tool roll that she always carried in the field: a leather pouch containing lock picks, multi-bladed knife, highly illegal mini cell jammer, Oasis monocular, a tube of Super Glue (useful for closing deep cuts), two pairs of forensic gloves, £200 in £20 notes and a tiny can of mace, just in case. The gun cleaning kit was still in the car, not that it was much use without a gun.

She didn't bother to dead-lock the door behind her. Ten to one she'd be back by three o'clock.

5

Phillip Shaw had no interest in the video link that appeared on the right-most of his three screens, set exactly thirty degrees apart on a desk devoid of anything not directly connected to his home-made computer. He glanced at the link, scanned some of the chat, then went back to what he was doing.

A few seconds later an alert on the left screen caught his eye. His mother had specifically tasked him to watch his sister, and this screen was his window into her life. He'd cloned every device she owned and had a running log of her activity. At fourteen, she was never far from her phone or tablet.

He opened the mirror of her iPad and watched Esther click on the link to the video. A sub-screen logged her browser routing through a series of servers before the video itself opened.

It was a single-camera movie of a hotel, probably in London, though Phillip was not familiar with much of the city. For five seconds nothing happened, then a ball of flame and dust erupted from an opening at the foot of a squat tower. The camera shook in the blast, then settled again as the dust cloud advanced rapidly towards it and the building began to topple forwards. The image grew darker, obscured entirely, paused for a moment, then cut to a view of the collapsed building across the road.

Esther replayed the video, but Phillip had seen enough. He ran a trace to see who had sent her the link (it turned out to be her best friend and neighbour JoLynn, who was more than likely sitting right next to Esther at the time).

His sister was safe, no need for concern.

He turned to the right-hand screen and maximised the top-most of the dozen or so chat feeds. The Dark Web was alive with discussion of the bomb video. It had, apparently, been shot just an hour and a half earlier in central London. Speculation was rife as to who had managed to get round the almost fanatical security of the city to mount such an audacious attack.

It meant very little to Phillip. Although his flat on the Broadwater Farm estate was just a few miles north of the city, it might as well have been on another planet. What happened in leafy central London was of little concern to him. Indeed, what happened more or less anywhere off the internet grid was of little concern to him.

Phillip Shaw, eighteen, unemployed and unemployable, was just another black kid on an inner city estate that meant nothing to anyone until it caused trouble. And since the heady days of the 1985 riots, the Farm had not caused enough trouble to warrant attention from anyone.

Phillip had never run with the gangs of the estate. Like many of his contemporaries, his education was limited but he had no interest in gang life. He had his own interests. As he drifted away from school and faded from the attention of social workers and teachers, his entire world became computers. Loose acquaintances in the Waterboys sourced bits of hardware for him (some legal, most probably not), and he built ever more sophisticated machines. He learned to hack, to spy, to subvert the efforts of the authorities around the world. He sold his countersurveillance software for pocket money. A routine that bypassed Chinese governmental spyware might earn him a thousandth of a bitcoin, but there were a lot of Chinese customers and he now had a decent little savings account, at least in the virtual world he called home.

But wealth didn't interest him. His mother didn't know he had the talents to be rich or she might have insisted that they move to a better neighbourhood. Phillip couldn't risk that. He felt safe in the Farm. He knew where he was. People planted bombs in other parts of the city.

If wealth, power, politics and the world in general didn't interest Phillip Shaw, there was one thing he could never resist: a challenge.

The internet was alive with the bomb video and speculation about who might have been behind it. If no one knew yet, the video must have been carefully cloaked and whoever was behind the events just a few miles down the road was trying to stay anonymous. *This* was a challenge.

Phillip logged on to the Dem0nAg3nt board and started to gather his team together.

6

Leila Reid stopped her anonymous blue Peugeot 208 right in the middle of Kensington Road. Parking was never easier than in a crisis. The uniformed officers at the De Vere Gardens cordon had been satisfied with her explanation that she was with CTC, sent by Lawrence on a preliminary scouting expedition. They'd slid the barrier aside for her then turned their attention back to the crowds who were trying to see what was going on a hundred yards further up the road.

She walked towards the wreckage of the Park Hotel. A steady breeze blew along Kensington Road from the west, low and laden with fine dust. She'd seen the aftermath of bombs in southern Lebanon during her time with the Foreign Office, but this was different. There was none of the acrid ammonia smell that hung in the air hours after a kitchen-table IED had detonated. Here the air smelled of burnt rubber and concrete. All the fires were out but trails of smoke still emerged from deep within the rubble that had been the west wing of the hotel.

Lawrence had told her the explosion had been at the Embassy. It had been *close* to the Embassy, but not *at* it.

Another lie to draw her interest? She should just to walk away, but she had already fallen into Lawrence's trap. They both knew that if he could get her to come this far, she'd be caught.

It was 2.17pm. There were still four ambulances parked a little way further along the road, along with two fire engines and half a dozen police patrol vehicles. Three Territorial Support Group vans were parked at the far barrier. They would be there principally in their Counter-Terrorism support role, but someone in Scotland Yard was also anticipating trouble. The TSG officers present at the scene were fully equipped for riot control.

Several pop-up tents had been erected on the pavement opposite the hotel. White-overalled forensics techs scoured the pavement along the line of shops behind them, carefully sweeping broken glass and fragments of wood away as the walked. There were only two things they could be looking for: bomb fragments and body fragments, one to piece together the cause, the other to piece together the effect.

With a clearer view around the TSG vans now she saw a number of S52 neo-Nazis were beginning to congregate beyond the barrier. 'Solidarity 52', a loose affiliation of disaffected former members of the English Defence League, Combat 18 and the BNP, had already decided this was a terrorist attack. And there was only one breed of terrorists these days.

Two uniformed officers emerged from the tavern directly across the road from the hotel and walked away towards a mobile incident truck parked by gates of the Embassy. Fine dust covered everything, and the ground crunched minutely as Leila picked her way through the debris towards the hotel.

The western end of hotel's five-storey tower had collapsed downwards and backwards into the subterranean parking garage and spilled across the entrance to Kensington Palace Gardens. A fire service ladder unit was parked close to the building, its ladder extended over the wreckage. Search and rescue were working their way upwards around the rubble, stopping, listening, moving on; a crane parked at the cordon fifty yards further along Kensington High Street was waiting to do the heavy lifting when the rescue of survivors turned to the search for bodies. At the moment the two German Shepherd sniffer dogs clambering over the building indicated there were still people to rescue.

A black man in civilian clothing jumped down from the back of one of the ambulances and walked towards the entrance ramp to the underground car park. Leila followed him. Something about him didn't fit.

'Hey, wait,' she called. He turned towards her. 'You police?' she said.

'No. Private security.'

'Then you can't enter the building. This is a crime scene.'

'TSG know I'm here. And you are?'

'Here to see what the hell's happened. What do you know?'

'I know we've got eight confirmed dead, forty-something serious injuries. It could have been a lot worse considering the location.'

'Most of the blast was contained underground.'

The man nodded. 'There's still about thirty hotel rooms we've not been able to enter yet,' he said.

'What about the Embassy?'

'They're not talking to anyone.'

'Foreign soil. If they don't want their casualties counting towards our totals, that's fine. Were you here when it went off?'

'Over in the park. I'm Ruth Morgan's body guard, Gavin Byers.' He held out his hand. Leila ignored it.

'And Miss Morgan's where now?' she said.

'I left her at the Palace.'

'Good.' She nodded.

'I'm going back inside,' Gavin said. 'You want to come along?'

'I'll catch you up if I need to. Just want to get a feel for the place first.'

Gavin took a hard hat from the back of the fire tender and stooped into an opening at the foot of the tower.

It was obvious that this had been a bomb. The rooms immediately above the car park entrance had collapsed, but the east side of the building was largely undamaged. Had this been a gas leak in the underground facility, the rolling ignition of gas would have directed most of the blast out of the openings in the building, and probably wouldn't have caused much in the way of structural damage at all.

But Byers was right: as far as deaths and serious injuries were concerned, it could have been a lot worse. If the bomb had been detonated at street level rather than underground it would have caused carnage.

She walked on a few yards towards the corner of the building. The blank, windowless wall that faced the Embassy of Israel on Kensington Palace Gardens had fallen outwards across the tree-lined road, crushing the sentry boxes but absorbing the bulk of the blast, leaving the Embassy itself intact apart from a few broken windows.

Despite the collapse, the entrance ramp to the car park was not entirely obscured. On the left was a service entrance for trucks serving the hotel. On the right, where Gavin Byers had gone, was the public vehicle access. That suggested two possibilities. Either this had been a truck bomb – which meant it could have been a home-made fertiliser bomb despite the unfamiliar smell – or it was a smaller, high-grade car bomb.

She took out the monocular and scanned the inside of the structure again. There were blast marks on the rear concrete wall down and to the right of the car park. A wheel, lying flat and attached to a suspension arm and stub of axle was the only evidence of the car that had been parked in that spot. Whatever else remained of it was buried.

It was the vehicle that had carried the bomb.

Leila backtracked through the rubble and dust and entered the main lobby of the hotel. A trail of blood led from the stairs on the left across the tiled reception area. The wide desk was strewn with fragments of rubble and dust, and sheets of paper had been swept into a pile at its foot. All the lights were off. She walked around the end of the desk.

A uniformed police officer approached from the bar as her shoes squeaked on the polished floor.

'I need to see a guest list,' she said.

'Who are you?'

'Detective Sergent Reid, Counter-Terrorism,' she said.

'Then you've got the list. Commander Thorne requisitioned it...' he glanced at his watch, '... two hours ago.'

'OK, I haven't been in the office for a while. Can you tell me anything about who was here? Military personnel, foreign dignitaries, anyone who might have been a target?'

'There wasn't anyone. This is a top tourist hotel, not a diplomatic club. Mostly Japanese and American visitors, a few Brits.'

'Any idea of casualty figures?'

'In here? Five room staff are missing, three confirmed dead, fifteen serious injuries, about thirty minor walking wounded.'

'Guests?'

'Mostly staff. Whoever did this picked the quietest time. Most departing guests had left and incomers don't generally check in until after two. Those staying over multiple nights would already be out and there were no conferences booked until one o'clock. There are only two keys unaccounted for from the entire west wing.'

'So it wasn't an assassination.'

'It was meant for the Embassy, wasn't it? This was as close as they could get.'

'Maybe. That's what I'm here to find out. Thank you.'

She picked her way back across the reception and out onto the main road. In the shade of one of the forensic tents she stood looking at the collapsed building. This wasn't an opportunistic crime. The infantile mentality of the average lone-wolf terrorist mitigated against their being able to source the kind of explosives that did this. They had neither the contacts nor the patience. But the alternative didn't make any sense. The Embassy had suffered minimal damage and there had been no high-profile guests in the hotel. There had been very few guests on site at all.

So why had the bombers planned such a sophisticated operation with no clear target?

7

Leila arrived at the Operations Room in New Scotland Yard a few minutes after three o'clock – outside the one hour window in which she was to give DCI Lawrence her answer, but in time for all but the introductory summary of the Tactical Command briefing. A dozen people, including James Thorne, Counter-Terrorism's Commander, and Mark Ross, the civilian head of CTC's internal hi-tech division, were seated around the large table. Another Detective Sergeant, Keith Butler, was talking quietly on a mobile phone in the corner. On a screen on the far wall was a still image from a CCTV camera inside the hotel car park. Leila stood just outside the open doorway. No one paid her any attention.

'So that's the situation on the ground as it stands,' Thorne said. 'The PM has stressed the need to get solid information quickly on this one. As you know, this is a particularly sensitive time. Politically, the optimum outcome would be for this to be a lone wolf strike. But until we get solid forensic data on the type of explosives used, we have to consider all possibilities.'

'We can rule out chapati flour,' Leila said. 'This was a

professional job. Probably PX.' Twelve pairs of eyes turned on her.

'DS Reid,' Thorne said. 'How did you get in here?'

'Charm?'

DCI Lawrence held his hands up. 'I asked her to take a look, see what her gut told her.'

'DS Reid is not currently operational,' Thorne said.

'Fine,' Reid said. 'I'll leave you to it then.'

'Just a minute,' Lawrence said. 'Have you been to the site?'

'Yes.'

'And?'

'This isn't the main event. There's another attack coming.'

There was a moment of embarrassed silence, then Commander Thorne stood up and addressed Leila directly.

'Unless you have good evidence of that, that is exactly the sort of speculation we can do without. The reason you're not currently active is your inability to think before you speak.'

'We do need to consider the possibility,' Lawrence said.

'It's more than a possibility,' Leila said without breaking eye contact with Commander Thorne. 'So do you want me on board or not?'

'Sit in on the briefing. We'll talk later.'

Leila took a chair and sat away from the table, close to the door.

'OK,' Thorne said. 'Let's start with the bomb. Mark, what have we got?'

Mark Ross opened a file on his laptop and sent the images to the large display screen. 'No delivery trucks entered the building in the forty-five minutes prior to the explosion, and

none have entered that have not also left. We do have this.'
He brought up an image of a Volvo V70 turning into the
parking garage. 'NCP use number-plate recognition on the
entry and exit to the car park. Although we've not been able
to rule out other vehicles, this is the only one that came back
as having a false number plate. CV55 GXA is a V70, but not
this one. The registered owner's confirmed that his is parked
in his drive in Middlesborough with a blown head gasket.'

'The time-stamp says seven thirty-eight this morning,'
Leila said. 'It had been there for four and a half hours. So
we're looking at a timer.'

'Yes and no,' Lawrence said. 'Mark and I have reviewed
the CCTV footage in light of a new piece of evidence. The
PM has sent his schedule in, showing that he had a meeting
with the Embassy at 1pm. His car would have driven right by
the garage.'

'So why did the bomb go off at noon?' Thorne said.

'Because of this woman.' Ross sent another image to the
screen. It showed a dark-skinned woman wearing a headscarf, walking down the ramp into the garage. He brought up
three other images showing what was clearly the same
woman, from several different angles, walking east along
Kensington High Street.

'What makes you think she had anything to do with it?'
Leila said. 'Apart from racial profiling.'

'We've tracked her back to High Street Kensington tube
station,' Ross said. 'We never once get a good look at her face.
She knows the locations of every camera.'

'And we can't trace her back beyond the tube,' Lawrence

said. 'We're working on the assumption that she altered her appearance on the train or somewhere in the station. We might get lucky and find something, but right now, it looks suspicious. Plus, a few seconds before the explosion, the camera closest to the parked V70 is disabled. We know from other cameras that no one else entered the garage, either from the street or the hotel, in the two minutes leading up to that moment.'

'Circumstantial at best,' Leila said. 'It makes no sense that she'd go back to the bomb an hour before it was due to go off.'

'No, it doesn't. But the meeting between the PM and the Israelis was only finalised at ten this morning, two and a half hours *after* the car entered the garage. We think the bomb was always set to go off at noon, but they saw a better opportunity once they knew the PM would be in the vicinity an hour later. She went back in to delay the detonation but accidentally triggered it instead.'

'Do we have any leads on who she is?' Thorne said.

'We haven't got a face,' Ross said. 'Nothing in any of the databases shows anything linked to PX, known active cells or unusual passport activity that ties up with what little we know of her so far.'

'Forensics are testing body fragments,' Lawrence said, 'but so far she seems to be a clean skin.'

'GCHQ have also drawn a blank,' Keith Butler said. He ended his call and slipped the phone into his pocket. 'There have been two minor surges in chatter in the last month. The first was after the announcements that the government were in discussion with Aaron David to establish talks in London. Again when the tabloids leaked photographs of Abu Queria here last month. It was not much more than a ramping up of the usual background. Nothing that led to any heightening of the threat. In fact, a lot of it seemed to be garbage – just noise, only louder. Another spike in the last two hours is similarly vague. Nothing we can tie to a name. GCHQ are combing the data with whatever filters we can give them from our end.'

'There's also been a video posted online of the explosion, but so far it hasn't yielded any direct clues,' Ross said. 'It was taken from the roof of a building opposite the hotel and a little way along the road. It's under renovation. Uniforms are interviewing there.'

'Anyone know who filmed it or uploaded it? Thorne said.

'That's a longer-term goal. It's all heavily cloaked. They knew what they were doing and right now everything points to it having been routed through companies and jurisdictions that are less than forthcoming with intel. Digital forensics are taking the video itself apart.'

'Are we still thinking there's a link to Harakat al Sahm?' Thorne said.

'On the surface of it, yes.' Keith Butler opened a file of notes and scanned them. 'Problem is, they're still all surface. They make claims of allegiance to ISIS, but there's no concrete intel that substantiates them. SIS are looking into it on the ground.'

'Anything from the Palace?' Leila said.

'The royal couple have been helicoptered out,' Thorne

said. 'They're going to Windsor tonight. HRH is flying to Australia tomorrow. There's no indication this was aimed at them. Why?'

'The PM's daughter's there. Probably not relevant, but something to keep in mind. Her personal security was assisting S and R.'

'Good. DS Butler, follow up on the al Sahm leads with SIS. The rest of you: the PM wants this tied down within the next twelve hours. Name, motive, arrests imminent. So keep focussed. DS Reid, DCI Lawrence, my office.'

Commander Thorne led them into a side office.

'Sit, please,' he said. He sat on one side of a huge desk; Reid and Lawrence sat opposite him. 'So why are you here, DS Reid?'

'DCI Lawrence thought you needed me.'

'And do we?'

'I think you've got a much bigger investigation here than you realise. I don't doubt you can find the cell, but I can do it more efficiently. And with the talks due to start on Friday, I think you need efficiency. This isn't over.'

'Why do you think there's something else coming?' Thorne said. 'Nine-eleven, seven-seven, Madrid, Paris, they were all linked clusters. If further attacks had been planned, they would have happened by now.'

'Only if they were a linked cluster,' Reid said. 'I don't think they are. I think this was a prelude – a signal if you like – to a specific, bigger event.'

'And that's where you come in?'

'It's what I do,' Reid said.

'Maybe.' Commander Thorne looked Reid in the eye for a long moment. 'OK,' he said, 'talk me through your reasoning.'

Leila leaned forwards and rested her forearms on the desk. 'It was a PX car bomb, but a car bomb like this could have done much more damage than this. ISIS – if that's who is behind this, and I'm on the fence with that – has got the means and the cash to source military grade explosives; they've got the planning to get it into place without leaving a trail, without arousing suspicion. But they're also ruthless. Their aim in everything they do is to terrify the enemy. So why did they just demolish part of a hotel, and at the quietest time of day for guests? Why kill a few people when they could have parked in the middle of Bond Street and caused carnage?'

'Because this particular hotel was next to the Israeli Embassy,' Lawrence said. 'Isn't that obvious?'

'Only to someone who's not been there. They barely scratched it. That bomb was not meant for the Israelis.'

'So who was it meant for?'

'Us.'

'The police?'

'Counter-Terrorism Command specifically. We've got the entire department focussed on this one event like it's all that's going on.'

'Well so far, you're the only one who thinks it's not.'

'Then let me find the cell, and we can find out for sure. But let's make it quick. I'm certain these people have a plan, and so far you've done nothing to derail it.'

'OK,' Commander Thorne said, 'let's say I am prepared to bring you in… you'll work with a partner; you'll be the brains, but you won't run the show. I'm not risking you compromising another operation.'

'No, Sir. You've got a team out there willing and able to do the leg-work, follow the rules, go through the grind. I work on this independently. No partner, no plan other than what I make up as I go along. If I mess up, kick me off the force properly this time, but if I'm getting results, let me do it my way.'

'You follow procedure.'

'I follow the evidence, but I'll do nothing that might compromise a trial. I report back to DCI Lawrence, I get updates from him. Don't put me on the Joint Operations Team, because I can't stick to a schedule.'

'I take it you'll want official police accreditation.'

'Only so I can do my job. That shouldn't be a problem: I'm still a fully qualified CTC DS. And I'll need a gun. My training's still up to date.'

'But your MI5 clearance isn't. Your only source of internal information will be DCI Lawrence.'

'That's all I'll need. Thames House are looking at what's already happened to cover their asses because they didn't see it coming; I'm looking for what's *going* to happen. It's up to you to decide whether you believe I can.'

'DS Reid, no one doubts your ability. It's your methods that are of concern.' He looked at her for a moment. 'But against my better judgment, I'm prepared to let this play out for a while. If you think you can get us anywhere near the identity of the bombers, go ahead. I suggest you start with the mystery woman on the CCTV feed. Walk the route, get inside her head…'

'I know how to do my job.'

'Then you'll also know I only want a name or a probable location. You don't approach the suspects, and you don't talk to anyone. You're on probation, one step at a time. From now on I'll be split between the Executive Liaison Group and COBR meetings at Downing Street. You're answerable to DCI Lawrence, and he'll keep me in the loop. Use your old desk while you're here; anything that comes in while you're in the field will be left there for you. And know this: I'll pull you out if you step out of line so much as an inch.'

'I'll find your bomber.'

'Good. Mark Ross will give you all the files you need. I'll authorise a gun and warrant card while you're with him. Collect them on your way out. And Reid?'

'Yes?'

'*Don't* let me down.'

8

Richard Morgan stared at his face in the mirror as a little light powder was applied to his forehead and nose. The press conference would be brief and to the point. Or, more accurately, brief and evasive about the point. It would go out live on the national six o'clock news programmes and although the bombing had been six hours earlier, there was still not much he could tell the country. The only thing they knew for sure was that the death toll was ticking upwards and looked certain to rise further over night. MI5 were working on leads; the Met were interviewing witnesses and raking through files, but no one really knew anything. By now they should have had a very public claim of responsibility, but so far no one was taking credit.

He stood, took a deep breath and walked out through the front door of Number 10. Cameras flashed and journalists pushed forwards against the temporary barrier. Siobhan Wiley, his press secretary, was standing behind a lectern placed incongruously at the edge of the strip of tarmac that was still legally a road. Only in England would the most powerful man in the country address his public from the gutter. Only in England would no one even consider it strange.

He tried to compose his face into something that was both reassuring and compassionate. All he could think about was that he had still not heard from Ruth. Since noon he had barely had two minutes to himself, and those minutes had always coincided with Gavin Byers' phone going to voicemail. Kensington Palace security confirmed that she had been expected there for lunch, but could tell him no more than that she had not been with the royal couple when their helicopter left for Windsor at three. He had no rational reason to worry: it was impossible that Ruth had been the target of this morning's events, and yet...

As soon as the press conference was over he would get one of his SO1 men to make enquiries. He had tried to avoid bringing yet another layer of confusion to the day's already chaotic events, unwilling to be seen to care more about his own family than he did about his 'people', but the time had come. There was probably a good explanation, but right now he knew he needed help to find it.

'Ladies and gentlemen of the press,' Siobhan said into the microphone, 'The Prime Minister, The Right Honourable Richard Morgan.' She stood aside and Richard took his place behind the lectern. He paused for a moment as flashbulbs illuminated the scene.

'This morning,' he said, 'London was once again touched by tragedy. My personal condolences, and those of my colleagues of all political colours, go out to the families of the fourteen people now confirmed to have lost their lives, and the hundred and eighty-eight who are being treated in hospitals throughout the city.

'It's particularly barbaric that this should happen just forty-eight hours before two people who know more about war and terrorism than most meet here in London to discuss a lasting peace in the middle east. I can assure you, and whoever planned this morning's tragic events, that such outrages will not stand in the way of that settlement. If anything, this has made us more determined than ever to find a way forward for the overwhelming majority of people who simply want to live in peace regardless of religion or nationality.

'Our security services, both here and around the world, will stop at nothing to find the people who did this, and bring them to justice. There can be no excuses, and there will be no hiding place for those who believe violence is the answer to their grievances.' He paused and glanced down at his notes. He didn't need to remind himself of the words, but needed a moment to compose himself.

'You will,' he went on, 'see a greatly increased police presence on the streets of cities throughout the UK, and the military has been deployed at ports and airports. However, it must be stressed that so far no group has claimed responsibility for the bombing of the Park Hotel, and I urge you all to be careful not to jump to any conclusions until the authorities have had a chance to do their jobs.

'We must also remember that what makes our city one of the greatest on earth is the tolerance and compassion of the people who call it home. The police have my government's explicit instructions that no acts of vigilantism, racism or violence against any communities within our city will be tolerated. We must stand together at this time, opposed only to that minority among us who seek to undermine our freedom and cohesion.

'Together we will get through this, and emerge stronger and more peaceful than before.

'Thank you. I will take a few questions, but am unwilling to speculate beyond anything that has already been released to the media by the Metropolitan Police in their last statement.'

A dozen hands went up and Siobhan pointed at a familiar face in the front row.

'Prime Minister; Colin Redman, Sky News. Does today's attack signal the start of a new phase in terrorist activities in the west?'

'Our security services are following up a number of leads. We have no specific claim of responsibility yet and as such we can not be certain this is even the work of an organised group. There is no indication that other attacks are in the planning stage, and we have not felt it necessary to raise the current threat level. We can be confident that London is as safe now as it was yesterday, and we urge everyone to remain calm but vigilant. These people had luck on their side this time; next time, if there is a next time, we will be ahead of them.'

Siobhan pointed at another journalist.

'Kate Mawson, BBC. Have you spoken to Prime Ministers Aaron David or Abu Queria?'

'I have assured both our guests that this will have no effect at all on our meeting. If anything, such acts should be an inspiration to all those concerned to make the talks work. As you know, my government has worked for two years to bring the Israelis and Palestinians together to forge a new understanding for a new generation of people in the region. We will not turn our backs on the middle east because of the views of a tiny number of extremists. If indeed today's events are in any way connected, which at this time, we have no evidence that they are.'

'Are you linking this with Harakat al Sahm?'

Richard tried to see through the sudden burst of flashbulbs. He could not see the face of the man who had asked the question. TV cameras and microphones were turning towards the shabby journalists who always lurked at the back of such press conferences, picking up scraps, scavenging for a juicy story to spin into a lurid headline.

'Please,' Richard said, raising his hands. Most of the cameras turned back towards him. 'Please. Speculation is the most dangerous avenue we can go down at this stage, so I would ask all of you to ignore the rumours and turn your attention to helping us discover the truth. Thank you.'

Quickly he turned and walked away from the barrage of questions. The heavy front door closed behind him and the voices became muted.

'How the hell did they get hold of that?' he said. His press secretary marched along the corridor behind him.

'No one outside of COBR and the security services knows about al Sahm,' she said.

'Well someone leaked it! This could be a PR disaster. The public are going to think we're hiding something and God only knows what the Israelis are going to make of it. Get me Jim Thorne on the phone and draft a rebuttal statement in time for the Channel 4 news. And find me the person that leaked this!'

He stormed into his private office and flung the briefing notes onto the desk. The pad on which his speech had been written slid onto the floor.

As he stooped to pick it up he noticed that in his haste to get away from the baying press mob outside he had also picked up the dummy notes that were always placed on the lectern prior to any address. They were there to make it look less blank and vacant, to give the impression that even the furniture was well-informed.

That he had taken it was of no consequence in itself, but as he picked it up to drop it into the bin he noticed that at the foot of the page was a tiny handwritten note. Maybe whoever had set the lectern up had been testing a pen, maybe one of the duty policemen had stood there to assist with lighting or sound checks. It was not of great importance, except…

What had been written made his blood run cold.

There was a mobile phone number and two words: 'Call Bunny.'

Bunny was what they had called their daughter between the ages of about two and two and a half, when she had been inseparable from her pink rabbit romper suit. No one outside of the family knew. No one had uttered the word in years.

Only someone with direct access to her, and the leverage to extract such specific information, could know that name.

Ruth wasn't at the Palace. And wherever she was, she was in serious trouble.

9

Richard Morgan dialled the number.

It was answered almost before it had rung at the other end.

'Prime Minister,' a voice said. Richard tried to pinpoint the accent but came up blank. Well-bred English, standard received Eton perhaps, or maybe just someone who had decided that was about the easiest one to fake. The voice had none of the inflection of the Middle East or South Asia, but that meant nothing. Over a fifth of US Islamist terrorists were white and American-born. Britain was catching up fast in its ability to radicalise its own.

'Let me speak to my daughter,' he said.

'In time, Prime Minister. We have something to discuss first.'

'The police are tracing this call,' he said.

'No, they are not. You're calling on your personal cell, which you have not declared to your security team. I too am using an unregistered pay as you go cell. Geolocation would yield nothing of use, and not in the time you have. Don't play games, Prime Minister. Time is short.'

'What do you want?'

'Your cooperation in a simple matter.'

'Go on.'

'The exact details will be revealed to you tomorrow.'

'Why not now? If the matter's that simple, it can be sorted out tonight and I can get my daughter back.'

'Tomorrow's better for us.'

'Have you planted more bombs?'

'We've already proved we can strike wherever and whenever we choose. Bombing's not our mission. It was merely a way of focussing your attention, showing you that we're serious and capable.'

'More so then kidnapping my daughter? You people are animals!'

'Everything has a purpose, Prime Minister. Now that we have your full attention, our purpose will become clear.'

'I want to know that Ruth is still alive.'

'Should we mail something to you? Something warm?'

'I'll kill you for this…'

'No one else needs to die. And if you cooperate, no one will.'

'So what is this? Ransom?'

'No. We need you to do one small job for us, then your daughter will be returned to you and all this can be forgotten. No one will ever know.'

'What makes you think the security services don't already know?'

'Because we've watched you, Prime Minister. We've studied your methods. You were clever in setting up the talks between two old enemies who've sworn destruction on each other for decades. Even cleverer in ensuring neither side knew quite as much about what was going on as you yourself did. You work in secret, you like to be in control.'

'I have no idea what you're talking about.'

'There we have it, Prime Minister. Secrecy, sleight-of-hand. You've made promises, stacked the deck, while all the time hiding your own agenda. So I'm confident that our arrangement can be kept between us alone. You'll see that it is the best way.'

'So what do you want?'

'You'll address the House of Commons at 9am tomorrow. Liam Treadwell, your Head of Corporate Services will be waiting for you outside your office. He's not part of our organisation, and knows nothing of us or our requirements. He's acting only as a courier, and interrogating him will produce no useful intelligence and will endanger your daughter's life. He'll hand you a sealed envelope.'

'Containing?'

'A simple instruction. If you act on it, your daughter will not be harmed.'

'And if I can't?'

'Then she dies.'

'I'm watched everywhere I go, I have to account for every move I make!'

'I hope that's not panic I hear in your voice, Prime Minister. This is no time for rash decisions. You need to think clearly. If you bring anyone else into this matter, we will know; if you deviate from your normal behaviour in any way, we will know. Your instructions will be simple and clear. Follow them, and we'll all come through this.'

'Except the fourteen people you killed this morning!'

'You must make sure it doesn't become fifteen by tomorrow night. Or fifty, or five hundred. Do not doubt that we're serious.'

'How do I contact you?'

'You don't. This phone will be deactivated after this call. We'll know whether you've complied with our instruction, so we will not need to speak again.'

The line went dead.

10

The Volvo used in the bombing was a dead end. The engine and chassis numbers had been welded off and the registration plate led to an off-the-road model two hundred miles away. With over a hundred thousand third generation V70s in production, and nothing to identify this one, that avenue of enquiries was going nowhere. In time someone would arrive back from holiday to find their car had been stolen from airport parking, but even that would get them no closer to finding the thief.

The car's arrival at the hotel also drew a blank. CCTV caught the driver's face as he turned off Kensington High Street and the hotel's own internal cameras watched him enter the lobby, approach the reception desk and leave an envelope with the concierge. Later enquiries showed that he was a professional driver. A motorcycle courier had arrived at the offices of his employer, Fleet of Foot, with the cloned keys and instructions to collect the vehicle from long-stay parking at Gatwick airport and deliver it to the basement car park of the Park Hotel, paying cash and parking it as close to the entrance ramp as possible. He was to leave the keys at reception, addressed to a Mr Alec Kochov. Kochov was a ghost; a one-night booking had been made by phone the previous day, but no guest of that name ever arrived and he could not be traced. The motorcycle courier who had initiated the vehicle transfer could also not be traced, but it was likely that even if he proved to be genuine, the trail leading back beyond his involvement would be similarly opaque.

It had been a clever and well planned operation. CTC knew the car had carried the bomb into position, but had no way of tracing where it had come from or who had booked the driver. Forensics had found nothing unique in the timer – it was nothing that could not be made from components bought on the internet for any number of innocent DIY projects. The explosives were C-4 plastic, usually associated with the US military, but chemically identical to that used in the USS Cole and Khobar Towers bombing carried out by al-Qa'ida. Given the vast quantity of military hardware the US had inadvertently donated to middle eastern terrorist groups in the last twenty years, this too yielded no useful information.

The key lay in the only clue they had so far discovered that was not completely obscured by careful planning: the woman who had returned to the car moments before the bomb went off. And despite Commander Thorne's doubts, DS Reid was the best person to trace her.

Leila Reid was old-school. She had joined the Met's Counter-Terrorism Command straight from a stint working for the Foreign Office, with placements in Syria, Lebanon and Turkey. She was fluent in Levantine Arabic and could make herself understood pretty much anywhere in the Arab world. Twenty-first century counter-terrorism had seemed like a natural move.

She knew the value of modern forensics and computer technology, but for her the greatest tool of all was not to be found in the microchip or the lab but in the human mind. Forensic clues told you what a person had *done*; an insight into their mind told you *why*, and that could lead to what they were planning to do next. The woman Leila was tracking was dead, but she had certainly not been operating alone. She was just one part of a cell that would itself be part of a much larger organisation.

With the CCTV footage loaded onto her iPad, she made her way along the now partially-reopened Kensington High Street to the Park Hotel. A group of about half a dozen young men ogled her as she passed. One wore a t-shirt emblazoned with 'S52' in a blue circle. Solidarity 52 – named in 'honour' of the fifty-two people killed in the July 7th terrorist attacks in London in 2005 – had been agitating for an excuse to take their grievances to the streets for months. Leila had no doubt there would be more coming out of the woodwork as night fell.

The police were still gathering CCTV recordings from local shops in case the bomber had been caught scouting the route to the hotel in the previous few days. They had canvassed staff and shown them the best of the images they already had. No one remembered seeing her and Leila was not hopeful that she would appear on any of the security tapes. Their suspect had been too careful for that.

The front of the hotel was now screened with temporary wooden boarding to a height of eight feet. She had no access to the parking garage, so she started her walk-through of the bomber's known movements from corner of the building.

The last camera to pick the suspect up was mounted high on the now-demolished wall of the hotel, pointing west. This had been at 11.57.45, a little over two minutes before the bomb exploded. If, as CTC suspected, the bomb had been timed to go off at noon, the mystery woman was already cutting it very close. She had avoided the number-plate recognition cameras, and another, inside the garage, went dead six seconds later without capturing her face.

Leila began to walk west. She glanced down Palace Green towards the Embassy. Tall green screening had been placed around the front windows and six Israeli Defence Force soldiers stood just within the perimeter.

She walked through the police cordons and on to the junction with Kensington Church Street seventy metres away. The bomber had moved into and out of shot of a traffic light camera on the junction. This was time-stamped at 11.56.16. The clocks were accurate, at least to a few seconds. The mystery woman was moving quickly, but calmly enough not to attract the attention of anyone around her.

Then there was nothing until she was caught on the forward-facing camera of the N9 bus as it passed her going west at 11.49.44. The low-grade image was insufficient to show her face from a distance and by the time the bus was close, she had turned to look in the window of Marks and

Spencer, just along the street from High Street Kensington tube station.

This was puzzling. Marks and Spencer at 11.49.44, Church Street at 11.56.16. It had taken her over six minutes to walk one hundred and twenty-five metres, knowing that she was on a tight deadline. At seven in the evening with light foot traffic, Leila covered the distance in under two minutes. Even allowing for the pavements being busier at noon, the walk should not have taken much more than three.

So where had she been for the *missing* three minutes?

Leila stood by the same shop window and flicked between stills from the two cameras. In both the suspect wore a long white shirt-dress over pale trousers. A white headscarf was pushed back to reveal her face from hairline to chin. Her face had not been caught on camera not because she had made any attempt to cover it, because she had been extremely careful. Dressed like this, no one would have given her a second look.

Crucially, in the bus image she was standing with her left side exposed to the approaching vehicle. In her hand she held a small package, probably a plastic carrier bag partly rolled down on its contents. Leila flicked back to the moving footage from the Church Street traffic camera. Their suspect ran a few steps, trying to make the lights before they changed. The bag in her hand flapped as she moved.

Quickly she went back to the bus footage. The bag hung as if its contents were heavy. Back to the traffic cam: the bag waved in the breeze. It was empty.

Between Marks and Spencers and the Church Street

junction, the suspect had dumped the contents but kept the bag itself to maintain consistency on the CCTV feeds.

Leila walked back along the south side of Kensington High Street from the tube station towards the traffic camera near the church. There she stopped and examined the images on her tablet again, trying to get inside the head of her quarry.

The assumption had been that since this woman did not appear on any of the Underground CCTV images, she had changed her appearance somewhere between leaving the train and entering the street. And if that was the case, she would be carrying whatever garments she had been wearing on the train. These would not be traditional Muslim clothes; the disguise would have been something contrasting, typically western. And carrying a bag of western clothes would have been highly suspicious if she had been caught and searched in the underground car park.

She had to lose whatever she was carrying before entering the garage.

She would have stashed them somewhere where they would be hidden from casual view, but be easy enough to retrieve when she had to reverse the walk and re-emerge from the tube in her original guise. That meant a building easily accessible to the public where she could enter and exit without being noticed. Somewhere that might account for the missing three minutes of her journey.

And Leila was standing right outside the perfect place – the exact place she herself would have chosen.

She turned the iPad off and crossed the road. St Mary Abbot's Church was still open.

Leila had not set foot inside a church since 2007, and not for nearly twenty years prior to that. She had been an agnostic until her brother had been killed in Baghdad as part of a two-year covert operation that took out three and a half thousand enemy insurgents but lost a good number of their own people in the process. After that she had found true atheism.

St Mary Abbot's brought it all back in a wave so sudden and vivid that for a moment she stood at the edge of the nave with her eyes closed. Clive had never been officially listed among the dead. Even in the secretive world of the SAS, the so-called Task Force Black was shrouded in mystery. He had not even been given a funeral. Leila had last been in a church attending the funeral of one of his fellow regular army victims, the closest she could get to a formal goodbye to her brother. Now, ten years later, it was the smell that hit her most forcefully, that brought back the immediacy of those long-buried emotions: bees' wax and turpentine, brass polish, dust, old paper and centuries of candles and oil lamps; smells that existed almost nowhere outside these houses of make-believe.

She opened her eyes. Had their suspect been in here just a few hours earlier?

Maybe.

In most churches in England a Muslim would have been noticed, but in the centre of London she would have passed easily as a tourist.

The church was huge and rather shabby. There should be a lot of places to hide a small bundle of clothes, and yet, as Leila stood staring at the altar, she realised that there would really be very few. Nowhere that had free public access would be suitable. The risk of its being discovered – possibly only moments after it had been planted given the state of vigilance against left packages – was too high. Yet the bomber would be highly unlikely to have access to any staff-only areas. The cell might have been able to infiltrate the church's staff or builders working on the renovations, but doing so would be far too high a risk for such a minor pay-off.

So that ruled out almost the entire body of the church, any open chapels and any rooms behind routinely locked doors.

Which left what? The kitchen was too busy, likewise the toilets next to it; the vestry would be locked; the south transept, sanctuary, and meditation area offered no hiding places. Nor did St Paul's chapel, directly opposite where Leila stood… but what was on the left of the chapel would have been prefect.

Work was under way to remove the old organ and an organ loft gives a small and very secret area where visibility of the church is good, but where almost no one ever looks. Here, with renovations under way, the organ loft was disused but intact. It would be the ideal hiding place for a small package for the few minutes the bomber needed.

Leila stepped quickly across the nave. There was builders' tape across the entrance to the steps up to the organ, tape which she ducked under as easily as she imagined their suspect had done in the missing three minutes of her journey to the hotel car park. The organ manuals were still in place, though by now they were not connected to anything. A pile of music still lay on the floor, along with a bag of tools and a workman's fluorescent jacket. Leila glanced down into the church; no one had noticed her ducking the tape, and no one was aware she was there.

She crouched by the pedal board and lifted the yellow jacket. Beneath it was a tightly rolled blue t-shirt. She slipped on a pair of latex gloves from her back pocket and gently unfolded the roll. Inside the t-shirt was a pair of light summer jeans. She had found the bomber's original identity.

She ran back down to the nave and along the pews to the gift shop. It was about to close and was busy with people buying last minute souvenirs – not only of the church, but of what had happened along the road from it that morning. She pushed past a young Chinese couple standing by the till.

'I'm with the police,' she said to the elderly woman behind the counter. 'I need a plastic bag, please, quickly.'

'Is there a problem?'

'I just need a bag. And get onto whoever's in charge here, make sure no one enters the organ loft.'

The woman handed a St Mary Abbot's carrier bag over the counter and was about to say something else when Leila raised her hand.

'There's no immediate danger, but no one must go beyond the tape by the organ. Uniformed officers will explain everything when they arrive in a few minutes.'

She quickly retraced her steps – again completely unremarked by the few people still in the church – and retrieved the clothes from beside the organ. As two church officials jogged towards the builders' tape, Leila walked out into the hot evening, one crucial step closer to understanding her quarry.

She handed the bag to a uniformed officer at the hotel cordon with instructions to take it to Scotland Yard and get a forensics team to the organ loft. She then walked back to her car and sat for a minute watching workmen in hi-vis jackets sweeping out the last of the debris from the hotel's main reception.

By now, it was possible that forensics would have found a DNA or fingerprint match for the bomber, but Leila doubted it. This was a meticulously planned operation, and the cell would have used clean skins for it. No one can remain untraceable for ever, but someone with no police record would slow the search down and buy some very useful time.

The clothes would enable the police to make up a likeness to canvas points back from the tube station, so there was no point in Leila trying to go further back than she already had. It had been a significant breakthrough.

One thing puzzled her though.

This was clearly not a suicide mission. That the bomber had left clothes in an easily accessible place meant she had intended to retrace her route back out of Kensington to wherever she had come from. That she had been able to avoid being picked up in a recognisable way on any of the CCTV cameras implied careful planning and a desire for living anonymity beyond this one operation.

Something else occurred to her as she watched the heavy crane trundling into position to start the bulk clearance of the wreckage.

The car had been collected from Gatwick airport at 6am, with the timer set for, they still presumed, a noon detonation. Some time after 10am the cell discovered that there was a better opportunity with the PM's change of schedule that would bring him to the area close to the bomb at 1pm. That meant there was a maximum two-hour period for the timer to be intercepted and changed. This would not have been enough for the mystery woman to scout a route from the station to the hotel and plan the change of appearance. But it *had* all been planned.

So there must *always* have been a contingency plan for the bomb to be intercepted after it had been driven into place.

And that made no sense at all.

Even if the bomb had been intended to detonate *earlier* than noon, and the woman was just going to check why it had not gone off, the same logical black hole still existed. There would have been no reason for the cell to plan for such a failure.

There was something she wasn't seeing. This bomb was big, it had got the attention of the country, it had performed the role that terrorist attacks were designed to perform, but it was not enough. This event had been important enough to build in a very elaborate fail-safe. Had it been parked under the Israeli Embassy itself, that would have been understandable. Entry to such a target would be incredibly difficult, and they would get only one chance to make it work. But this bomb was under the hotel. Fail today, they could just try again.

It confirmed her hunch that this bomb was not the end.

It was either a signal to other cells that they were to commence further strands of the plan, or it was a smoke-screen for something far larger: focus attention on this while they got on with the main event.

The problem was, nothing she had discovered so far got her any closer to knowing just what that main event might be. She needed to trace their one known suspect back to her source, before the next stage of the operation could begin.

11

When Leila got back to Scotland Yard there was already a stack of papers on her old desk and a slew of memos reporting tip-offs that had come in from the public. She didn't read the latest police reports, preferring to get all her information direct from DCI Lawrence. She scanned the tip-offs but quickly dismissed them. It had been a mistake to publish CTC's phone number online. The sorts of people who look up the phone numbers of Special Operations organisations on the internet were generally the sorts of people such organisations could do without.

There were a dozen CTC officers in the briefing room when Leila took a seat near the back. More arrived over the next couple of minutes. Even this late in the evening, very few of the core staff had gone home. Mark Ross sat at the side of the room, flicking through images on his iPad. DCI Lawrence arrived on the dot of nine o'clock, still in hushed conversation with Keith Butler.

Leila opened the meeting with her report of how she had come by the bomber's primary identity. It was the only significant breakthrough so far. The department was drowning in false leads and back-checks on historic intelligence, none of which were going anywhere. When she had finished, Mark Ross sent a series of images of the t-shirt and jeans to the screen on the wall at the head of the table.

'The clothes yielded nothing useful,' Lawrence said. 'They were all western, low-grade garments that could have been bought anywhere. Forensics are going through them for secondary trace but they're not hopeful. Both items were brand new. She probably put them on moments before leaving her primary location.'

'What about the body? Leila said.

'We've only got fragments, mostly badly degraded by fire. We know from the CCTV that she was wearing a simple thob and a headscarf, nothing that would stand out in London. Cloth was cotton. Again, could have been bought anywhere. As for the body, forensics are looking at what we've got, but it's not much. The only unique identification found on the body was this ring.' Another image appeared on the screen.

'It was on the middle finger of her right hand,' Keith Butler said. 'We got lucky: the finger was embedded in the driver's seat. The bone stopped the ring being flattened. However, we're not sure exactly what it is.'

'It's an old-fashioned key,' Leila said. She walked to the front of the room and peered closely at the screen. 'See how it's been looped around so that the shaft forms the body of the ring and the bitting and bow meet at the upper side of the finger. It's probably home-made. My guess is that it was fashioned out of an older piece of jewellery. I doubt it was ever a real key.'

'You've seen this before?'

'Similar. This points to her being a native Palestinian, or a close sympathiser. The key symbolises return from exile, literally opening the doors that were locked to them in 1948. I spent time in the camps of southern Lebanon. Keys were quite popular.'

'That doesn't fit with the ISIS angle,' Lawrence said.

'I'm just telling you what I see.' She took her seat at the back of the room again.

'OK. Preliminary DNA tests have not given us an identity. We'll run comparisons with known Palestinian samples and we might get something. Forensics are doing isotope analysis of bone fragments, see if they can find out where she spent the last few years.'

He nodded to Mark Ross, who sent another image to the screen. This one was a hastily updated spider diagram showing the latest intelligence on Islamist groups active in the West.

'The wider issue,' Lawrence went on, 'is one of attribution. It's nine hours now, and we've not had any claim of responsibility.'

'Nothing?' Leila said.

'We've had Animal Liberation, Occupy, Combat 18, some guy with a Birmingham accent who said he was al-Koran. Nothing remotely plausible. Do you have any thoughts?'

'With the Palestinian link, I'm still open to this being about the peace talks.' She nodded at the diagram on the screen. 'Your ISIS evidence is circumstantial at best.'

'Harakat al Sahm is real enough. GCHQ's intel amounts

to something too solid to be just someone playing the fool.'

'Is there any third-party corroboration on the online forums?'

'No.'

'And surveillance threw nothing up in the last few weeks?'

'No. What's your point?'

'My point is that al Sahm's only link to Islamic State is what they themselves claim. Has al-Baghdadi ever even formally accepted their bayah?'

'The claim of allegiance? No, but that doesn't mean they're not acting as agents of IS.'

'Except that without al-Baghdadi's consent, they wouldn't have access to IS weaponry or support. And they're clearly being supported by someone. I agree, everything about this points to a sleeper cell of a major organisation. I'm just not convinced we've got the right organisation.'

'We'll find the link.' Lawrence drew breath to move on.

'I don't think you can ignore the possibility that this whole IS thing could be a smokescreen,' Leila said.

'For who?'

'Someone who has reason to put us onto the wrong path. Look at it: we're chasing shadows inside one of the most complex affiliations of insurgents and terrorists the world has ever seen. It's like looking for a piece of mud in a swimming pool full of shit. We're wallowing around in there while they have a run at the main event. Which I think is the peace talks.'

'Then get me evidence.' He turned his attention back to the room in general. 'Whether this is about the peace talks or not, it's all about how it looks, and right now, that's not good. There's a formal welcoming dinner for the delegates at seven on Friday evening, which means we've got less than forty-eight hours to get on top of this. The PM is adamant that this should not be used as unfair leverage by either side.'

'There is one more thing,' one of the uniformed officers said. 'Things are starting to kick off on the streets. Response officers are reporting a higher-than-usual number of 999 calls-outs.'

'GCHQ have told us there's an abnormally large number of emails and tweets inciting retributive action,' Ross said. 'Trouble's brewing in all the major cities, especially here.'

'Solidarity 52 were out near the bomb site,' Leila said.

'Territorial Support are deployed,' Lawrence said. 'I think we can keep a lid on this. There's never been serious unrest following a terrorist incident before. But we need to be seen to be making progress. What counts is perception. I'll brief Commander Thorne and see if we can get the PM to do something in time for the morning papers even without a concrete attribution. The rest of you, you know your duties. Let's get this thing contained, and quickly.'

Lawrence left. Leila caught him up as he was about to enter Commander Thorne's office.

'Can I say something?' she said.

'I'm sure you're going to anyway,' he said.

'You've got to stop trying to make this fit an extant pattern. If you spend time chasing after an organisation as diffuse as Islamic State, you're going to get nowhere.'

'COBR concluded that the ISIS angle should be the main

focus. That's not CTC, it's all the intelligence agencies. The PM backs them.'

'Because he wants to believe this is a one-off, a new skirmish in his ridiculous war on terror. We find the culprits, shoot some people, it all goes away again. Or maybe we could just shoot some people anyway. Brazilians have funny-coloured skin.'

'Be very careful, Reid,' Lawrence said. 'This is not a cover-up. The PM, no, *all* of them, want us to start with the most likely scenario. We've got to have something to hang our theories on. We've foiled dozens of plots in the last decade by using exactly these methods. This time one got through, but we stick to what we know and we'll find the culprits. If you're right and there's another bomb coming, this is the best way to stop it.'

'But you've got no intel. This is like a jigsaw puzzle and someone's given us the wrong box. There's no point trying to hammer the pieces together to make the picture you think you should be making. We'll find the real picture if we work with the pieces we do have. And the first piece we've got is a solid Palestinian lead.'

'And we're following it up. If you have other ideas, be my guest. That's why I brought you in. Get me more pieces. I'll call you when we've got anything new here.'

12

Faran Jaafar sat in his beaten up armchair in front of his beaten up TV with his feet on the beaten up coffee table between the two. In his right hand he had a can of beer, his left rested on a tatty second-hand copy of Anderson's *Imagined Communities: Reflections on the Origin and Spread of Nationalism*. He could have bought it new, but that wasn't his style. He was using his years at SOAS both to get his degree and to rebel a little against his over-privileged Kuwaiti upbringing. Living in a run-down top floor flat that had mould in the bathroom and cockroaches in the kitchen was the most fun he'd had in his life.

He had been unmoved by the bomb that morning. London was a big place; his flat in Tower Hamlets and the hotel in Kensington were in the same geographical city, but culturally they might as well have been on different continents.

He had watched the video of the explosion with little interest; he'd watched the early evening news with even less. But what began to come through as evening fell was much harder to ignore.

At eight o'clock the first twitter feeds had started. At first Faran ignored the chirrup of his phone. There had been a lot of talk about the bombing since noon and this seemed to be just more of the same.

But the tweets kept coming, more and more frequently.

Around nine, he scrolled down the list and felt a chill even in the stuffy atmosphere of his flat. People he knew – people he would have said were as emotionally disengaged from today's events as he was – were starting to post some disturbing stuff.

'#reclaim our streets. the fightback has started. youtube of #mosque gatherings.' That was from Sarah Gerrard, a fellow IR student he knew vaguely, who had never been particularly political before. It was typical of a slew of some thirty tweets that had stacked up in the last ten minutes.

'#enough-is-enough. We all stand together or we all fall apart. #reclaim our streets at your local mosque.' David Corby-Arras, probably the most liberal (and gay) man Faran knew. He had either retweeted it by mistake or someone had hijacked his account. Or maybe the bombers really had gone too far this time.

He felt his pulse beating hard in his neck.

He clicked on the #reclaim hashtag and there were thousand of posts. Selfies of skinheads in S52 t-shirts standing in front of mosques; images of 9/11, 7/7, Madrid, Paris, Tunisia; sinister white text on black flags that read 'Je Suis #Reclaim'; declarations of war that boiled with urgency and hate.

For the first time, he became aware of voices down in the

street. He couldn't hear much, and the tingle in his spine may have had as much to do with what he had just read as with the voices themselves, but he couldn't shake the feeling that these sounds were somehow more pressing, more immediate, than the usual background.

He woke up his computer and logged into Facebook. If the twittersphere was hot, FB was on fire. There were hundreds of messages, links to videos, images of the bomb site, cartoons of obviously Muslim men with dynamite in their turbans or AKs sticking out of their robes like cold, skinny penises.

He closed the computer's lid. He needed to speak to someone, anyone. His phone whistled and he tapped the screen. A new image filled it. A photograph – faked, he assumed – of a person sitting, head back, on a bus. A shard of glass protruded from her neck and her shirt was a slick of glistening red. The woman's eyes were open, staring blankly at the camera.

What shocked him most was the caption that had been added at the foot of the image. In faux-arabic script, it said 'This Is Islam'.

As he scrolled through the contacts list on his phone he heard the screech of tyres in the distance. In a street where traffic noise was the norm, it took something special to stand out, and this did. He drew the net curtain aside as the blaring horn grew louder.

Driving a high speed down the wrong side of the road was a white Ford Transit. A man sat half-out of the passenger window, two others stood just inside the open back doors.

They were chanting something Faran could not make out and beating a rapid, heavy salvo on the van's walls. It turned right at the end of the road and disappeared.

Other vehicles followed. Groups of men in the familiar S52 t-shirts, some wearing Occupy masks, most brazenly bare-faced, ran along the pavements.

They were heading for the mosque on Whitechapel Road.

Faran glanced at the time on his phone as he put it in his pocket. It was 9.20. Maghrib prayers would be under way. Raised voices seemed to surround the building now.

He locked the front door behind him and looked out of the window at the rear of the buildings. Below was a small car park and a row of houses that were mostly occupied by Pakistani and Bangladeshi families. A group of white youths had crowded around an old Nissan Micra, rocking it from side to side. Inside, a woman in a hijab was frantically trying to get the car started. She succeeded and reversed, hitting a Mercedes parked on the other side of the car park, before screeching away. The men jeered. One of them looked up towards where Faran was standing and he let the curtain fall back into place.

On the first floor, directly below Faran's tiny attic flat, lived a group of three, sometimes four, women. As he passed, he knocked on the door. No one answered.

'It's Faran from upstairs. You all OK in there?' he shouted. He heard a movement inside but no one spoke. He would check on them again when he returned.

Outside it was still hot, the air heavy with an approaching storm. Faran looked along Vallance Road before slipping out, keeping close to the wall as he made his way towards Whitechapel Road. He ducked into an alleyway thirty yards or so from his front door as another van sped past.

At the junction he stopped. From just beyond where he stood the street was gridlocked. Several drivers were already trying to do three-point turns to head back out of the chaos.

The mosque was about two hundred yards away on the other side of the road. A crowd of a hundred or more people had gathered outside and more were joining all the time. There were a few placards and banners, but most of the people there were happy just to shout abuse at the building and leave it at that. It was those joining the back of the group who looked more intent on mayhem. Most wore balaclavas or scarves pulled up over their faces. One had a grainy enlargement of the 'This Is Islam' image taped to a placard.

He took out his phone and began to film the scene.

Police sirens approached from behind him. A riot van peeled off down Turner Street to get to the far end of the mosque while a patrol car stopped near the back of the crowd. The two uniformed officers abandoned their vehicle and began to run towards the building.

Faran followed, keeping close to the shop fronts, always alert for escape routes. He held his phone out in front of him, trying to keep a steady image on the screen.

At Davenant Street he stopped again, moving behind a petrol pump on the Shell Garage forecourt. From here he was barely twenty yards from the back edge of the mob across the road.

The two policemen were fighting their way through the

crowd towards the closed door of the mosque. A bottle arced high above the mob and came down just behind the rear officer. The crowd cheered and closed in behind the two policemen. A few seconds later the doors of the building opened a crack and the two men disappear inside.

More bottles began to fly.

Across the road a window smashed. The Islamic bookshop on the ground floor of a tall, forlorn-looking building had been spotted by a group of half a dozen youths, some wearing the distinctive S52 emblems on their t-shirts. Two of the gang tore the shattered window out and began to throw books out into the street. Another set fire to the pages of a book and threw it into the shop.

That was the catalyst that turned what had been a rowdy demonstration into a full-scale riot.

Three men ran along the pavement with a metal barrier between them and charged at the car showroom next to the bookshop. They battered it until the glass shattered. With no interest in the cars inside, they ran off with their weapon between them and began to attack a clothes shop for no reason other than that no one tried to stop them. Others poured into the showroom and petrol-bombed the cars within.

Faran retreated. He'd seen enough. If he wanted to see any more, he could turn on the TV. There were at least a dozen people who, like him, were standing back from the main group, holding mobile phones above their heads.

By now the violence was spreading down Whitechapel Road, cutting off his escape, so he crossed Davenant Street to make his way home the back way.

Along the road that led to the back of his building a group of two men and two women had stopped a taxi. The car's tyres were flat and the windscreen was shattered. The passenger door of the vehicle was open.

He was trapped. The two men smashed the driver's side window and wrenched the door open. They pulled the Asian driver out into the road and punched and kicked him as he tried to crawl under the car. When he made it far enough under the vehicle to be out of range, one of the men climbed onto the car's roof and jumped up and down on it. The other lay beside the vehicle trying to drag the driver out. While the women ransacked the driver's cash box, the taxi's passenger decided to make her escape. She opened the door and made a run for it towards the main road.

Faran scrambled over a six foot wall and stood on a bin on the other side. He could do nothing to help the taxi driver, but he could get make sure his attackers would be unable to just walk away. He zoomed in and got a perfect image of the hate-filled faces of the men.

There was a scream from further along the road. Faran risked leaning over the wall, one eye on the road, one on the image on his phone.

Half way along Davenant Street the two women had caught up with the taxi's passenger. She was dressed in a chador, which was all the encouragement her attackers needed.

They shoved the woman back and forth between them, all the time becoming more and more enraged by her screams for help. One of them pulled the veil up over the woman's head and punched her in the face. The other took hold of the skirt part of the garment and began to rip it down.

Faran stopped filming and moved through the back yards behind the wall. When he had gone as far as he could – he hoped, far enough that he was out of sight of the taxi – he climbed back over the wall. By now the two female attackers had torn the top half of the chador to shreds.

Faran ran towards them. He caught the first of the women with a fist in the back of her neck. She immediately crumpled to the ground. Her accomplice screamed. Faran scanned the street for help. A small grey door had opened some fifteen feet further along the road. A terrified old man looked out, beckoning to the now almost naked Muslim woman. Faran pushed her towards the door just as the second attacker launched herself at him. Although not a big man, he was a rower and swimmer, and was more than a match for her. He threw her to the ground and began to run as he heard feet approaching him from behind.

He glanced over his shoulder. The two men had now given up on the taxi driver and were closing in on him fast. He shoved the grey door but it didn't move and he had no time to wait for it to be unlocked again.

He easily outpaced his pursers as far as the main road. The sky was now almost dark, and the increasing number of fires cast huge shadows of the restless mob across the road. More police vans had arrived and officers in riot gear were breaking the crowd into smaller sections, herding them along side streets and trying to get to the mosque.

Faran ran towards Vallance Road.

He thought he heard a gunshot, but he couldn't be sure. It may just have been fireworks or a car's petrol tank exploding.

He made it almost to the corner of his road when he ran into a group of youngsters running towards the mosque. One of them caught him on the chin with a lucky hit before running on.

He staggered back against the fence of a derelict lot just yards from Vallance Road and safety. From his right the two men from the taxi attack bore down on him. One was carrying a long metal bar – a piece of scaffolding or a part from one of the market stalls that lined this part of the street, Faran never knew.

The last thing he knew for sure was that he had been hit.

The first blow struck his stomach; a second took his legs out from under him. He tried to crawl under his attackers. He made it a few feet along the pavement before a third blow smashed the side of the head.

He lost consciousness then.

If it hadn't been for the volley of gunshots that rang out from Vallance Road a few seconds later, momentarily distracting his attackers, he would have lost his life.

13

At a little after 10.30, Richard Morgan left the Cabinet Room on the ground floor and slowly climbed the broad staircase to the second floor. He couldn't face the flat at the top of the building yet. As long as he wasn't 'home', he didn't feel the need to phone Kate in Brussels to tell her Ruth was missing. His wife was away on business and would probably be in meetings herself until midnight. With luck, the crisis would be over by the time he had to speak to her. With luck, he may not have to mention it at all. His marriage was a sham, a front maintained for the sake of the public images. They had barely spoken for the last three years.

He pulled the chair away from the desk and kicked his shoes off. With his feet on the desk he stared out of the window that looked out over St. James's Park. The sky was dark and heavy, the night hot. They had made progress today: the intelligence services were directing all their efforts at finding the culprits and the general consensus was that this was an isolated event. Audacious, effective, but isolated. Of course, Richard knew that it was not entirely a one-off; Ruth's kidnap had been somehow bound up with the plan, but even there there was no indication that further public atrocities would be coming. If the bombers wanted to kill more civilians, they didn't need Ruth to do it.

So what the hell were they playing at? Had the bomb really been nothing more than a distraction to cover Ruth's kidnap? Had it been a very public retribution for his support of airstrikes in Northern Iraq?

Or had it simply been to prove they could?

He read through the briefing he had been handed as he left the COBR meeting. London was volatile. Some rioting, a few disturbances. Reports were sketchy. He would receive another briefing in half an hour or so. In the meantime the departmental and service heads would deal with the situation on the ground.

He turned on the TV and, like millions of others throughout the country, wondered what was happening to his country. He got at least some of the answers by flicking between Sky News, the BBC's rolling 24-hour coverage and al-Jazeera.

The disturbances on London's streets had started peacefully enough. Crowds of protesters had gathered around the capital's principal mosques: Tottenham, Stoke Newington, Kilburn, Paddington, Shepherd's Bush. East Ham and Forest Gate inevitably attracted a lot of attention, as did the mosque on the Whitechapel Road. The fact that the mosques being picketed covered the full spectrum of Islamic tradition, and as such targetting many of them would be like targetting a Jehovah's Witness meeting to protest against the pope, was lost on those gathered together to make their point.

As the evening went on, the mob became more vociferous in their attempts to make that point, largely thanks to the convergence of two factors. The first was social media's ability to spread a compellingly simplistic message widely and quickly. The second was the coverage given to one man – a man who could make all the tweets and Facebook nonsense somehow seem perfectly rational.

Among its coverage of today's events, the London Evening Standard had run a quarter page op-ed by Professor Peter Lacey, a 'terrorism expert' from London University. His theories were nothing a reasonably well-educated member of the public could not have come up with, but the media loved him, largely because he was certain to provoke a heated debate.

Sky News and the BBC quickly co-opted Lacey into their news feeds. Just minutes after Richard had turned on the TV Sky re-ran an interview with Lacey that the anchor described as having been recorded 'earlier'. What he said could not have been calculated to be more inflammatory.

'Bombing incidents like the one we saw this morning are indicative of a new phase of Islamist terrorist activity,' he said, speaking half to the interviewer, and half to the camera, emphasising his key points by directing them straight at the viewer. 'And as our political institutions are paying lip-service to prevention, the real threat continues to rise. Since 7/7 counter-terrorism officer numbers have more than tripled, MI5 has doubled in size and the Prevent programme has ushered in a new fanaticism to find political subversion and rebrand it radicalization.'

'The security forces have foiled dozens of plots in the last three years alone,' the interviewer said off-camera. 'Do you not consider that a success?'

'Far from it. Like the McCarthyite pogroms in the US, they have utterly failed. The reason is simple: they are hide-bound by political correctness and bureaucracy and they have no understanding of the culture that underlies such political views. A quarter of British Muslims sympathise with the motives behind the Paris massacre and fully ten per cent state that the Charlie Hebdo staff deserved to be killed.'

'But the same survey also found that ninety-five per cent feel loyal to Britain. How do you reconcile these incompatible statistics?'

'I don't see them as incompatible. And even if ninety-five per cent of British Muslims do feel loyal to Britain – a figure which I would dispute anyway – that still leaves five per cent – in excess of a hundred and thirty five thousand individuals – who are extremely corrosive to our national values.'

'Stop now, you idiot,' Richard whispered.

'So what strategy should we be using to defeat this minority view?'

'These radical groups,' Lacey went on, 'represent the biggest threat to liberal democracy that we have seen in modern times, precisely because they have a belief structure perpetuated by their leaders that liberal democracy is incompatible with their faith. And faith can not be tackled from outside. It can only be tackled from within. The cause of, and the means to prevent, attacks such as the one we saw this morning lie squarely within the communities themselves.

As long as mainstream Muslims do not stand up and denounce what they claim is an unrepresentative minority, the situation…'

Richard changed channel.

By now, al-Jazeera had pieced together a cohesive narrative of events at the East London Mosque and were showing it like a mini-movie. Compressed in time, the events took on a terrifying inevitability.

Early in the evening a small group of protesters had gathered on Whitechapel Road, but did nothing more than talk to the worshippers coming and going from the mosque, sometimes handing out leaflets, sometimes walking a few steps with a chosen individual. No violence, no real attempt at intimidation.

As dusk had begun to fall, a coincidence of events quickly turned the mood ugly.

Feeling particularly under the accusing gaze of the world's media, the worshippers gathered in greater than usual numbers for Maghrib prayers at sunset. By then, most of the UK's TV coverage was interspersing footage of the bombing with interviews held with Imams distancing themselves from the event. But no one listened to the words, they just saw the juxtaposition of images: bomb/mosque. And Peter Lacey was there to make sure no one missed the point.

And into this mix came one final element that made riots all but inevitable.

Amateur footage taken from high up in a building almost opposite the East London Mosque at around 9.30 showed two uniformed officers pushing their way through the

growing crowds. Within minutes of their entering the
building and corralling the worshippers back inside for their
own protection, battle lines had been drawn. If the police
were protecting the terrorists, they were, once again, fair
game. Petrol bombs began to fly.

The situation changed so rapidly and on so many fronts
that the professional news crews were ousted from the
screens by amateur video, which was being uploaded to
Youtube and the like at a rate of almost two hours of
coverage a second. The news channels regurgitated the feeds
verbatim while the reporters tried to run a meaningful
commentary on the events. As with the Mark Duggan riots
in 2011, unedited rolling TV coverage was showing what fun
the riots could be. Soon reports were coming in of looting
and violence in areas with no Muslim population at all.

In January 2015 Paris had come together; now, London
was tearing itself apart.

There was a knock at the door and Jane Marks, his night-
shift aide, peered into the dimly lit room.

'Prime Minister,' she said quietly, 'the eleven o'clock report
has been collated. You need to see this.'

He motioned her in and she handed over a sheaf of
papers.

Richard's heart sank.

'Jane,' he said, 'do something about Lacey.'

'The Home Secretary put out a rebuttal half an hour ago,
but the news agencies are not interested right now.'

'Have him shot then. Or hung. Or something. We need
the treason statute back on the books. He's a bloody liability.'

He waved her away. As she closed the door he began to flick through the reports sent in from the police, fire and ambulance services.

Thunder rumbled overhead and the first big raindrops of the gathering storm pattered against the window. Richard glanced at the clock on the desk. 11:34.

The emergency services' reports confirmed what was already clear from the TV: London was in chaos. Major fires were being fought in Hackney, Southwark, Islington, Ealing and Tower Hamlets. Large crowds had surrounded an appliance in Gresham Road in Brixton, preventing the crew reaching a fire at a shop a few doors away from the mosque. Mounted police charged the area but were driven back by fireworks, bottles and bricks. The fire engine was commandeered by rioters and driven into a wall outside the mosque.

In Kilburn an Indian shopkeeper (Sikh, Richard noted) had been dragged from his shop and beaten unconscious while his shop was looted and torched. Ambulance crews came under attack as they tried to rescue him. Six Pakistani youths had been hospitalised in Forest Gate after a car drove into them near a shop owned by one of the men's uncles. A taxi driver and his passenger had been assaulted in Tottenham, just fifty yards from where another man had been beaten almost to death with a length of scaffolding pole. There had even been reports of gunshots fired.

The list went on, and Richard had no doubt that another would be growing faster than he was reading this one. Uniformed crews of all services were immediately targetted wherever they went. Police especially were taunted and provoked into action that was then filmed and uploaded, acting as a further call-to-arms.

The city was spiralling out of control.

Richard would have to address the House tomorrow. His own Backbenchers would call for troops to be deployed; the opposition would call for mediation and tolerance. Investigations would begin, plans to prevent the situation spreading nation-wide, reports and meetings, demands for extra funds, the whole circus of crisis management. And all the while Richard would be trying to keep the peace talks on course and the delegates sheltered from what was happening all around them.

He turned the TV off and placed his glasses on the desk beside him.

Amongst all the film, the talking heads, the editorial commentary being rushed out for tomorrow's papers, among the need to protect one side without infringing the rights of another, one person had been lost. Ruth was out there somewhere, made to disappear into the chaos.

And right now Richard would do just about anything to get her back.

14

Leila arrived at the Vallance Road crime scene at ten minutes past midnight, two hours after the shooting. Although forensics had been through the place, she still needed to see it for herself before any major clear-up took place. Context was everything. She had been in the office when the reports of a triple shooting and fire had come in. Lawrence considered it irrelevant, but Leila was intrigued. The crime was unusual.

Armed Met officers stood at the cordon around the building. A few onlookers braved the rain and stood watching, but with the cloudburst over this part of south London at eleven thirty, most of the rioters had melted away. That had been the police's first lucky break. Their second had been that fire crews were already on their way to the area when the flat went up in flames, so most of the evidence had been preserved.

Leila examined the front door as she passed. It was a simple blunt-force job, probably a boot to the flimsy woodwork. The ground floor was a disused shop that had not yet been investigated. Above it was the flat of the building's owner, one Martin Thomas. He had been taken to the hospital for checks and a little gentle interrogation. The last Leila had heard before going to the scene was that he was less than cooperative.

On the stairs up to the second floor, the scene of the shooting, she was passed by three forensic investigators carrying plastic boxes of evidence. Water trickled down the bare stair treads from the dead fire above. A single bloody footprint remained amongst the ash and dirt.

She stopped on the landing and looked around. There was another flight of stairs to an attic, which had not yet been investigated.

So this was nothing to do with the riots. This was one house in a row of houses; three flats. The first floor flat had been ignored, the top floor likewise. The middle flat had been specifically targetted. It was possible it was drugs, but unlikely. This wasn't a big drug area, and it would have been unusual for hired hit men from that world to do their calling during a full-scale riot.

She slipped on a pair of latex gloves and shoe covers and entered the second floor flat.

'What have we got?' she asked. There were four officers in the flat, and the question was directed at whichever of them was senior enough to consider himself qualified to answer it.

'And you are?' a bearded man in civilian clothing turned to her.

'DS Reid, CTC.'

'The big guns! You think this is terrorism?'

'You tell me. You are?'

'Inspector Colin Davis. As you can see, I'm not officially on duty, but Major Crime's spread thin. This is being handled as a firearms incident.'

'It's a start. You've got three dead, yes? Shot; attempt at burning the scene. Robbery?'

'You think there's anything worth stealing here?'

Leila smiled. 'Fair comment. So fill me in.'

'Three woman. Late thirties, early forties, Middle Eastern appearance. Each shot twice in the chest and once in the head. Hollowpoint, fragmenting bullets. Ballistics guesses…'

'Don't guess. It matters.'

'Ballistics says they were almost certainly 9mm. They won't know until the autopsy, but right now they're stumped. They've never seen ammunition that can do this much damage at close range without leaving an exit wound.'

'They'll be custom made or adapted from hydra-shoks.'

'Terrorists don't make their own bullets.'

'No they don't,' Leila said. 'Keep that in mind. Do we have identities?'

'Getting there. We've collected all the physical evidence, we're now beginning to trawl through what's left. Why's CTC involved?'

'They're not. You've just got me.'

'OK, then why are you involved?'

'Execution-style shootings are rare. Executions of three women are unheard of. This wasn't a random shooting, so I'm working on the theory that it could be related to this morning's events. Unless you have anything else?'

'Crazy boyfriend?'

'Are you seriously pursuing that as an option?'

'Right now we're open to anything.'

'Then you need to focus. There were two attackers. The boot-print on the front door is different from the bloody print on the stairs. There were exactly nine shots used in the executions.'

'Witnesses say there was a single gunshot, followed some minutes later by a sustained round of gunfire.'

Leila walked to the window and looked out. It was single glazed and looked out directly onto Vallance Road. Plenty of people would have heard the shots. Plenty had probably seen the gunmen.

'Right, so... two men – not more, it would have been inefficient – broke in on the ground floor,' she said, turning back to Davis. 'They mounted the stairs to a flat they knew, or knew of. They shoulder this door and enter the hallway. A single shot gets the women's attention. You need to establish whether that was a warning tenth shot or whether one of the victims was hit straight away. There'll be a bullet in the wall somewhere if it was a warning.

'There's a pause. That suggests this was not a straight-forward execution. The gunmen wanted information...

'They then execute the three women. Both men fired. There was no time for a gun to be reloaded, and while it is possible that an extended clip might have been used, I think we can rule it out.'

'Are you guessing, or do you know?' Davis said with a faint smile.

'A hit like this would have seen both men armed. Bullets were 9mm hollowpoint. These people knew what they were doing, so they're not going to risk a jam, which for quick-fire is a high probability with HP ammunition.'

A uniformed officer ran up the stairs behind them.

'Martin Thomas has given us names,' he said as he entered the flat's sitting room. 'Said there were two women on the lease, but he knew there were three living here most of the time, and a fourth who came and went.' He handed Inspector Davis a sheet of paper.

'Kalela and Nagham Chalabi, sisters,' Davis said. 'Probably two of the deceased.'

'He doesn't know the names of either of the other two,' the messenger said. 'Or claims he doesn't. They may have been illegals. The top flat was occupied by a single male, Faran Jaafar. Thomas thought he heard him knock on the women's door before he went out around nine-thirty.'

'Do we know where Jaafar is now?' Leila said.

'Not yet. Top flat's locked and there's no reply. He's not known to the police. We're trawling records, but if he'd been on the radar, we'd have found him by now. Immigration might get something.' His radio crackled and he excused himself.

'You still think you're needed here?' Davis said.

'Where are the bodies?' Leila said.

'Tagged and bagged in the bedroom. We're stretched thin with the riots, so transport'll come when they can.'

'I'll make a call, get them moved. We need confirmed identities as soon as we can.'

'What are you not telling me?' Davis said. 'You think these people were part of the group behind this morning's bomb?'

'When we know who they are, then I can tell you. I'm going upstairs. Alone, please. Give me five minutes.'

She mounted the stairs to the top floor. So far Jaafar's flat had not been opened by the police, and that was how she liked it. She could view this one fresh.

She crouched and felt around the black plastic bin-bag outside the door. It contained the usual kitchen detritus, but what interested Leila most were the cans. She tore a small hole in the bag and saw the distinctive red and gold logo of Stella lager. There were at least ten cans in the bag.

So that ruled out the first likely place Mr Jaafar might have been tonight. He had not got locked down in the mosque.

She had left her lock picks in the car, so she shouldered the door open instead. The wood was old and riddled with rot, and it might as well have been left open anyway.

Inside, a short corridor with one room off to each side led to a sitting room at the front of the building. A lamp was on, casting a soft yellowy glow up the hallway.

Even in the low light she could tell this was a flat occupied by a single male. The carpet was dirty, and there was a pervasive smell of beer, old pizza, a bathroom that had never seen bleach, and that underlying odour of maleness.

It was not, however, the flat of a pauper.

Against the wall was a bicycle, a Scott Addict carbon fibre thing that must have cost three grand. The back tyre was flat.

The door on the left opened onto a bathroom. For now, she did not flick the light switch on. Opposite it, under the eaves of the roof was a bedroom. Again, a lamp was burning on the bedside table. The furniture was old and scratched – probably supplied at minimum cost by the landlord – but scattered around the room were top-end clothes. Nothing too flashy, just quality: Hilfiger sweatshirts, Armani jeans, Nike trainers on the floor. She backed out of the room.

'Oh, sorry Ma'am, I didn't know you were up here,' a voice said from the open door behind her. She turned to the silhouetted constable.

'Give me a minute, will you? Unless you've found Mr Jaafar?'

'No, Ma'am. I'll let you know when we do.'

The constable left and Leila tried to get back inside the head of the flat's occupant.

The name was middle eastern, possibly, she thought, Kuwaiti. The wealth suggested it. Yet he wasn't working in England; there were no suits, and this was not an address to give a prospective employer. Student, slumming it a bit maybe – the pseudo-intellectual left-wing variety rather than the Islamo-fascist kind.

Kuwaiti meant Muslim, three to one a Sunni, but this guy was not devout. He might drag himself to Friday prayers if there was nothing else to do, but he preferred a beer. If they were thinking Islamist extremists for the bombing this morning, this man was nothing to do with it. She doubted he'd give a shit if someone made a crack about his beliefs any more than if they spilled beer on his three hundred pound jeans. He lived in that buzzy, youthful zone where everything was disposable.

In the sitting room was a single armchair, a coffee table, TV, dining table with two mis-matched chairs and a sideboard. Again, all supplied by the landlord. The right side of the room had been partitioned off to form a basic kitchen. In the light of the single lamp on the table it looked as if it saw very little use. There were a couple of boxes of breakfast cereal in the corner, a bowl and a plate on the drainer. The cooker was clean and there was no sign of pans or cooking utensils. He was eating somewhere else. University canteen? Take-away? Downstairs with his neighbours?

On the table, a laptop stood with its lid open, the screen blank. Beside it was a Canon G30 digital video camera and a GoPro mini camera. Two external hard disks were almost buried by papers, and a stack of political and cultural textbooks were piled against the wall. The iPhone – for there most certainly was an iPhone in this guy's arsenal – was missing.

Still wearing the latex gloves she had put on downstairs, she tapped the laptop's keyboard. The screen instantly came to life (latest version of the OS – the older versions never woke up this quickly). There was no password, so he hadn't intended to leave the machine unattended for long.

Scattered across a virtual desktop as untidy as his real one were files: PDFs of research articles he had downloaded, a couple of game shortcuts, and a few videos with numbers rather than file names. There were eight or nine folders labelled as containing more video files. She double-clicked on the hard disk icon and the main disk was displayed. She opened the icon on the right labelled Movies, and was not surprised to see dozens of folders, mostly labelled only with dates. She closed the disk window. The forensic techs could wade through this lot if it turned out Jaafar was worth investigating.

Her logical mind had already dismissed the owner of all this Western capitalist detritus, but her gut had not. He was nothing to do with the bombing, but he was something to do with the women downstairs – if nothing else, he'd checked on them before he went out this evening – and something had been important enough about *them* that they had been subject to a professional hit.

She opened a video at random from the desktop. It was small, probably taken at low resolution on his phone, not one of the cameras. It was a static shot taken inside a lecture theatre, showing more of the head of the girl in front of him than the lecturer. She scanned through the file, but it was just more of the same.

She tried another. This time it was an action movie, full screen, the camera just inches from the road surface as it sped along London streets. She had no doubt that if she went back to the bike in the hall she'd find a mount for the little GoPro.

The third file was taken in a park. The camera was hand-held, initially unsteady, pointing at a Jungle Gym in the middle distance. After a few seconds the image zoomed in on two little boys playing on the ropes. It held steady for a few seconds as one hung upside down, revealing his skinny white torso.

There had to be something, Leila thought.

But she was wrong.

Into the frame walked two women. Jaafar must have waved to them. They began to walk towards him, one slightly in front of the other.

Both were dressed modestly, in a style that suggested the influence of the middle east rather than a slavish adherence to principle. The front one – clearly a friend of Jaafar's – spoke to him. Leila did not turn the sound up. She could form a much more accurate first impression of the relationship between them by watching them rather than listening.

Both women were in their late thirties, early forties. The more reluctant of the two carried a plastic carrier bag with green vegetables poking out of the top. Both carried small handbags. They were not fellow students and were probably not old enough to be his mother and aunt. Jaafar said something and both women laughed. They were comfortable with him, at ease. The first was happy to maintain eye contact during their brief talk, and smiled freely. They knew him well, met him often, always in informal surroundings. There was none of the awkwardness that might suggest this meeting was out of the usual context.

There was a very good chance that these were Jaafar's neighbours from downstairs.

The first woman knelt down in front of Jaafar and may have made some comment about the camera. For a moment it turned away. When it turned back, it had been placed on the ground and the image was no longer that of an experienced cinematographer. He was just keeping the camera rolling because that was his habit. The woman's knees, tight together beneath a thin skirt, filled the lower right corner of the shot. Her friend also knelt down, a little further back, on the left.

Leila was about to turn the video off and go back downstairs to ask Davis to make an identity match with the bodies in the bedroom when something caught her eye. Quickly she hit pause and peered at the screen.

The second woman had moved her hands to her knees – a movement not of comfort but defence. She was nervous, of the cameraman or of his camera Leila could not tell. But it was what else that gesture revealed that made her heart beat a little faster.

On the middle finger of her right hand was a ring, crudely fashioned out of a key.

They'd got their bomber on film, and this time they'd got her face.

15

Keith Jordan parked his car some way from Martlesham on the edge of Broadwater Farm. He refilled the 7-shot magazine of his stubby Kimber pistol and walked quickly along the road to his target's building. He had been hired to do just the one job tonight, but things change. The message had come through on his disposable cell a little after eleven o'clock. Just an address and a simple instruction. One more job and another fifty thousand wired into his account in St Kitts. By the time it had been laundered out it would only be half that, but twenty five grand for a hit on some trash family in the Farm was unbelievably good money. Whoever his ultimate paymasters were, they obviously didn't care about driving a hard bargain.

He had taken James French with him to the Vallance Road job, but out here two white guys walking into the middle of a black man's ghetto might be remembered. Anyway, this should be an easy job. Get in, collect the goods, eliminate witnesses, get out.

He jogged up the concrete steps to the top floor. It was almost midnight. Thunder rumbled and the air was thick and charged. A couple of kids hung over the balcony walkway watching fireworks lighting the sky beyond the next block, but there was surprisingly little trouble here – they didn't party like it was 1985 in the Farm any more. One of the kids looked at him as he passed. He didn't care. The best description the police would be able to get would be *big white dude*. One white dude looks pretty much like any other when you're eight years old and black.

The target flat was at the far end.

He knocked on the door and listened. Footsteps inside. Too quick to have got out of bed. Whoever was in there was already awake. That could mean there was a whole bunch of them sitting around smoking ganja and talking bollocks. He slipped his hand into the back of his jacket and wrapped his fist around the pistol's grip.

The moment the door opened, he shouldered it, hard. There was a startled cry as he pushed on through, kicking the door closed behind him. He grabbed the short wire-haired woman by the throat and drove her back towards the living room.

'How many?' his whispered.

'Wha…?'

'How many of you here?'

'Just me. And my daughter.' She was telling the truth: the sitting room was empty. 'Oh, please, Mr, you got the wrong people.'

He took the pistol out and shoved the woman backwards. She tripped, but the first bullet slammed into her chest long before she hit the floor. He stood over her for a moment.

Stupid bitch. Should have brought your kid up to keep out of other people's business. Teach a bit of respect. He put a second bullet in her forehead.

There was a photograph of the woman on the wall beside him. With the gun still in his hand he tore it off its hook and peered at it. On the woman's left was a girl, fourteen maybe, thin, with her hair all straightened and highlighted like a Beyoncé mini-me. On her right was a bigger kid, or possibly – they say black don't crack, after all – her husband. Big face, big dumb grin, but keen eyes. He smashed the frame and stuffed the picture into his jacket pocket.

Someone screamed just behind him. A girl in baggy pyjamas, long straight hair, headphones around her neck, stood in the doorway blinking hard in the light. For a moment she just stared at him then turned and ran for the front door. In an instant Jordan was on her. He wrapped her hair around his free fist and dragged her towards the living room.

'Where's the computer?' he said. She tried to shake her head and pointed at the passageway leading to the bedrooms.

As he passed, Jordan kicked open the bathroom door, then the door to the first bedroom. Both were empty and dark. His third kick revealed the room he was looking for. Three computer monitors stood on a desk, their screens alive with rolling text. A single low energy bulb burned in a lamp, angled down on the keyboard. He shoved the girl against the desk.

'This all of it?'

'What?'

'This what you've been working on?'

'It's not…' she said. Her voice was tight with terror. He pushed her to the wall and smashed one of the monitors with the butt of the gun.

'Talk to me and you might live,' he said. 'I'm only interested in files that were put on here in the last twenty four hours.'

'I don't know what he's got. He was working on the print out.'

'He?'

'My brother. This is his…'

'Where is he now?'

'I don't know. He went…'

He raised the gun and shot her down through the right shoulder. The bullet was a custom low-velocity hollow-point, designed to be slow and extremely disruptive. The girl doubled over, clutching at her chest. Blood began to seep from her mouth. The wound would be fatal in ten minutes or so, but he could work on her until it was.

'He went where? Next door? The city? *Fucking Africa?*'

She coughed a glob of blood onto the carpet. Lightning illuminated the room and the girl flinched when a sharp crack of thunder rattled the windows.

'When's he coming back?' Jordan said. 'Talk to me.'

The girl was getting unsteady on her feet. He lifted her head with the barrel of the pistol and looked into her eyes. There wasn't much left in them.

'Shit. You're not going to die on me, are you?' He'd nicked something important with that bullet. Something that was going to take her out in a lot less than ten minutes anyway.

She coughed and more blood poured down her chin. A volley of firecrackers exploded close to the building and he could hear people shouting.

The girl retched and coughed again. Jordan stepped backwards, narrowly avoiding being sprayed. She gasped for breath and looked up at him with pleading, wide eyes.

'I can make this stop if you tell me where he is,' he said.

Her eyes grew even wider and her chest hitched as she tried to draw more air into her lungs. Her left hand waved in the direction of the window.

'I know he's fucking out. *Where?*'

Her hand dropped and she took a half-step towards him. 'Fuck you then.'

He threw her backwards and put a bullet in her chest and another in her head before she even hit the bed. In the low light the red pool that blossomed around her Beyoncé hairdo looked black as oil.

Rain began to patter against the flat's windows. He needed to move. He might not be in the middle of a proper riot, but he was in the middle of some wide awake nutters who could seriously slow him down, and they were going to be swarming all over the building in a few minutes. No one parties in the rain.

He crouched and turned the computer side on. It was in an old mac case: easy to open. He dropped the side and located the hard disk. With no need for subtlety, he simply smashed it out of its housing with the grip of the Kimber.

He heard footsteps running along the concrete walkway outside.

'Shit,' he hissed. He stood up and scanned the desk. A knock at the door. He took the external hard disk and yanked it away from its cable. He stuffed the pistol into his belt and a disk into each back pocket and grabbed the pile of papers from beside the computer.

He reached the end of the short corridor as fists pounded on the front door, much more insistently this time.

'Hey, you OK in there?' a voice called. 'Miz Shaw, you in there?'

The door was shoved. Jordan heard whispered voices against the background hiss of rain.

There was no other way out of the flat, so he backtracked to the first bedroom on the left. He slipped into the darkness, leaving the door open. If whoever was outside decided to come in, they would make a less thorough search of a room with its door left open than one that looked as if someone was trying to hide in it.

There was another knock at the door, then it burst open. As the door bounced off the inside wall, Jordan slipped under the bed in the far corner of the room.

'Hey, anyone home?'

The question was met only by another crack of thunder.

'There's no one here,' the voice said.

'That was muzzle-flash, sure of it,' a second man said.

Two sets of footsteps crept along the hall to the living room. There was a pause. Jordan could hear nothing over the sound of the rain, but they couldn't have avoided finding his first kill by now.

A shadow passed along the corridor. He slipped the gun

out and aimed it at the open bedroom door but the figure did no more than glance into the room. He had no intention of shooting these guys. He'd kicked the wasps' nest now. The more he killed the more of the bastards would turn up, and he had no way of outgunning or outrunning them.

He heard the door at the end of the corridor creak open.

'Hey, Bones, get in here.'

The second man jogged past. Jordan heard whispered voices from the computer room.

He had about ten seconds to get clear of the building before one of them came back out and started examining the flat properly.

With the stack of papers clutched to his chest, he ran from the bedroom and along the short passage to the open front door. Behind him he heard one of the men speaking to the emergency services. There seemed to be some debate about whether police or ambulance was the more important. *Bit fucking late for either*, he thought as he swung around the door and out onto the concrete walkway. He ran down the steps and along the road back to his car. Within fifty yards he was soaked to the skin.

He slammed the car door and beat the steering wheel with the heel of his hand. There was no point in waiting for the kid to come back. He knew what the boy looked like, but there was very little chance he'd be able to get close enough to finish him off tonight. If he was caught, the police would find the hard disks and the entire mission would go south. Prison would be the best he could hope for: anyone prepared to pay through the nose to get those disks wouldn't hesitate to erase the idiot who cocked the job up. He'd have to leave it. Hope. Without the disk or the printed evidence the missing kid was of little importance anyway. He might have read the file, but he wouldn't be able to remember it. Anything he could say would be purely circumstantial.

Sirens in the distance. He took the gun from his belt and wiped it over with his shirt. He pushed it deep under the passenger seat and started the car.

He'd drop off the disks, papers and photo then head out to Heathrow with the pre-packed case he took on every job. The gun would stay in the car and the car would be picked up from airport parking in the morning. Nothing could trace back to him. By 9.45 he'd be sipping margaritas on a flight to Miami.

James French could come back to the Farm tomorrow and try to find the missing kid. Just to be sure.

16

The attack on Faran Jaafar had been witnessed by over two dozen people. Only one of them called the police. Amid the jeers of S52 thugs and guarded by a police escort, the paramedics loaded the unconscious and bleeding man onto a gurney and drove him to the nearby Royal London Hospital. There his expensive clothes were cut away, his few possessions bagged and tagged, and he was taken for emergency cranial surgery.

They established his identity very quickly. Although he carried no wallet or identity papers, a call to the first person listed in his phone's directory gave them a name, and that quickly led to an address. The information, however, was not considered of immediate importance, so it was filed while the evening's main event was still number one priority.

Only when the storm broke at eleven thirty and the riots began to quieten down was the incident formally logged.

It took until 3am before a connection was made between the injured man's address in Vallance Road and the shootings at the same building.

Leila Reid arrived at the Royal London at 3.30. Jaafar was

sedated but his injuries had not proved to be life-threatening. A shattered orbital socket and severe concussion were the worst of his problems, and he was expected to make a full recovery, even if he would never quite regain his perfectly symmetrical looks.

Two armed officers stood at the door to Faran's private room. Leila flashed her ID at them and let herself in.

A nurse was adjusting the drip that fed sedatives into the young Kuwaiti's arm. One of his eyes was heavily bandaged.

'Can he talk?' Leila said.

'Who are you?'

'Counter-terrorism. I need to speak to Mr Jaafar. Now.'

'Whatever he's done, while he's in our care he's a patient. He's been through a lot tonight.'

'He's not a suspect. Please, I need to speak to him, alone.'

'You've got five minutes.'

The nurse pressed the call button into Jaafar's hand then left. Leila approached the bed.

'Mr Jaafar,' she said. The man grunted quietly but did not open his one exposed eye.

'Look at me, Mr Jaafar. I need you to answer some questions.'

His eye opened a little and he turned his head.

'Good,' Leila said. 'I need to ask you about your neighbours. The women who live in the flat below you.'

'Why?' he said. 'They were…' His eye drifted closed again.

'Mr Jaafar. Look at me. Look at me.' He did, slowly. 'I know you're in pain, but you're not going to die, so stay with me, OK? The women who lived below you…'

'They are nothing to do with this,' he mumbled.

'We're investigating your attack, Mr Jaafar. The police have examined your mobile phone and found the film of the run-up to it. We'll catch the people who did this to you. I'm here about another matter. What do you know of the women who lived downstairs?'

'Are they all right? I stopped by on my way…' He fell silent.

'Three of them are dead,' Leila said.

'What?' His one good eye opened properly. Now she had his full attention.

'They were shot tonight,' she said.

'You think I had something to do with it?'

'We know you didn't shoot them. Did you have anything else to do with it?'

He shook his head minutely and winced in pain. His hand twitched on the nurse's call button. Leila took it from his weak grip and laid in on the bed just out of his reach.

'Tell me about them,' she said.

Jaafar tried to sit up, winced again, and lay back.

'Kalela is a mature student at SOAS,' he said. 'We got the tube in together sometimes. That's how I know them. Kalela told me about the flat. Her sister did casual kitchen work.'

'Where?'

'She's been at Maroush for the last couple of months. Connaught Street.'

'And the other woman? The one who wasn't on the lease.'

'That could have been Ghada or Sireen. God… they're all dead?'

'Yes. Who was the other woman?'

Jaafar's eye slowly closed again. Leila was tempted to slap him awake but he spoke before she was fully decided.

'What did she look like?' he said.

'I can't tell you.' Leila had spent only a few minutes looking at the bodies, and as each had been shot in the face she had very little idea what they looked like. She thought for a moment then said: 'She was the one who *wasn't* wearing a ring in the shape of a key.'

'You mean Ghada.'

'Ghada was in the flat, or she wore the ring?'

'If she wasn't wearing a ring, it wasn't Ghada. She always wore it. I don't know why. She would fiddle with it constantly.'

'Did any of your other friends have a ring like that?'

'I don't think so. Why?' He looked at her again. 'I thought this was about the women who were killed?'

'We're trying to get information on all of them. Tell me about your friends, your relationship with them.'

'They cooked for me, did my laundry sometimes, shopping, that sort of thing.'

'And what did you do for them?'

'I looked out for them, made sure they were OK.'

'Come on, Mr Jaafar. They didn't wash your clothes and feed you just so you'd glance their way now and then. What did you do for them?'

'Yeah, OK, I sometimes gave them money if they needed it.'

'Money for what?'

'Food, rent, the usual.'

'They never asked you for large amounts?'

'No, a few pounds here and there. Why would they need a lot of money? Were they mixed up in something?'

'That's what I want you to tell me.'

'I don't know. What is this about?'

'Did you ever discuss politics?'

'Politics? Like what?'

'Like the situation in the Middle East.'

'Oh, right. They were Palestinians so you think they were terrorists. Is that why they would want money?'

'You tell me.'

'You're wrong. They were just trying to make a new life for themselves. Live in peace. They lived modestly, but none of us were exactly devout.'

'And what about Ghada?'

'I hardly met her. She was a friend of Sireen's. She was cold, very quiet. But she was no terrorist. If all you've got on her is racial stereotyping, I'm not sure she was even Muslim; certainly not one that gave any indication of adherence.'

'Do you have a last name for her?'

'No. I said, I hardly met her.'

'Not good enough, I'm afraid. Mr Jaafar, you really don't want to get caught in this net. If you know anything, you'd be wise to tell me now. We investigate your attack, you go home, everyone's happy. Obstruct me, things might get more complicated. So, I ask you again, what was her name?'

'I don't know.'

'Fine. We'll do this the hard way.' Leila turned to leave.

'Wait,' he said. 'I know where you might find out.'

'Go on.'

'In my flat, at the back of the closet that's built into the bedroom wall, there's a safe. I keep my papers and cash there. Kalela asked me to keep her and her sister's passports and so on. They didn't have anywhere to keep them and they were terrified of being burgled.'

'And you have Ghada's papers too?'

'I don't know. About a week ago Kalela gave me a brown envelope, asked me to put it in the safe. It had Ghada's name written in Arabic on the front.'

'Lock or combination?'

'Combination. 24-12-56,' he said.

'Thank you. We'll look into it. Someone will come and take a formal statement from you tomorrow.'

She left without speaking to the guards on the door and walked quickly out into the hot night.

17

Leila phoned DCI Lawrence as she left the hospital. She gave him the safe combination and told him she'd be there in fifteen minutes.

'We can handle that,' Lawrence said. 'There's been another shooting.'

'You think it's connected?'

'We can't see why, but the MO's strikingly similar. Inspector Davis asked for you and we can't spare anyone else from here. If it looks to relevant, we'll follow it up.'

'Where?'

'Flat in Broadwater Farm. I'll send the address through to your system.'

'What's the situation on the ground?'

'Still some running battles with the police, but not much. Seems most of it's come in from outside the estate trying to relive the old days. So be discrete when you get there.'

'Why?'

'The dead are black. Mother and daughter.'

'Then it's nothing to do with what's going on. It's just a drug hit, isn't it?'

'Davis says it might interest you, so that's good enough for me. Take a look. If you don't agree, come back. Just be careful up Kingsland Road. We've still got a serious battle at the Turkish Centre. Gangs of youths on both sides and our lot somewhere in the middle.'

'Noted. I'm on my way.'

She retrieved her car from behind the hospital and drove north. There were police road blocks half a mile from the Suleymaniye Mosque and palls of black smoke in the still damp air. Flames reflected off the buildings as she turned off the main road and made her way around the battle through deserted back streets. Without waiting to find trouble at the North London Mosque, she again took a slower detour through residential streets.

She arrived Broadwater Farm at 4.15am. It was mostly quiet, but if the gangs patrolling the estate's streets got wind of a double murder of two of their own, that could change very quickly.

She passed two uniformed officers guarding the stairwell and ran up to the top floor where Davis was waiting for her.

'Good work with Jaafar,' he said.

'They got the safe open yet?'

'They have, and they've got a name. Ghada Abulafia. British passport, decent but not extravagant bank balance.'

'Got an address?'

'No, but we'll find it.'

'So what have you got here?'

'Double execution. 9mm hollowpoint head and chest hits. Forensics have been in to photograph the scene and secure it, but they've not touched anything, except to put the light on in the bedroom. I wanted you to take a look.'

'Who are they?'

'Neighbour named them as mother and daughter Marie and Esther Shaw. Time of death is around midnight.'

'Anything in the files?'

'No, they're clean. There's a son too, Phillip, about eighteen. Odd chap by all accounts. Missing.'

'Kidnap?'

'He may have been in on it for all we know. Take a look at the scene, see what you think.'

Davis called the two forensics techs and SOC civilians out of the flat and motioned for Leila to enter. He did not follow.

The bodies were still in place. The older woman, Marie, lay face up in the sitting room. She was in her night clothes. Near her head was a broken picture frame and shards of glass. Leila peered at the glass. The frame had contained an ink-jet print and enough of the cheap colour had stuck to the glass to leave the ghosts of three faces. She didn't touch it; she didn't need to confirm who was in the photo.

Off the sitting room was a short corridor that led to a bathroom and two bedrooms. One was in darkness, but Leila could see two single beds arranged at ninety degrees along the far walls. The other bedroom was lit by a bare incandescent bulb that smelled of burning dust.

The daughter, Esther, was lying against the bed, again in pyjamas. One shot to the chest, one to the head. Leila leaned over the body. There was evidence of the third shot in her shoulder – the shot that got her talking. There were several pools of blood near the desk under the window.

This was not her bedroom. She would share with her mother and the brother would be in here. The only thing that suggested otherwise was that the room was immaculately tidy. There were no posters on the plain cream walls, no clothes strewn across the floor. The focus of the room was a long desk on which stood three computer monitors, one of which had been smashed. A computer stood on the floor with all the cabling neatly coiled and fastened together with black electrical tape. All but one cable went somewhere, no loose ends. An anglepoise lamp lay on the floor, its bulb smashed.

She stood for almost a minute staring at the desk. She could feel this boy, his obsession, the attention to an environment he could control. He didn't use the computers for work: the lack of any paperwork mitigated against it. He wasn't a gamer either. The monitors were small, mismatched, basic. The kit on the floor looked home-made, which suggested either someone with very limited means, or a requirement for the sort of system not available off the shelf. Or both. It was a classic hacker set-up.

She flinched when Davis entered the room behind her.

'What do you think?' he said.

'Not the same MO.'

'Head and chest executions… unusually low velocity bullets.'

'By a single shooter this time. There were two gunmen at Vallance Road.'

'Why do you think there was only one here?'

'Mother is in the sitting room. Let me walk you through it. I'm still calculating…'

She led Davis back to the front door.

'Door has been broken in,' she said.

'The call-in said he'd smashed the lock to get in.'

'That fits. So there was no initial forced entry,' she said. 'The security chain is also intact, which means when the mother opened the door, she was expecting someone she knew and trusted. The Farm has a very low crime rate now, but that still seems highly incautious. Who would you open the door to without precautions at midnight?'

'No one outside the family.'

'Exactly. So I think we can say the boy was out, but expected back. But the person she sees when she opens the door is not him.'

'Person, singular?'

Leila nodded. 'I'm coming to that. One thing at a time.' She walked back into the sitting room.

'Gunman forces Mrs Shaw back here, asking whatever he needed to ask. She either yields or fights back. Either way, he has no further use for her so he kills her. Esther hears this and tries to escape.'

'What makes you think she wasn't being held by a second gunman? She would have had plenty of time to escape between the attacker, or attackers, entering the flat and the final shot unless she was being held.'

'She's got headphones around her neck. She'd have been oblivious to the initial entry. Anyway, two attackers would have brought the women together, played one off against the other. The leverage of torturing one would have yielded quicker results. Ester was shot in the shoulder, not fatally, but it happened in the boy's bedroom.'

'So he grabbed Esther as she makes a run for it. After her mother was dead.'

'Yes. Note the single bullet to the chest. It's execution-style, but not the kind of overkill we saw at Vallance Road. Your assassin here just wanted to kill them. So he gets Esther and she takes him to her brother's bedroom.' She led Davis along the corridor and into the room. 'He's the key to this. Whatever the gunman wanted, it's something to do with the boy, and it's something to do with this room. And whatever it was, Esther told him, or as much as she could.'

'How do you know she told him?'

'Because it all ends here. She was standing here when she was first shot. Single to the right shoulder, designed to inflict pain. Your gunman is left handed, incidentally.' Leila stood against the desk with her back to the broken monitor. 'He then pushes her out of the way, against the bed and shoots her twice more, fatally. Very quick.'

'That agrees with what the witnesses tell us,' Davis said. 'There was a gap of about a minute and a half between the first and second groups of shots.'

'They heard them?'

Inspector Davis shrugged. 'The initial call-in was for muzzle-flash, seen from a flat over in Northolt tower. Witnesses closer in all say the same thing: they thought heard something, but they can't be any more specific.'

'Then they're being willfully deaf. Low velocity bullets, yes, but no silencer. This guy likes to work close up and discretely. A five inch silencer on a five inch barrel, he couldn't have got the angle needed to shoot down into her shoulder. Unless he was seven feet tall, and then I'd hope even here he might have been seen. *Did* anyone actually see anything?'

'This is the Farm – what do you think? They keep crime low here by dealing with it themselves, not by talking to us.'

'He was here maybe two minutes. He knew exactly what he was looking for.'

'Impressive. Any chance you can you tell me what that was?'

'I take it you're being sarcastic, but yes, I can. Or some of it. Look at the void on the desk. There's blood spatter, except here,' she indicated a clear rectangle near the front of the desk.

'Forensics saw it. There's another smaller void at the back.'

Leila shone her torch towards the right rear of the desk. There was a light spray of blood droplets, then a space of about four inches, then another couple of tiny red marks. She leaned over and saw a firewire cable slumped on the floor – the only untidy cable down there. The computer had been moved and opened.

'External hard disk,' she said. 'It's what we would have expected. He probably stripped the internal one as well; you'll have to get one of your techs to check.'

'But you think this larger void is more important?'

'Yes. There were papers here.'

'Or a book.'

'The boy doesn't have any books. The void is the size of

A4 paper. There's a fast laser printer in the corner.'

'OK. Paper.'

'Which is curious. A computer geek is working on a something: what does he need to print out?'

'Whatever he's finished.'

'No. A finished file has a purpose. It gets uploaded, or run, or shared. It's done. He printed something he was still working on, something he needed to see in black and white.'

'A complex bit of the programme he was writing? You think he needed to work something out on paper?'

'Maybe. It might just have been a to-do list. But it was important to him, and it was important to whoever shot his sister and mother. The gunman took the hard disks; he also took those papers. And he made no attempt to disturb any of the other equipment, other than to break one monitor, which would have been just to intimidate the girl.'

'Right. So the million dollar question is: do you think this was this one of the Vallance Road gunmen?'

'I have no idea. It does seem to be too much of a coincidence that the methods are so similar, though the motivation was slightly different. At Vallance Road they were fast, triple-tap executions. That means there was a message being left. This is more like aggravated burglary. There was no intent to intimidate other people in this community, just to steal the computer kit and eradicate witnesses. Plus, there's no obvious connection between the women who knew our bomber, and this family. And you say there's no sign of the brother?'

'No.'

'Canvas the area. This doesn't feel like a kidnapping. The most likely explanation is that he was absent throughout.'

'Rioting?'

'No. This boy's a computer geek. Most of his friends, if he's got any at all, will be on line. If he's got any political leanings, they'll be of the conspiracy theory type. He trusts his computer, not people. He won't have gone far. He's either hiding on his own or is being hidden close-by. And it'll be dawn soon. He'll move at first light.'

'We'll get onto it.'

'Right now. If this is connected to the Vallance Road shooting, it's connected to the attack on the hotel this morning.'

'You think he stumbled onto the identity of the cell?'

'It's the only thing valuable enough right now to kill his family for.'

'Why? Terrorists aren't concerned with anonymity. They'll tell us themselves who they are soon enough.'

'This lot are going to a lot of trouble to conceal their identity, and there's only one reason why they'd do that.'

'Because this is an ongoing operation,' Davis said. 'Phillip Shaw's a threat.'

'Exactly. And your gunman took a picture off the wall. He knows what Phillip looks like now. We need to find the boy, and quickly. If we don't find him before they do, there'll be nothing to stop them.'

Day Two

18

Leila was woken by a tap on the window above her head. She'd arrived back at Scotland Yard at 5.50am and had taken the opportunity for an hour's shut-eye in the passenger seat of her Peugeot.

Another tap.

'DS Reid,' a voice said. She turned her head stiffly and looked up into the face of DC Steve Jones. He was holding a paper cup of coffee. Reid wound the window down.

'Thought you might need a liquid refresh,' Jones said, handing the coffee to her. 'DCI Lawrence is coming in at eight.'

'Thanks,' she said.

Leila took the plastic lid off the cup and threw it behind the seat. Jones was a man who knew how to further his career in CTC. In the office she always took her coffee black, no sugar. Breakfast was the exception: cappuccino, plenty of froth and a couple of sachets of demerara. She took a sip. Jones would go a long way with attention to detail like this.

She drained the last of the coffee as she walked down the corridor to Commander Thorne's office. There were already a dozen officers milling around, and plenty more in the other offices she had passed on the way. She couldn't wait another hour for Lawrence to arrive.

She tapped on the Thorne's door and went in before he could stop her.

'DS Reid, I didn't expect to see you here,' he said. 'I thought you'd phoned all your intel in last night. Is there a problem?'

'I'm hoping you can tell me. Have we found Phillip Shaw yet?' she said. She sat down opposite her boss, again before he had chance to tell her not to.

'Shaw?' He spread the files on his desk. 'The second shooting…'

'Double assassination in Broadwater Farm last night. I said we needed to find him as a matter of priority.'

'It's… in the system. We're stretched thin on leads that are going nowhere.'

'Well this one isn't going nowhere. We need to get Shaw out of the system and into action.'

'You think he's something to do with this?' He opened the file and scanned the first page of the report that Inspector Davis had copied through to CTC.

'Yes, I think he's something to do with this,' Leila said. 'His family wouldn't have been killed if he wasn't.'

'But what's the connection? They're black, they're not Muslim, they've no political affiliations. They're just ordinary people.'

'All terrorist operatives are just ordinary people. That's how they do what they do.'

'You think the Shaw boy's part of the cell?'

'No, I don't. I'm just saying his ordinariness doesn't mean anything. He's not a terrorist, but I think he knows about them. I think he found something and someone needed to make sure he didn't tell us about it. We need to get to him before they do.'

'OK. I'll get the Gang Unit onto it. They're our best chance at Broadwater.'

'Let me know when they find him.'

'Your shift ended about six hours ago, DS Reid. You've done what DCI Lawrence asked you to do. I don't remember recalling you for today's shift.'

'My shift doesn't end until this does. We're closing in and I need to be here. So, where are we with the bomber?'

'Remember who you're talking to, DS Reid.'

'My apologies, Sir. Can you tell me if we got anything from Jaafar's safe?'

Thorne sighed deeply.

'His tip-off was good,' he said. 'Ghada Abulafia kept her passport and a small amount of cash with him, along with a bank deposit book with a balance of two hundred and eighty pounds.'

'What do we know of her?' Leila said.

'Immigration have confirmed she was a Palestinian national who came here with her father, Ibrahim Abulafia, in January 1988, age thirteen, claiming refugee status. She became a naturalised British citizen in 1990 and lived with him until 2006, working agency shifts for various hospitals as an orderly. She had an address in Wembley for six months, then left when the tenancy was up for renewal. After that, we've got nothing. She went dark.'

'For nine *years*?'

'Jaafar has confirmed that she spent some time at the Vallance Road flat in the last year, but was not a permanent resident. We've got nothing else yet. The murdered women may have known more, but Jaafar himself had hardly spoken to Abulafia.'

'OK, so they came here early 1988. That's the beginning of the first intifada,' Leila said. 'Where did they come from?'

'Silwan in East Jerusalem. It would account for the level of politicization.'

'Except Ibrahim emigrated. Hardly the actions of a highly politicized man. Plus they were legal: background checks would have thrown anything up when they were naturalised.'

'The father's background is murky.'

'Meaning what?'

'Just that. It's a sealed file. SIS deny any knowledge of him, but it's possible he was an informant. Either way, he's been a model citizen since he arrived here.'

'Are we giving any more credence to al Sahm in this?'

'It's a working title. SIS are reporting anything they've brought in on the ground overnight at the eight o'clock briefing. I'm assuming you won't be there.'

Leila looked at him but he gave nothing away. She wasn't sure whether that was an order or just an acknowledgment that she was working to her own timetable. Not that she cared either way. She had no intention of being at the briefing.

'So what are we doing with the father?' she said.

'His flat in Ealing's under surveillance. He's a cleaner for London Underground. His shift starts at eight. There's nothing in his record to suggest he knew anything about this, so for now we're just watching him.'

'Why not bring him in?'

'If he is operational, he'll clam up or give us deliberate false leads. Watching him is far more useful right now. Whether he just clocks on for work as normal or tries to make contact with anyone else, we'll be there. We can pick him up if necessary.'

'Come on. You can't kid a kidder. If this was anyone else, you'd have him in the cells by now. SIS are doing more than denying him, aren't they?'

'They assure us he's not involved. If we want any more than that, we'll need a warrant from the Home Secretary. My guess is even then they'd delay us until next Christmas.'

'So he was an informant. How interesting.'

Thorne shrugged. 'We're strictly hands-off. Of course, if he was ever working for SIS, it makes it highly unlikely he'd be involved in this.'

'I agree. Even if they screwed him over, this would be way out of proportion. Send his address to my cell. I want to go and check out the flat.'

'You might think you're still on duty, but I'm telling you, you need to take a break. And I expressly stated that I don't want you hands-on with anything sensitive. You're acting as a consultant for now, nothing more. Dyson and Page are on the ground at the flat. They'll go in when he leaves.'

'Dyson and Page'll go through there like a couple of

elephants,' Leila said. 'Right now, we don't want to spook him. If you're right and he's an ex-informant, he'll be hyper-aware of being watched. Get them to tail him. You don't want me anywhere near suspects, so I'll make sure I don't see him when I go in.'

'You are unbelievable.'

'But I'm what you need right now. Sir. Let me take a look at the flat. He'll never know I was there. I can get a handle on him if I can see where and how he lives. He's the only live link we've got back to al Sahm, and even that's tenuous.'

'What makes you think there's anything worth finding there? Surely if he knew anything he would have been targetted by the assassin too?'

'He may be on their list. Or it may be that they daren't risk taking him out because it would lead us to look into his family. They don't know we've identified Ghada yet.'

'Or more likely SIS are telling the truth and he knows nothing at all.'

'Maybe not, but there are two reasons why it's worth me taking a look. Firstly, you say there's two hundred and eighty pounds in Ghada's bank account. That's a decent float to keep you alive day to day, but not to run an operational cell. There's more money somewhere. Secondly, what did the passport tell you?'

'Nothing. It had never been used.'

'That's what I thought. She has it so she's got ID. But she's travelling on another one. There's probably a whole other identity.'

'And you think it'll be at the father's place?'

'It's a long shot, but it's the only shot we've got. Send a copy of her passport photo and details to my phone so I've got a point of reference. We need to move fast on this.'

'You still think they're going to strike again?'

'I've no evidence for it, but I'm sure they're planning to. They haven't done it yet, so they're waiting for something, something significant. We're less than four and a half hours to the time the first bomb went off yesterday. If they are going to strike again, that would be a symbolically powerful time to do it.' She stood to leave.

'And please,' she said, 'get Trident to find Phillip Shaw. He might just be able to tell us who al Sahm is, and what they're planning to do next.'

19

Raha Golzar woke in her cell in Low Newton Prison at six, exactly as she always did. At eight she ate breakfast, showered, then returned to her room. Same as always. She waited, but this time she knew what she was waiting for. If she was being moved, the unit's Clinical Director, Dr Penhalligan, was going to have to sign off on the transfer.

He arrived a little before nine.

'Good morning, Raha,' he said from the door.

'Good morning,' she said.

'Are you well?'

'Fine.'

'Taken your medication this morning?'

She looked up at him. 'I'm not medicated. I'm on anti-allergy drugs for my... challenged immune system, not anti-psychotics.'

'Your file says you're a paranoid schizophrenic,' he said with just a hint of a smile. Golzar just looked at him.

'Still not talking?' he said. 'Raha, I know you're not a schizophrenic. I know you shouldn't be here. I know Thorazine made you shake like an old man and flaked your skin quicker than the lupus. But I'd rather sign you off with a clear conscience than throw you into general population with the slightest doubt that you still need our help. So talk to me.'

'Do you know anything about my transfer?'

'Enough. Please, come down to my office and we'll have a chat.'

Golzar followed the doctor to a small, softly furnished office. None of the nurses paid her any attention. Never in fifteen months had she been violent or even disrespectful. They had even less idea why she was there than she did.

'Please, take a seat,' Penhalligan said. 'As you know, we've had a request from the CPS to transfer you to Holloway. You're to be rearrested, but your papers have already been marked restricted, meaning the exact reason is classified. I'm afraid I can't tell you any more than that. Hopefully your lawyer will be given a bit more courtesy than we are.'

'They think I'm a terrorist,' Golzar said. 'All very hush-hush.' She smiled.

'Indeed. And that's why I just want to go over your file one more time. What you said to me when you first came here was puzzling. We have never been able to corroborate any of it, and I'm afraid that's largely the reason the security forces have insisted you stay with us. I must say, your case is curious. Have you ever read 'One Flew Over the Cuckoo's Nest'?'

'No.'

He nodded. 'Anyway, in order to certify you of sound enough mind to be transferred, we need to revisit your statement. Which I am sure you are clever enough to realise might be a perfect opportunity for you to evade your trial, but…'

'I will tell you the truth. If nothing else, you've given me a lot of time to think.'

'Good. Then we'll start at the beginning. I'm going to work through your transcript and I want you to stop me as soon as anything I say troubles you. If you now think any of it should be changed, please tell me. OK?'

Golzar nodded.

'Your name is Raha Golzar, born 15th August 1973 in Qon, a hundred miles south of Tehran in the Islamic Republic of Iran.' He looked up; Golzar nodded.

'Good. Your mother was a nurse, your father an engineer, you were educated latterly at Tehran University, doing a masters in biochemistry.'

'Nursing.'

'Sorry?'

'I was training to be a nurse.'

'Really?' He wrote something on her file. 'OK. Let's continue for now. In 1996 you were seconded to a facility in Kazakhstan associated with a Russian military organisation called Biopreparat?'

'No. A nurse would not get work with the Russian military.'

'But you do know the name Biopreparat, an ex-Soviet weapons facility. That's real?'

'It existed. Iranian students are not so very different from any others; we were curious about the world. I don't know if it's still there now though. Obviously, I've never been there.'

'So you know nothing about bioweapons.'

'I know which end of a hypodermic to put in a patient's arm. Someone better paid than me filled the syringe.'

Dr Penhalligan flicked through the remaining pages of the statement.

'A nurse,' he said, almost to himself. He leaned back.

'I'm confused,' he said. 'Were you arrested here in Britain or…'

'Jerusalem.'

'Jerusalem. So that much is true. Why were you in Jerusalem?'

'Humanitarian volunteer work in the West Bank. I was taking a short holiday before the job started. You can verify my placement.'

'Not my job, Raha,' he said. 'I'm sure you'll be questioned more thoroughly in Holloway. All I'm here to do is assess your mental state. It makes no difference to me whether you were on holiday, where or who with. And to be candid,' he leaned forwards and tapped her file, 'it makes no difference to me whether what's in here is lies or the truth. If you're in trouble, if you need to stay here, tell me. They can not move you unless I sign you off, and what's in this file is a textbook case of paranoid delusional behaviour. If you tell me you still believe it, neither I nor anyone else can prove otherwise. Do you understand what I'm saying to you?'

'I was a nurse, Dr Penhalligan. And my mental state is fine.'

He nodded.

'Then can I confirm…' he turned his attention back to the printed transcript. 'The CIA have no interest in you?'

'Why would they?'

'According to your first interview, you were in Israel with their backing,' he said.

'Of course not.'

'You were never shot and kidnapped by British agents?'

'No.'

'And no one's coming to break you out of Low Newton?'

'No.'

'I really don't understand. You're saying this was all a fabrication?'

'I think I knew it wasn't true, but maybe a part of me wanted it to be. Maybe I believed some of it in those first days. I had lived my whole life in Iran. Suddenly, I'm in here. I'm in the West; I'm important. So yes, maybe I told you what I thought you wanted to hear; what I wanted to believe.'

'But you were really a nurse?'

Golzar nodded again. 'On holiday.'

'Then how the hell did you end up here?'

'Wrong place, wrong time, wrong face. I had a couple of days in Israeli-controlled West Jerusalem, that was all.'

'Can you do that? Move between east and west, I mean.'

'I did. The Qalandia checkpoint in Ramallah allows medical staff passage. Maybe that was my mistake. I guess someone thought I was someone else. I was picked up as a terrorist suspect and brought to England. Then they discovered I was… not entirely sane. As you saw yourself, back then they might have been right.'

'So why did you keep the pretence up? You could have retracted this statement at any of your sessions. You never said a word. To anyone.'

'I was safe here. I haven't felt safe before in my life. I thought maybe I could get political asylum. If not, even being here was better than going back to Tehran. Can you imagine what VAJA would have done to someone who'd spent this long mixed up with the British security forces?'

'VAJA?'

'Iranian secret police. Don't look at me like that. Everyone in Iran knows about them. Anyway, I guess it's time to, what do you English say? – "face the music"? I know I've done nothing wrong; maybe I can persuade your courts of that too. I might even be able to spin out my deportation long enough to grow old in peace.'

'Well, I wish you luck. They asked me to decide whether you're sane, and nothing you've said or done persuades me otherwise. I have to release you. To be honest, I'll be quite sorry to see you go. You've never been easy to work with, but you've never caused us any trouble.' He smiled and closed the file. 'I'll draw the papers up and you'll be on your way south by this time tomorrow. Is there anything else you want to say to me?'

'No. I'm ready. Thank you, Dr Penhalligan.'

Golzar walked to the door then stopped. 'Tell me,' she said, 'is this file going to used against me?'

'The courts can apply to have it released as evidence, but so far we've not had any request. As I told you when you arrived, this part of F Wing is technically a medical facility.

Our talks are confidential until otherwise authorised, and the doctor the government sent here for your first interview made no notes. Do you want it to be made available?'

'Until two minutes ago, I was a paranoid covert CIA agent. Now I'm a nurse. What do you think?'

'Probably best not. I'll make sure it disappears into the black hole that is the NHS computer system. Whatever your legal problems are now, they don't seem to have anything to do with this.'

'Good. Thank you again, doctor.'

Golzar was returned to her cell. She asked one of the new orderlies to see if the library had a copy of 'One Flew Over the Cuckoo's Nest', then dealt herself a hand of Patience. Her chess opponent had been hospitalised after slamming her arm in a door – intentionally – and no one else came even close to giving her a game worth playing.

She thought she'd played her interview it about right. Some truth, some lies, some of her original statement confirmed, some denied. Just enough to get her out and heading south.

But why had all this happened now?

If the British wanted her safely out of sight, what could they possibly gain by putting her on trial? The only logical answer was that there was no trial. They were keeping up the act of due process – legal transfer, access to counsel – but an act was all it amounted to. For now, at least, no one from Human Rights Watch would have her in their sights.

After fifteen months of silence, she was now a pawn in a new game, and other than Donald Aquila, she had no idea who the players were.

Either someone was trying to tidy up loose ends… or Black Eagle were operational again.

20

Richard Morgan slipped into the bathroom next to his office on the top floor of the Palace of Westminster. He had shooed his aides and various ministers out after a scant good morning and an assurance that his 9am address to Parliament was in hand. Liam Treadwell, his Head of Corporate Services, had passed him an anonymous-looking brown envelope as he walked along the top floor corridor five minutes earlier. There had been no sign of anyone paying undue attention, but he knew his caller hadn't been bluffing when he had said the exchange would be monitored.

Morgan had taken the envelope and put it with the other papers under his arm. A minister from the Home Office had been at his shoulder, bringing him up to date with the latest on the investigation, and his new SO1 protection officer, hand picked by the Met Commissioner himself, had dropped back a little. Richard dismissed the minister and looked over his shoulder. The SO1 man was talking into a radio. Was he confirming that the PM was safely at his office... or that the handover had gone without a hitch?

'Give me a minute,' Richard said. He slipped into the quiet

of the executive bathroom and bolted the door behind him. He took the papers over to the vanity unit. It was lit by fluorescent tubes, a light that made his face look even paler and more washed-out than he felt.

The envelope wasn't a bomb, and it wasn't anthrax. Killing him now would achieve nothing, and whoever was behind Ruth's kidnapping needed him alive to further their plan. There was no risk in opening it. He might still report it to the police, but he had to know what the demand was first.

He tore the envelope open, ripping the back of it nearly in two, and pulled out a single sheet of paper. He could see the ghosts of barely a dozen words printed on the other side.

Carefully he unfolded it.

Something fell into the sink and for a moment his attention was distracted from the text printed on the sheet.

Moved by pity and revulsion in equal measures, Richard picked up the thumbnail that had fallen from the envelope. It was Ruth's – expensively manicured and varnished with a subtle shade of pink that accentuated her skin tone rather than fought against it.

The nail had been ripped out. There were marks from the jaws of a pair of needle-nosed pliers in the varnish. They had done this for no reason other than to authenticate the message. If there was any doubt before, there was none whatever now that they would kill her unless he did exactly what they said.

He scanned the text.

It was a simple instruction. Bald, precise and shockingly easy. He'd expected something far more: the immediate repeal of a law, a high-profile prisoner pardonned, the revelation of clandestine military secrets. But this was not only easy to do, it was something that had crossed his mind as an option anyway. It could even be turned to the government's advantage with the right preparation and management. Whoever these people were, they had not done their research. They had not reckoned on the combined force of some of the best military, intelligence and police forces in the world.

'Prime Minister?' his SO1 guard knocked again on the door. 'Are you all right, Sir?'

'Yes, I'm coming.'

He folded the note around the bloodied fingernail and dropped the lot into his inside jacket pocket. He hit the hand-dryer with his elbow, paused for a moment, fixed a confident smile, and stepped out.

He could do this. He just needed to make the COBR Committee think it was their idea and not his. The fire service had attended nineteen blazes last night in Tottenham alone, almost two hundred across Greater London. Tonight was going to be the same. The Met police had officially launched Operation Orchard to investigate the cause of the riots, and the open sores that ran along racial and ethnic fault-lines would be inflamed again. London was no place for talks of peace.

So the talks of peace would happen somewhere else...

It was not ideal, but it was going to work.

21

Faran Jaafar lived in a dump, but at least his dump was on a reasonably decent street. Ibrahim Abulafia just lived in a dump.

Leila parked a hundred yards away on a quiet residential street and walked to the block of council flats. There was a burned out car on the grass verge in front of the single storey services building and half a dozen boarded-up windows on the ground floor. A council road sweeper was making slow passes up and down the far end of the road, collecting up the remains of last night's mayhem.

Leila checked her phone and made her way along the concrete walkway to the stairs at the back of the block. The lift had lost its 'out of order' sign, but the badly dented doors rendered it redundant anyway. Even if it had been in service she wouldn't have risked it. The stairwell stank of urine; the lift was probably considered to be a private cubicle.

She mounted the stairs to the third floor. A rash of newly sprayed anti-Islamic graffiti adorned the walls, the spray cans abandoned amongst the used needles and broken bottles.

A train rattled past and the building rattled in sympathy.

That could be the only reason Ibrahim stayed here. Its proximity to South Ealing tube station, and therefore free transport to work, would not have been enough for most people, but she guessed compared to his native Silwan, this was OK.

The lock was a simple Yale. Picking it would take no more than a few seconds, but she was not alone. A woman with a pushchair approached her along the walkway. Leila knocked on Abulafia's door and pretended to wait for an answer.

'He's at work,' the woman said.

'Do you know when he'll be back?'

'Tonight. Why you looking for him?'

'It's his daughter Ghada I'm after. Is she still living here?'

'Ain't seen 'er in months. Don't think she lives here no more.'

'OK, thanks. I'll leave a note.'

The woman walked on as Leila felt around her pockets for a pad of paper and pen she knew weren't there. When the sound of the pushchair bumping down the stairs had faded, she took out her lock picks and swiftly opened the door.

The flat was a tiny one-bedroom affair with the front door opening straight onto the living room. It was clean and tidy, with a minimum of furniture and very little decoration. On the wall above the dining table – already laid out for dinner for one – was a hamza, a five-fingered amulet popular in the middle east as a defence against the evil eye. On a 1960s teak sideboard against the far wall were three birthday cards. Leila leaned over to read them. Two were from friends – signed only with British first names – the third was from Ghada.

There was no note giving her father her current whereabouts, only 'Happy Birthday Baba, your Ghada'. A little stiff, written in a hurry maybe, but genuine.

On the opposite wall, over an old-style CRT television was a picture of Jerusalem. It was nothing more than an image cut from a magazine and framed in a cheap wooden frame with thin glass, but it was a beautiful picture. It showed the golden Dome of the Rock at sunset with the Mount of Olives in the background.

On the settee in the middle of the room was last night's Evening Standard, folded back and open at page four. A half page image of the search and rescue operation at the hotel was uppermost – the last thing Mr Abulafia had looked at.

He had no idea his daughter was behind the bomb. This was as much news to him as it was to the rest of London.

Ibrahim Abulafia was a modest man. There were a few books, mostly paperback novels probably picked up in his work as a cleaner on the underground or given to him by friends. There was no non-fiction, and nothing remotely related to his homeland. Other than the picture of Jerusalem, there was nothing that hinted at any nationalistic leanings. The lack of a computer suggested that he got all his news from the TV or the slightly right-of-centre, British establishment Evening Standard. He was not a political animal. His daughter had been radicalised some time around 2006 when she left this Ealing flat for a brief stint in Wembley, then an address unknown. She had not tried to bring her father into the fold.

She had, however, maintained contact with him. She

thought enough of her father to send him a birthday card.

She had moved around enough that she had been off the grid for nine years. That meant a stream of temporary addresses, never for more than a couple of months at a time, never putting down roots. Yet she did have roots, here in Ealing. She had only trusted her Vallance Road friends with her 'official' papers. There had to be more.

She opened the cupboard and drawers of the side board but quickly dismissed their meagre contents. Same in the bedroom. The bedside cabinet contained a box of tissues, an out-of-date bottle of Nitrolingual (the man had heart trouble) and a remote control for a TV that was no longer in evidence. She moved the clothes aside in the wardrobe and examined the frame, but again, it just didn't feel right. Ghada was clever: she was hiding her whole identity, not just a few pounds she didn't want the taxman to know about.

She went into the kitchen. The police often found small items hidden in the freezer compartment of a refrigerator. She did not expect to find anything this time, but opened it anyway. Ibrahim's dinner was ready for the microwave when he came home: a bowl of mashed potato, some carrots in a Tupperware dish and four slices of cooked beef in a sealed container on the top shelf. Other than a bottle of milk, with its top sealed with clingfilm, and some chocolate biscuits, the fridge was barren. The freezer compartment contained nothing but a thick layer of white frost built up over many months.

The drawers and cupboards likewise contained nothing out of the ordinary so she returned to the sitting room and stood looking out over the grass quadrangle at the centre of the block.

Would Ghada ask her father to hide papers for her? If she thought enough of him to keep in touch, she would surely think enough of him not to drag him into her world by association. Anything she had left here would be hidden even from him.

She did a slow pass through the bedroom and bathroom and back into the sitting room, examining the edges of the carpet for signs that it had been disturbed. These modern blocks of flats would not afford the luxury of a recess beneath floorboards, but it would be possible to hide papers under the carpet. While the walkways of the carpet were threadbare and tatty, the edges were still firmly attached to the gripper rods and even a close examination beneath wall-hugging furniture did not yield anything.

So what was secure from burglars, was not going to be disturbed by her father and was permanent enough that it would always be here when she needed it?

A faint smile crept across her lips. The Dome of the Rock.

She took the picture off the wall and examined the back. It was too thin to contain even a passport, let alone enough papers to furnish an identity, but what struck her as odd was the amount of masking tape that had been used to attach the backing board to the frame. She ran her fingers very lightly along the edges. In the bottom left corner she felt a slight bump.

She peeled the tape away from the board, a millimetre at a time, careful not to tear or distort it.

And there was the one thing she should have thought of.

Under the tape, tucked hard against the frame was a key, about two inches long and perfectly flat. The multiple teeth on the blade suggested a complex lock, something high-end, ultra-secure.

She replaced the tape and hung the picture back on the wall. She then examined the key.

On the shaft was a tiny four digit number followed by three letters.

3289GBI.

Gould's Bank Incorporated.

It was a safety deposit box.

22

Richard Morgan was driven back to Downing Street at 9.45. He fidgeted through the MI5 and CTC briefings in the ten o'clock COBR meeting. Lord Silverton was at pains to stress the nervousnesss of the Diplomatic Knights. These powerful behind-the-scenes figures were ready to call for the peace talks to be abandoned in the face of the current crisis.

Commander Thorne didn't make things any more comfortable with his report of the rioting the previous night. Three Territorial Support Group vans had been destroyed, seven officers injured unable to work and thirty regular uniformed police out of action. Civilian casualties were unconfirmed, but the BBC were reporting around a hundred hospitalisations. The trouble had been widespread, organised and extremely violent, concentrated around mosques but with increasing levels of looting and arson that was controlled more by the weather than by the police. They were expecting more of the same tonight and were bussing in support from surrounding forces.

No one seemed to have any good news.

Richard made a few notes. Burning his chest was the

kidnappers' letter and his daughter's painted fingernail, tucked into his jacket pocket with his wallet and the Montegrappa pen she had given him when he had been elected Prime Minster. What he would give for the resources that were being wasted on the riots to be directed at finding her. But at least he had another way: he could give in to the kidnappers' demands. He could let it play out, buy some time. The damage could be contained, minimised. Wasn't he sitting in a briefing about precisely how good the British security services were at limiting damage? After all, what had the kidnapper said? 'You've stacked the deck, all the time hiding your own agenda?' *Too damn right*, he thought. *And if I've done it once, against two of the most paranoid governments in the world, I can do it again. Then I'll grind you bastards into the dirt...*

'Prime Minister?'

Richard looked blankly at his Home Secretary.

'Do you have anything else to add?' Whitehouse said.

'Yes. I do.' He paused for a moment, cleared his throat. 'I want to hear your thoughts on how this all affects the peace talks. Cancelling is not an option.'

'We have increased security around the Israeli Embassy,' Commander Thorne said. 'Whitehall has additional guards stationed on the roof, both CTC and regular firearms officers. The Mission of Palestine is, I believe, receiving extra assistance from Five.'

'It is,' Sir Malcolm Stevens said. 'Abu Queria is already in residence and has been very amenable to having our agents within the building. The Israelis, not so much. Prime Minister Aaron David is due in this evening. His people are nervous, but we've not had any indication yet that he won't be attending tomorrow's opening dinner.'

'I'm less concerned about a specific terrorist threat than I am about appearances,' Richard said. 'The riots last night cast London and our government in a very bad light, especially as they were specifically targetted at Muslim areas.'

'I agree,' Emma Whitehouse said. 'I spoke to the Palestinian Ambassador early this morning and he feels that the mood has taken an unfortunate swing against his cause. The Israelis are inevitably being seen as the victims of Islamist aggression. And the US media are not shy about putting such a spin on it.'

'If we have the same tonight and tomorrow,' Richard said, 'we could end up driving the delegates right through what is going to look like a war zone on the way to the dinner. A war between the West, including Israel, and the Muslim world. It will make our government look both biassed – for allowing it to happen – and weak.'

'There is another option,' Whitehouse said. She opened a manilla file and glanced at the printed sheet inside. 'We always had two other locations lined up as back-up positions should security dictate a change of venue.'

Richard nodded. 'Mapleton House,' he said.

'That was our second choice.'

'Which means,' Richard went on, 'that it would not be an obvious target should al Sahm wish to strike again.'

'If we're still assuming that this wasn't aimed at the talks, a move isn't necessary, surely,' Thorne said.

'I'm inclined to agree with you, but as I said, this is also about appearances. A war on the streets of London is not an appearance I want to expose our guests to.'

'Prime Minister,' Stevens said, 'Mapleton's just not possible at such short notice. The conference starts in little over twenty four hours. It would be impossible do the necessary security vetting in time.'

'I disagree. All the staff have already been passed, and nothing need change there. We use all the same people, just in a different place. The delegates can be flown straight to Mapleton by helicopter. The house is surrounded by parkland so we can get even more security in place outside the building than we could have done here in the city. No one could get within half a mile of the place without being seen.'

'Except from the air. Mapleton's nine miles from Gatwick and seven from Redhill. We can't lock down air traffic and the risk's just too great of trouble coming in from the skies.'

'No,' Richard said. 'If Mapleton wasn't secure, we would never have passed it as an option.'

'It was an option if we'd had two weeks' notice!'

'Well times have changed! You have twenty four hours' notice. That should be enough. Does anyone else think that Mapleton's viable?'

'I think it is a very good choice,' Lord Silverton said. 'It's out of the way of any civil unrest, and whoever's behind the bombing will have no chance of getting another attack in place.'

'And of course,' Richard said, 'with your help Lady Thatcher almost bankrupted the special contingency fund turning the place into a fortress.'

'And you yourself installed Goshawk MLs inside and a six hundred thousand pound doppler fence outside.'

'Quite. So we should announce the change,' Richard said.

'And you think the Israelis'll accept a last minute change of venue?' Whitehouse said.

'I can deal with the Ambassador,' Lord Silverton said. 'MI5 will have to deal with Mossad.'

'We can sell this as an advantageous move,' Richard said. 'Mapleton's more secure than central London precisely because we've only chosen it as the location twenty four hours before the talks begin. If al Sahm, or whoever we're dealing with here, have any plans in the pipeline, they're unlikely to be able to change them as quickly as we can change ours. They caught us off guard yesterday. Now we need to catch them off guard. So, if there are no further thoughts?'

There was a general murmuring of approval around the table. No one raised any further objections.

'Good. We may never get another chance to make these talks a success, and Mapleton gives us the best chance of a conducive atmosphere.'

'We will look into the feasibility and report back to you by noon.' Whitehouse said.

'And I expect you to report that it is feasible. I'll brief our people, get things moving. Now, if you will excuse me…'

23

Greg Stiles was one of six Trident Gang Crime officers who were working the Farm that morning. He was the one who got lucky.

Ten in the morning was a bad time to be digging for gang intel. It was downtime for the dealers, pimps and players of that world, but Scaz Bones was waiting for him in the car park beneath Martlesham when Stiles walked in.

The Waterboys were just low-level drug pushers, middle men for importers higher up the food chain. And Bones was just a middle-ranking foot soldier. He'd had the misfortune to be arrested for possession of crack with intent to supply three months earlier, on the back of intelligence gathered by Stiles himself. The two had something of a history, but it wasn't all bad. Although Stiles was white, he had grown up dirt poor in a Croydon sink estate, and he had a certain sympathy, admiration even, for the likes of Bones. They were an irritating disease on the estates, but were rarely fatal. At worst they killed each other now and then. They only gave trouble when they got trouble.

Stiles unlocked the car door. There was a whistle behind

him and he turned. Leaning against one of the concrete pillars was a familiar dreadlocked figure. Bones stood with his hands in his pockets and looked nonchalantly out across the road. Stiles approached him.

'Let me see your hands,' he said.

Bones looked at him briefly, then began to walk away. Stiles followed across the open grass area towards the tower block at the centre of the complex. He stopped to tie his boot laces as Bones entered the building, then followed.

Bones was waiting for him in the recess beneath the stairs.

'Word is you're looking for someone,' Bones said.

Greg nodded and motioned for Bones to take his hands out of his pockets. He was almost certainly carrying a gun, and Stiles would have been happier if he had at least known which hand it was in. Bones let go of something in his left pocket and pulled his hands out.

'Seems you're not the only one,' Bones said. 'Some white dude was here 'bout an hour ago. Some of our guys let him know we were taking pictures then crowded him.'

'He's gone?'

'Yeah, he's gone. Any more come, we'll get them gone too.'

'You know anything about what happened last night?' Stiles said.

'Yeah. Some guy shot the place up,' he nodded upwards, indicating Phillip's flat. 'Our man tried to go back, but we stopped him. We got him safe now.'

'Where?'

Bones shook his head.

'Did you see who the shooter was?'

'Some white dude.'

'Very helpful.'

'Our man's shitting himself, says he can't trust none of you.'

'He can trust me. I've always played it straight with you.'

'With the Waterboys, maybe. We got no complaints. But our man ain't one of us. And he's got some big trouble.'

'So how do we get him out of it?'

'There was a woman came to his place last night.'

Stiles nodded. He'd seen the report.

'He wants to talk to her. Only her.'

'Why?'

'Because that's the way this is going down. You get her here, we'll make the introductions. She don't show, you think you'll ever find him?'

'I'll see what I can do.'

'You send her to my place, alone. Someone'll make contact, then if our man's happy, they can meet.'

'Keep him out of sight,' Stiles said. 'We need him.'

Bones nodded and walked away.

Stiles walked back out into the hot June morning. He hated the idea of handing this over to another department, but as he looked up at the towering building above him he knew that there was no choice. If Shaw had asked for DS Reid, they were going to have to give her to him. Even in the small area of the Farm, one terrified kid could vanish without a trace for years if he wanted to.

24

Leila parked her blue Peugeot between a Bentley and a Panamera on St James's Square off Pall Mall. There was very little to indicate the presence of Gould's Bank across the road other than a discrete brass plaque that had been polished so diligently that the words were now just ghosts against the gleaming metal. It had been clever play by the bomber: private banks were discrete and choosing a Jewish bank to hide her operational identity would have made her extremely difficult to find using routine investigations. The security forces would have been tied up for weeks questioning Sharia and western banks before they ever thought of crossing this particular cultural divide.

She had taken the precaution of requesting a search warrant for Abulafia's safety deposit box when she had sent through her report of what she had learned from her visit to the Ealing flat. DCI Lawrence had told her to stand down and wait until the warrant – and someone Commander Thorne trusted to do the search – arrived. Leila was not waiting. If the cell behind the bomb knew CTC were on to them that safety deposit box would not be safe for long. They could well have someone watching the bank right now.

She walked up the steps into the lobby. A guard dressed in an expensive suit and looking more like the maitre d' of a gentlemans' club than security nodded and bid her good morning.

At the desk – also polished to within an inch of its life – a woman greeted her. Leila showed her ID and laid the key on the desk.

'Is this one of yours?' she said.

The woman examined the key.

'I am not at liberty to discuss any matters concerning our customers,' she said.

'Did you see the warrant card?' Leila said. 'Counter-Terrorism. The owner of this key is dead, and the clock's ticking before whole lot more people join her. Now, is this one of yours?'

'I will bring the manager.'

'You do that.'

The woman disappeared into a side office. It was 10.37am by the clock on the wall. There was no way of knowing when the second attack would come, but it would be symbolically powerful if it was at noon today. Hitting exactly twenty-four hours after the first strike would underline the point that the security services were doing nothing to keep the city safe. That gave CTC less than ninety minutes to figure out where the attack might come… and stop it.

Leila was about to ring the desk bell when an elderly gentleman opened the door to the side office.

'Please,' he said, motioning her towards the door.

Leila stepped into the oak-panelled office. The manager sat down behind a leather-topped desk and studied Leila for a moment before speaking.

'3289 is a deposit box in this bank,' he said. 'But unless you have a warrant, I can not tell you any more than that. There is a reason people choose to bank with us.'

'There's a warrant on the way, but we're short of time. I need to see that box, now. The owner is a prime suspect in yesterday's bombing in Hyde Park.'

'I will be happy to assist you in any way I can. When your warrant arrives. Now, would you care for a tea or coffee?'

'No. Look,' she glanced down at the name plate on the desk, 'Mr Menkes, you are going to take me to the vault right now, or the blood of dozens more people could be on your hands. Time is running out.'

'I'm sorry. There's really nothing I can do.' Joseph Menkes shrugged and continued to stare at Leila across the desk.

Leila reached into her shoulder holster and pulled out her Glock 17 service pistol.

'Take me to the vault. Now,' she said.

'You threaten me in my own bank?'

'To focus your attention. Now that I have it, please take me to the box. I won't ask you again.'

'Very well,' Menkes said. 'As you wish.'

He led Leila out of the side door of his office and down a flight of stairs to the basement. She slipped the Glock back into its holster. She could do without the security guard spotting it and sounding an alarm.

Menkes unlocked a barred door and led her into a small

room, at the far end of which stood the huge circular door to the vault. He tapped in a six digit code and leaned towards the iris scanner. A small light above the door changed from red to green and there was a faint hiss as the room's seal was broken. Menkes hauled the door open. The inside of the vault was already lit.

'3289 is in the right corner,' he said.

'I need you to get whatever information you have on the owner. Everything: dates, times, accounts, images if you have them.'

'It is not permitted to allow customers to remain unsupervised inside the vault. You will be able to examine the box in that booth…' he indicated a screened desk on the far wall, 'but I must remain within the vault while you do so.'

'Then get someone else to dig up the file. I'll want it as soon as I've finished in here.'

'Or you will threaten my staff with your weapon?' Menkes said.

'I'm just trying to do my job. Unlike you, I don't have all the time in the world for niceties.'

She walked to the far corner of the vault and scanned the box doors. There were two sizes: 3289 was one of the smaller ones – eight inches wide, four high. She opened the door and slid out the heavy inner box.

She glanced at Menkes and slipped on a pair of latex gloves. Despite his insistence on remaining in the vault he was now outside in the corridor, talking to the woman who had been on the front desk. He held a sheet of paper in his hand, probably the warrant. Leila caught the word 'file' then the woman left. Menkes turned and stood in the doorway.

Leila opened the lid of the box. Inside there were three rolls of coins, twenty in each little skin of brown paper. She picked one up. One ounce Krugerrands, the most widely accepted currency in the world, coins of choice for shady deals from Argentina to Zimbabwe. That accounted for the weight, and somewhere around fifty thousand pounds in untraceable, liquid cash. At the back of the box were neat bundles of bank notes. She flicked through one of them: around twenty thousand dollars in used, clean fifty dollar bills. Four bundles of ten thousand pounds sterling in used tens, another four of twenties. There was well over a hundred thousand pounds in total. The box still had space for at least as much again, and Leila had an idea that until very recently it had contained a lot more.

The cash was impressive, but ultimately irrelevant.

What she had been hoping to find was underneath it.

In an unmarked envelope was a black passport: a US passport

She opened it. It was Ghada Abulafia's all right. Same photograph as the unused British one they had found in Faran Jaafar's flat, same date of birth and birthplace. The surname had changed to Mussan, but other than that only the number and issuing country were different. She had made very little attempt to create an alias. She had simply obtained a passport from a different nationality and altered her family name to confuse casual searches.

The only way Abulafia could have obtained such a passport was if she had dual nationality, and they had discovered nothing in her history to indicate that that was the case. This was not, therefore, a legal alias. It was an identity specifically created to enable their bomber to stay under the radar.

She flicked through the pages. Abulafia was a traveller, as they had suspected. There were stamps for New York, Chicago, and Los Angeles as well as a few for Washington DC. More intriguingly, there were several for Ben Gurion International in Tel Aviv, spread evenly approximately six months apart.

Ghada Abulafia might have been born a West Bank Palestinian, but she had found a way to move about freely in Jewish Israel.

And someone in the US government had enabled her to do it.

25

Daniel Peretz and Harel Cohen had arrived at Mapleton House just before noon as part of the Israeli delegation's security. They were kept waiting at the rear entrance for nearly two hours while officers from CTC and MI5 swept the building with bug-detectors and sniffer dogs. When Peretz and Cohen were finally allowed inside, uniformed Met constables were trawling the grounds around the building. Nothing out of the ordinary was found either inside or out.

Mapleton House had been built by Sir George Mapleton – he of the tobacco and slaving fortune made in the eighteenth century – as a country retreat. With crippling death duties in the 1960s it had been seized by the treasury and converted for governmental use. It was used for conferences, visiting dignitaries and meetings too secret or sensitive for central London. It had been a favourite of Margaret Thatcher and in her time as PM she had converted the vast drawing room into what was effectively a Georgian bomb shelter. The walls were reinforced with sheet steel and lined with lead to make them impenetrable to radio or listening devices. The windows were half-inch-thick toughened glass said to be good enough to repel an RPG. They had never been put to the test, and no one currently in the vicinity had any intention of having them tested in the next three days.

Harel Cohen had always been on the roster for the Peace Talks. He was Mossad, though his day-to-day work was done with the Embassy in London. His cover as a diplomat was good enough that his name had not been flagged by any of the security searches performed by the Palestinian delegation. London knew who he was, and having him on site was a condition of Prime Minister Aaron David attending the talks. MI5 didn't like it, but these talks would require bigger sacrifices of principle than that.

If the Palestinians would not have been happy about Cohen's presence, they would have been livid if they had known anything about Daniel Peretz.

Officially Peretz was with the caterers, a simple government man tasked to keep an eye on the food and make sure everything was Kosher – literally and meta-phorically. In fact he was something much more than that. MI5 suspected he was Mossad; even Harel Cohen thought he was Mossad. Only a tiny number of people in the very highest echelons of the Israeli Defence Force knew who he really was.

'I'm going to have another look round the kitchens,' Peretz said.

'You want company?' Cohen replied. The two MI5 officers glanced at him. They had barely spoken since the two Israelis entered the main building.

'No. I think better alone,' Peretz said. He slipped out of

the drawing room and along the corridor towards the servants' part of the house at the back.

There was no one in the kitchen.

Mossad had been using the same detailed plans of the building as the British, but they had a little more experience of the many and devious ways unwelcome visitors could find to infiltrate a building. There was something Peretz needed to see for himself.

He slipped on a pair of thin leather gloves and moved down the bare stone treads into the wine cellar so silently that even a stray agent in the kitchen would never have known he was there.

The wine cellar was just that: rack upon rack of bottles. Nearest the door were the cheap ones used for general meetings; beyond lay the dusty Petrus and Yquem bottles that were the preserve of visiting heads of state and royalty. Peretz never touched a drop, but his training was thorough enough that he could spot a fake dignitary by his choice of vintage from any of a dozen or more Grands Cru. Only a junior agent acting a part would pick an '81 Lafite-Rothschild off a menu if an '82 was being offered as well. Details: Peretz understood the value of details.

Beyond the wine racks was a second large room, now empty. This gave onto two smaller rooms at the far east end of the building, former cold-stores back in the days before electric refrigeration. He opened the first door and shone his pen torch in. The room was empty except for a few bundles of newspaper in the corner. The walls were all blank Victorian brick, leaching lines of white salts from the ancient mortar. He closed the door and opened the other one.

This room was whitewashed and had racks of wooden shelves against the far wall. He stepped in and tested one. It was not attached by anything more substantial than fifty years'-worth of cobwebs. On the wooden slats that once might have held the winter's supply of apples were boxes of bottles, demijohns, pickling jars and huge copper pans. None had seen use in decades.

Behind one of the racks was the almost invisible outline of a door, bricked up and painted over decades ago and detectable only because of the too-regular edges of the bricks where they met the old frame. Unless he had been looking for it he, like everyone else who had been down here, would not have given it a second glance.

He closed the entrance door behind him. With the torch in his teeth, he carefully unloaded the shelf and piled the glass and copper junk against the left wall. He then slid the fruit rack away from the wall.

He did all this with the same stealth as he had moved into the room, conscious that the slightest sound might be heard upstairs. This small room was directly beneath a wide corridor that ran between the kitchens and the drawing room, and on to the main banqueting hall. A dumb waiter in the corner behind the door confirmed Peretz's suspicions regarding the original purpose of this space. The Georgians loved their icecream, and it would have had to make the shortest possible journey from the cold store to the kitchen and awaiting guests.

With the shelves emptied, he took his Entourage automatic knife from his back pocket and ran the blade around a brick about five feet from the ground. The mortar was soft; poor quality in the first place and now rotted out by damp.

He worked the tip of the blade into the mortar for several minutes. He sliced it through all around the brick then dug out a small hole at each end. Dust and flakes of paint rained onto the floor. He stopped, allowing the complete silence of this underground world to resume. Then he eased the tips of his fingers into the tiny holds and began to draw the brick out.

It took him almost three minutes to get it free.

The 1978 plans the National Trust had drawn up showed this wall as being completely solid. Mossad had got hold of much earlier plans that MI5 had either not found or had considered so out of date as to be irrelevant, and even these showed only a gap in the brickwork, not what lay beyond.

None of this part of the cellar had been used since the 1930s, and as Peretz shone his torch through the hole he had made, he saw why.

The old doorway led into a tunnel, about two feet wide and five feet high. It had collapsed and he could see no more than six feet into it before the rubble completely filled the space. Not even the faintest trickle of a draft came through the blockage.

This abandoned and derelict tunnel, shown only on the very earliest, hand-drawn building plans, led to an icehouse about four hundred yards away, buried deep in a wood. Ice would have been brought from there to the house where it could either be used or transferred up through the dumb waiter to the kitchens or reception rooms above.

Peretz nodded to himself and slid the brick back into place. It was a snug fit: not invisible, but tidy. With the torch still in his mouth he moved the shelves back into place and left the room, aware that by now his long absence might have been noted.

He met one of the MI5 officers in the grand entrance hall a couple of minutes later.

'What's perimeter security like?' Peretz said without preamble.

The MI5 man looked at him.

'We're on the same team,' he said. 'I want to know no one is going to sneak up on us. You've got heavy woodland cover less than four hundred yards away.'

'Fifteen of our people will be patrolling the grounds twenty four hours a day, plus uniformed Met police, high profile. ASU with infra-red in the air when the delegates arrive. If a mouse breaks cover, they'll see it.'

'Tech?'

'Doppler microwave sensors ringing the area.'

'You're using fast-switching quad wireless?'

'Unofficially. You know your stuff.'

'I live in Tel Aviv; it pays to. Main gate's the only way in or out?'

'Yes, heavily guarded. And before you ask, water comes in through a four-inch main. Sewage goes out through six-inch pipes to a fifteen thousand gallon septic tank under the rear lawn. Air's covered by radar, anti-aircraft guns and two Typhoons on standby. Apart from the jets, everything's within the sensor perimeter, so it's tamper-proof.'

'And there's no way it can be bypassed?'

'Shit, were you born this paranoid or is it just practise? No, it can't be bypassed, unless you can hack the government mainframes. The protocols are switched randomly every thirty minutes with four-core overlaps. You'd need a computer faster and smarter than anything commercially available to get round it, and someone to drive it. No, the perimeter's secure. And even if anyone could get past it, we've got the best security devices in the world inside the building.'

'Your famous Goshawk MLs?'

'No. These.' He pointed at his own eyes and turned to go. Peretz watched him jog down the wide stone steps to the drive.

Pride before a fall, he thought. *Pride before a fall*. He actually had a lot of respect for British intelligence, as far as it went. It just wasn't far enough for his taste.

Peretz himself had been schooled in a much tougher way of working. After national service he had signed on as a regular in the IDF and quickly risen through the ranks to a point where he had to start lying to his family about just how he spent his days. At twenty-eight he was recruited into Sayeret Matkal, a Special Forces unit not unlike the British SAS or the US Deltas only with fewer screw-ups. For six years he had worked around the world tasked with counter-terrorism and hostage rescue. Then he had been head-hunted again and life started to get very interesting indeed. To the very few people with whom he could talk freely he was part of Kidon – a unit of secret service spooks who specialised in simply assassinating the bad guys rather than waiting to rescue the good ones.

But even that was only part of the story.

As the British agent's black BMW crunched away down the drive, Peretz walked along the front of the building. The afternoon was hot and unpleasant – not the dry heat of Tel Aviv, but the clammy, stifling heat of an island under an approaching front. There would be another storm tonight.

Checking the locations of the uniformed officers who were wandering somewhat aimlessly around the croquet lawn or standing on the ha-ha watching swallows soar and dive over the meadow beyond, Peretz walked along the edge of the camelia borders towards the woods in the distance.

The wood was old growth, a mixture of ash and oak, and not natural. The trees were all the same age, most likely planted to give the impression of a royal hunting forest for the delight of guests at the house. It would also have been a very good shelter for the ice house.

All the ground plans showed the presence of the ice house, but even the earliest ones Mossad had sourced gave it only as a vague spot some twenty yards beyond the edge of the wood. That was not a problem; finding it was not Peretz's concern. He just needed to be sure that no one *else* would find it. He wandered through the trees, constantly checking vantage points, views of the house, sight lines to the various security men patrolling the grounds. He knew he must still be inside the ring of doppler motion sensors: had he strayed over the invisible line there would already be a shit-storm rumbling up the slope towards him. That was good. The ice house, wherever it was, was as protected from intrusion as the main house itself.

After fifteen minutes picking his way through the trees he came to a fence with wheat fields beyond. He must have passed right over the hidden structure without seeing it. And if he hadn't found a single clue as to its position, no one else would either.

He walked slowly back to the house.

Cohen asked him why he had been poking around so far from the house when he was detailed to look after the catering arrangements, but Peretz just said he needed some air. Nothing to be concerned about.

Everything was just as it should have been.

26

Commander Thorne was waiting for Leila when she arrived back at the CTC offices at Scotland Yard. The operations room was alive with activity. The junior detective who had brought the warrant to the bank took one look at his boss and quietly slipped into a side room.

'DS Reid,' Thorne said, 'my office. Now.'

He led her into the glass office and closed the door.

'I've got the passport,' she said. She placed the evidence bag on her boss's desk.

'That's what I wanted to speak to you about. No, remain standing, DS Reid.' He sat behind his desk and consulted a pile of papers.

'Half an hour ago I received a call from a Mr Joseph Menkes at Gould's Bank.'

'OK...'

'Anything I should know?'

'Like what?'

'He said you threatened him with a gun.'

Leila did not reply.

'Is this true?'

'Menkes was obstructing a time-sensitive search,' she said. 'He was aware of who I was and what my reasons were for visiting the bank but he refused to cooperate.'

'He was waiting for the warrant. That is his legal right.'

'I told him the warrant was on the way and asked him to show me the suspect's safety deposit box. He refused. I had reason to believe that he was stalling in order to obstruct my search. It was a Section 17 judgement.'

'You were only preventing serious damage to a person or property if your outlandish theory about another attack is correct. Which so far no one in this building believes it is. Any defence lawyer will rip you to shreds!'

'The warrant was on the way, and reasonable force is permitted by TACT Section 114.2'

'You threatened to shoot him!'

'No. I drew my weapon, with the safety on at all times, to focus his attention.'

'And you've blown the whole of that side of the operation! That was an illegal search. Any evidence you gathered will be inadmissible.'

'I disagree, Sir. I saw Menkes in the corridor outside the vault with the warrant in his hand before I opened the safety deposit box. My actions in his office enabled me to access the vault more quickly, but the warrant enabled me to make the specific search.'

'DS Reid, you are on very thin ice. Against my better judgement I allowed DCI Lawrence to bring you in on the peripheries of this investigation. You're given a lot of leeway because you're a talented investigator, but with this Menkes business you've shown yet again that you're a liability to sensitive cases. You've screwed up an investigation before because of your disregard for the law. I won't stand in the way of a prosecution if you've done it again now.'

'Understood. Did my intelligence lead to discovering who in the US government has been helping Abulafia?'

'Harris and Field are on their way to the Embassy now. They're meeting with the Special U.S. Liaison Officer.'

'Special Liaison? CIA?'

'Unofficially.'

'I need to be there.'

'No. DS Reid, you need to take a break. Go home.'

'Not when we're this close, Sir.'

'It's not a request. Get some rest. Your imaginary noon deadline has passed and there's been no further attack. Come back tomorrow, and I'll reassess your position. The peace talks have been moved to Mapleton House; we're going to need all the bodies we can get to cover it.'

'They've been moved? Why?'

'Downing Street decision.'

'That doesn't make any sense. They can't have done proper security checks.'

'We work with what we've got, DS Reid. The PM's happy, so we've just got to make sure he stays that way.'

'No. There's more to it than that. There has to be. There must be a connection between yesterday's events and this sudden change of venue.'

'There is! The PM's got nervous about exposing his guests to any danger in the city.'

'Do you really believe that?'

'It's not about what we believe. It's about working with what we know.'

'Al Sahm are going to attack the peace talks.'

'Then they're going to have opposition. We've got CTC and MI5 in there, as well as uniforms. The Palestinians and Israelis are bringing their own people too. Mapleton's far more secure than London was.'

'And this was a decision made by the PM's office?'

'It was decided collectively through COBR. I was there. If there's a plot, then everyone's in on it: our own security services, government, the PM, diplomatic corps... though strangely I seem to have been left out of the loop. I think you're right that the attack was aimed at disrupting the talks, but al Sahm have showed their hand too soon. They've created a problem for us, but if anything they've focussed attention on how important it is that the talks succeed.'

'Maybe.'

'Definitely.'

'I want to talk to Jaafar again,' Leila said. She sat down; Commander Thorne did not stop her. 'He led us to the passport; he may have more useful information that he doesn't realise is important.'

'Jaafar's dead.'

'What?'

'He was killed this morning.'

'How? We had an armed guard on the door!'

'But no one thought to check the food. The doctors can't say for certain until after to post-mortem, but they think someone managed to spike his breakfast with Xarelto. He suffered a massive brain haemorrhage and there was nothing anyone could do to stop it. Warfarin they could have flushed; the effect of this stuff's impossible to reverse.'

'Professional job. But how the hell did they know where he was? We made the connection between him and Abulafia, and as soon as we did he was locked down.'

'We have no idea. Again, it seems they were one step ahead of us.'

'Then we need to move faster. Did you get anywhere with finding Phillip Shaw?' Leila said.

'Trident are down there now. If he's there, they'll bring him in.'

'Anything on his computer?'

'Nothing of any use. The hard disk was missing. Forensics techs say there were fragments captured on a RAM drive when the machine was destroyed, but nothing that leads anywhere. Cyber Crime hasn't found anything that ties him to yesterday's events.'

'They will. Whatever he was doing, he's got enough that someone killed his family.'

'Until we find him, we can't say more than it is a coincidence. Probably a case of mistaken identity. You know what the Farm's like. The gunman could have got the buildings mixed up, or misread the flat number, anything.'

'Then why did he take papers from Shaw's desk?'

'We don't know, and we're not in the business of guessing.'

'I'd like to see him when he gets here.'

'Reid, go home. You're seeing conspiracies where there

aren't any. We've got people here who can interview Shaw.'

The phone on Thorne's desk rang. Leila stood to leave but he held a finger up at her.

'Yes?'

His brow furrowed as he listened. He glanced up at Leila then wrote a few words on the notepad on his desk.

'What? That was over three hours ago...' he said. 'No, you send intel up here and let *us* decide what's relevant!'

There was a long pause while Thorne listened again.

'I'll send someone over, if it's not too late,' he said and put the phone down.

'Trident *have* found Phillip Shaw.'

'Good. I guess I'll be staying then.'

Thorne looked at her across the desk.

'What?' Leila said.

'The Waterboys have got him hidden. Apparently he says he'll only talk to you.'

'Why me?'

'God knows. Is there something else I should know, Reid?'

'He must have seen me in the flat last night. He must have been within sight of us all the time.'

'And you're not exactly discrete. Anyway, Stiles's contact insists the boy has something worth hearing after all.'

'You said they found him over three hours ago.'

'Somehow the report ended up in Major Crime as a low priority. They only got to it ten minutes ago.'

'Give me the address...'

'I seriously doubt your ability to handle this, DS Reid. No, I'll send someone else. He'll come.'

'Yes, I'm sure he will, but it'll take longer. We don't have time to negotiate and we can't exactly arrest him. I'll go. If he's asking for me, then it's the quickest way.'

'OK. But I'm warning you, Reid: stick to protocol. If you mess up once more, you'll be off active duty for so long the next time you set foot in here will be for your retirement party. Are we clear?'

'Yes, Sir.'

'Go and get Shaw. Bring him here. Nothing more. Then go home.' He handed Leila the note from his desk. 'This is the address. Ask for Scaz Bones and he'll take you to Shaw. I'll expect you back within the hour.'

'Yes, Sir.'

'And DS Reid,' Lawrence said. 'Leave your gun here. Bones is gang material. You go in there armed you're likely to start another war. God knows, we're going to see enough of that again tonight as it is.'

'Understood.'

She turned to leave.

'DS Reid,' he said.

'Sir?'

'Have you spoken to anyone outside this investigation about what's going on?'

'Like who?'

'The press? Bloggers? Your Facebook friends?'

'Of course not. And I don't have Facebook friends. Mark Ross still has to show me how to do email.'

'Then you know nothing about this?' He motioned her round to his side of the desk and brought an image up on his computer. It was a gruesome photograph of – Leila assumed – one of the three people who had been killed on the bus outside the hotel. A shard of plate glass still protruded from the victim's neck and her eyes were open in a look of mute shock. Death must have been instant. The image itself was shocking, but it had been altered before being posted online. Someone had added the words '*This is Islam*' in quasi-Arabic script.

'You seriously think I'd do something like that?' she said.

'Not the wording, no. But this is a forensic photograph. No one outside this investigation has access to the digital archive.'

'I didn't leak it, if that's what you're driving at. I've never even seen the Scene of Crime stuff.'

'OK.' He closed the image. 'You know why I ask.'

'Of course. I'm going to be your prime suspect for the rest of my career, aren't I?'

'Go and get Shaw, DS Reid. Then clock off.'

'Sir.'

Leila left the office and walked quickly to the stairs.

She did not check in her gun.

27

Leila parked in the same car park beneath Martlesham that Stiles had left a few hours earlier and walked across the open green space to the Northolt tower block. A group of men sat by a low wall passing a two-litre plastic bottle of cider around. One, a white skin-head who looked about sixty but may have been in his twenties, eyed her suspiciously as she passed.

It was stultifyingly hot: ninety degrees and high humidity. The sky was so pale it was almost white. What little breeze there was only made it worse.

She walked slowly, sure that she was being watched. She doubted she would make it as far as the address she had been given. In their own way, the gangs were as cautious as the police, never giving full information where partial would do the job.

She began to climb the stairs. A couple of black men passed her going down but did no more than glance at her. Despite the heat she kept her thin leather coat closed to conceal the gun nestled under her left arm. She wore nothing else that would identify as her police, though she knew people around here had a sixth sense for anyone who was not their own.

She reached the address she had been given on the sixth floor and still no one had approached her. She banged on the door and waited.

It was almost three o'clock, some five hours since Stiles had first made contact with Scaz Bones. Shaw had probably been moved. The Waterboys would not risk the fact that the delay in getting anyone out here might mean trouble for them and the boy.

She banged again but there was no sound of movement within the flat.

After another thirty seconds, she turned and retraced her steps down the stairs and out across the open area between Northolt and Shaw's home block. She reached her car and wondered what to do now. She could not leave without him – he was their best lead right now. She was about to get back into the car to phone Lawrence to tell him she would be delayed when there was a rush of footsteps behind her.

She didn't even have time to turn around. A hand grabbed her around the mouth and she was hauled backwards towards the stairwell. She tried to kick out behind her, but she was moving so fast that she could get no backwards momentum.

She and her attacker came to a stop against a wall and a hand reached deftly into her jacket and stripped the gun from its holster. She was pushed forwards and turned to find herself looking at a short, very dark-skinned boy of about fifteen, pointing the gun at her head. He had already clicked the safety off.

'You Reid?' he said.

Leila nodded.

'You come alone?'

Again she nodded.

The boy looked indecisive. He waved the gun in the direction of the stairwell and Leila walked into the enclosed space that led up to the flats above.

'Stop there,' the boy said.

'I've come for Phillip Shaw,' Leila said. 'I was given an address for a man called Scaz Bones. Is that you?'

'No. Why you bring a piece?'

'I'm counter-terrorism. We always carry a gun.'

'You ever kill anyone?'

'Not yet.' Leila looked him in the eye. The kid was doing his best to look intimidating, but neither of them was fooled. 'I'm not here to cause trouble. Just take me to Bones. Shaw asked for me specifically.'

'Gimme your mobile and radio.'

'Here.' Leila slowly took her mobile phone from her jacket pocket and handed it over.

'This all you got?'

'Yes.' She opened her jacket then ran her fingers through her hair to show she was not wearing an earpiece. 'The radio's in the car.'

The boy removed the battery and sim card from the phone and slipped the lot into this jeans pocket.

'This is a lot of trouble for one lost kid,' Leila said.

'He got himself in some bad CIA shit or something.'

'I'm British police. We're your friends.'

'You ain' my friend, bitch. Now go back up where you came. Bones's waiting.'

'What about my stuff?'

'I'll send it over when we clear you're alone. Now get going.'

Leila jogged across the area between the buildings and up the stairs. This time when she banged on the door it opened immediately.

'Come in,' the man said.

'You Bones?'

He nodded. He was tall, skeletally thin, with long dreads in a bunch down his back and a straggly beard that failed to be entirely convincing. He looked about thirty.

'What the hell was all that about?' Leila said. 'You ask to see me then give me that shit?'

'We just checkin you came alone. Checkin you not *talking* to anyone. Our man's nervous, and that makes us nervous, yeah?'

'Fine. Where is he?'

'Out the back.'

The flat was almost dark; curtains had been taped across the windows and only a little of the strong summer sunlight lay in shafts across the bare floor and mismatched furniture.

Bones opened a door to a bedroom at the far end of the flat. Two black men, neither more than twenty, looked up at her. One was sprawled on a bare mattress, the other leaned against the windowsill facing the door. A boy with a shock of curly hair like an Afro on the way to full maturity sat with his back to her, leaning on a desk. Only when he looked around did she see he had an open laptop in front of him.

'Mr Shaw?' Leila said.

'Phillip,' the boy replied. 'With two ls, Shaw, S-H-A-W, not like next to the sea.'

'Right… I'm Detective Sergeant Reid,' she said.

'You were at my house last night. I saw you looking at my sister.'

'I'm sorry for your loss.'

'I didn't lose them,' he said. He turned back to the computer and began typing.

Leila looked at Bones.

'We can see right into the flat from here,' he said. 'We been keeping an eye on the place. The shooter ain't been back.'

Leila stepped back to Bones, who had remained on the threshold of the room. She spoke to him in a whisper.

'How is he?' she said.

Bones shrugged. 'He's Phillip. He's always the same.'

'But he knows someone killed his family.'

'Sure. But you seen him. Phillip's… not like us. He's… a good kid, but odd.'

'Drugs?'

Bones laughed. 'Phillip's eaten nothing but fish finger sandwiches since we brought him in. He only drinks water. If anyone wants a smoke they've got to leave the room. Like I say, he's odd, but he was born that way.'

Leila approached the boy. She crouched down beside him and put her hand out. The man who was leaning on the windowsill stood and shook his head.

'He don't like it,' he said.

'Sorry.' She watched Phillip for a moment. He was totally absorbed in what he was doing on the computer. She had no idea what it was.

'Mr Shaw, Phillip, I need to ask you some questions, then I can take you somewhere where you will be safe.'

'Safe here,' he said.

'OK, yes, you're safe here, for now. I need to know what you found last night. A man downstairs said something about CIA involvement? Is that what you found?'

'In the Langley mainframe, there's a file cluster…'

'You've hacked the CIA?'

'Of course.'

'Why?'

'The person who uploaded the video used a screen name. He'd set up the account using an anonymised IP and he was disguising his movements with routing cloaks. I followed him around for four hours until I couldn't go any further.' His fingers never left the keyboard as he spoke.

'Just like that?' Leila said. 'You traced this file thing just like that?'

'Yes. DemonAgent wrote the source code for the cloak. Someone's tried to customise it but they've not done a very good job. Then I had help from other people from DemonAgent to probe the American servers and we tried to locate the original source of the ID for another four hours. We didn't get very deep into the system. The Americans have better security now. Better than the Chinese but not as good as the Koreans.'

'Hold on…' She held her hands up in the boy's peripheral

vision. He didn't look at her but he did stop typing. 'Please, just slow down a bit. What exactly did you find in Langley?'

'I don't know yet. I printed out what I had and went for a walk. I think when I walk.'

'And that's when the man came to your flat?'

Phillip nodded.

'OK, let's back up a bit. You say you traced whoever posted the video from his screen name, right?' Phillip nodded. 'Does that mean you know who he is?'

'No.'

'But you know he works for the CIA.'

'No.'

'I thought you said you found the origins of his name at Langley.'

'I traced it back to the Langley servers. I'm not saying that was where it started. At some point beyond that, branch data associated with this ID was encrypted using a system none of us has been able to crack yet. It's based on something we wrote for Chinese hackers last year. Once the Chinese government got hold of it it makes sense the Americans would get it too. But it's been customised using a key system that can't be hacked from the outside. They did this one properly. So we've found the algorithm, but not how it works.'

'And that algorithm is also in the CIA?'

'Yes.'

'OK, look... there's a lot riding on this. You're making some pretty serious accusations, and, excuse my scepticism, but if all this only took you few hours, why haven't our people been able to do it?'

'Because you people ask permission,' Bones said from behind her. 'And because it's what Phillip and his crew do.'

'Fair enough,' Leila said. 'Phillip, I can't pretend to understand ten per cent of what you're telling me, so strip it down for me: is there anything you found that might get us closer to finding the bomber?'

'I don't know yet,' he said. His fingers hovered over the keys and he stared at the screen as he spoke. 'I don't know what would help you.'

'Nor do I. Anything, some little clue we've not found yet.'

'We got the name of the hidden partition where the data is stored.'

'Really? Yes, OK, that would help. Tell me it's al Sahm...'

'No.' His hands returned seemingly involuntarily to the keyboard. 'Al Sahm's just what the people on the TV are calling it. The partition is called L I Z H I N...'

'What? I don't understand...'

'Look.' He wrote the character string down – LIZHI NATS1BIY11ZH – and turned back to the screen.

'Phillip, I haven't mastered email yet. I don't know anything about computer code.'

'It's not computer code. There are seventeen characters. It's a code used by the Americans during the war. They used it now because it would be virtually impossible to find unless you knew what you were looking for. We only found it because we had some of the code used by the encryption system, and that's stored in the partition. We found the outside by knowing a little bit about what's on the inside.'

'This code: it's Navajo, isn't it,' Leila said.

'Yes. It was used in the war because no one understood it. But Google does, with a bit of help. Well, a lot of help. Well, actually it's total crap, but I tried some searches and got a translation in the end.'

'And it's not al Sahm?'

'No. It's *Black Eagle*. Is that what al Sahm means?'

'Al Sahm means *The Arrow*. We're linking it with Islamist extremists. Does that seem to fit?'

'I don't know. I linked whoever posted the video to a Langley partition called Black Eagle. That's all I could do before someone stole my disks. And the police have taken away the rest of the computer. This one's very slow.'

'Right. We need to get you out of here. We've got people who can work through what you've found.'

She stood up. Bones was now standing right behind her.

'Phillip ain't going anywhere with you.'

'I have to take him in. He's got information that could stop another attack. And he needs to be somewhere safe.'

'Like he says, he's safe now. Out there, he's not.'

'I really need to get him where he can talk to someone who understands this.'

'Maybe, but not now. If he's going anywhere, we'll do it tonight,' Bones said.

'Tonight? Why tonight?'

'There'll be trouble tonight. We can get him out so no one sees him go. That man that kill his fambly, he's going to be back. But he's a white dude. He gonna show up at night.'

'Fine. Ten o'clock, I'm coming back here for Phillip. You stand in my way, I'll arrest you. Aiding a terrorist organisation and obstructing an investigation. Phillip has his ways of getting things done: so do I.'

'You come back here without trailing anyone behind you, you got him.'

Bones stepped back and Leila pushed past him.

'Detective Sergeant Reid?' Phillip called after her.

'Yes?'

'In the cupboard at the top of the wardrobe in my bedroom I have a box. I need it.'

'A box? Why? What is it?'

'I need a better computer. I have some parts there; I can build one.'

'Why do you need a better computer?'

'I want to know what Black Eagle is. Don't you?'

28

Security had been massively increased around the US Embassy in Grosvenor Square. What had long been armed roadblocks now bristled with security staff toting machine guns. British police were flagging down vans and trucks approaching along Park Lane and checking drivers and cargos. Others pulled over seemingly random cars to quiz their drivers. They were planning for a car bomb that went off yesterday.

Leila had retrieved Phillip's box of esoteric computer parts from his room (she told the constable standing guard at the flat door that she was collecting evidence) and exchanged it for her gun and phone back in the Martlesham car park. She had not called in the fact that she was leaving without the boy, but had driven straight down to Westminster, parking as close to the Embassy as she could. By now Harris and Field could already have left, but she doubted it. The Americans would have kept them waiting. It was possible they hadn't even started their meeting yet.

As she approached she looked up at the huge gold eagle that stood, wings outstretched, above the Embassy's main entrance. Would anyone plotting from within the US government really be stupid enough to codename the operation 'Eagle'? Or was this just the fantasy of a socially retarded, conspiracy-mad kid with too much time on his hands?

Reid handed her warrant card to the guard in the east pavilion.

'I've got a meeting with the Special Liaison Officer,' she said.

The guard radioed through her credentials for scrutiny within the building. It was confirmed that Harris and Field were still inside, but the meeting had started some time ago. The guard handed back her warrant and directed her across to the main door. She glanced up as she jogged up the steps; she still couldn't decide which of the eagle explanations seemed the more implausible.

She was checked again by a plain-clothes security officer at the door of the huge pale stone lobby then directed over to the reception desk. A young man strode purposefully from the lifts towards her.

'Sorry I'm so late,' she said before he could speak. 'I was meant to be here half an hour ago. CTC, with your Political Liaison Section.'

She handed over her warrant card and he examined it minutely. The officer offered neither a name or position, but everything about his bearing and manner suggested an ambitious junior diplomat. The British diplomats who occupied the ground floor office of 10 Downing Street looked like men on a break from their gentleman's club; the

US diplomatic corps looked like men on a break from a black-ops assassination job. Seemingly satisfied with her credentials, he handed back her ID.

'I think you've missed most of the meeting,' he said. 'Please leave your gun, mobile phone and any electronic devices at reception, then follow me.'

She handed her stash of contraband to the concierge on the front desk then followed her escort to the lifts. On the fourth floor, he directed her through hushed corridors to a door towards the rear of the building. He knocked and opened the door.

Inside, Harris and Field were sitting at their leisure with a man wearing a pale linen suit.

'DS Reid?' Field said.

'Sorry I'm so late. Got caught up on a transfer.'

'Were you scheduled to be in this meeting?'

'Of course, didn't Commander Thorne text you?'

'No.'

'Well, you can call him if you need to check.'

She walked over to the American and held out her hand. He stood and shook it.

'Detective Sergeant Reid, Counter-Terrorism Command,' she said.

'Michael Holt,' he said. He did not offer either rank or department.

'DS Reid,' Harris said, 'if you're going to sit in on this, please take a seat.'

'I won't be staying,' she said. 'I just need to clarify a couple of points that have come up in the investigation.'

'I was just telling your colleagues here that our Embassy has put itself at your disposal, anything you need to find whoever's behind this outrage. Our government will offer whatever intelligence we have that might prove relevant.'

'Which amounts to what so far?'

'Both Langley and the Pentagon are collating data on Harakat al Sahm as we speak.'

'That'll be useful.'

'As I said, whatever we need to do.' He seemed entirely oblivious to the sarcasm.

'What can you tell me about a woman by the name of Ghada Mussan?'

'Who?'

'Originally Abulafia, but her US passport has the name Mussan.'

'Should I know anything about her?' Holt was still looking at the two men sitting opposite him.

'It seems she's one of yours,' Leila said.

Holt laughed. 'There are upwards of a hundred forty million currently valid passports in the US. You must forgive me if I don't recall the name on every one of them.'

She glanced at Field who was smiling at the American's wit.

'That's not quite what I meant by 'one of yours',' she said. 'But never mind. We'll find her.'

'And anything we can do to help you, we will be more than happy to do. Now please, unless there is anything more… pertinent… we were in the middle of a discussion.'

'OK. There is one more thing. Tell me about Black Eagle.'

'Black Eagle?' Holt said. He sat up a little straighter in his chair. His eyes met Leila's for the first time and she let him size her up. 'You'll have to help me out there again, I'm afraid,' he said.

'It's what got an innocent family killed last night. I just want to know what it is.'

'I can't tell you anything...'

'DS Reid, this is not part of our enquiry here,' Harris said. 'Mr Holt has agreed to see us as a courtesy, not to be interrogated.'

'So you're confirming,' she said to Holt, 'that you know nothing of a covert CIA operation by the name Black Eagle.'

'You think that's what this is?' Holt said. 'I can assure you, Detective Sergeant Reid, that if the US government were operating on British soil, your people would have been fully informed. And if you are implying that the we are in any way complicit in the deaths of British citizens, you are treading on very sensitive diplomatic ground.'

'I'm not implying anything,' Reid said. 'I just want to know if Black Eagle is real.'

'And do you?' Holt said. She looked at him for several silent seconds.

'Yes,' she said. 'Thank you.'

29

DCI Lawrence sat at his desk drumming his fingers on the arm of his chair. Like Commander Thorne, he was beginning to think that bringing Reid in had been a big mistake.

It was not that Leila was incompetent. Far from it: she had an intuition that had on many occasions saved them days of painstaking trial and error. It was more that she never knew when to stop, when that intuition for the truth slipped silently into fantasy. And in a delicate and fast-moving investigation like this, fantasy was the last thing they needed.

He had just got off the phone to Commander Thorne who had been the last in a cascade of trouble that had started right at the top echelons of the US Embassy. Michael Holt had contacted David Bates at SIS who had contacted Sir Malcolm Stevens at MI5 who had contacted CTC. Reid had thrown a grenade into already frosty negotiations and no one was happy.

Lawrence took his personal mobile from the top drawer of his desk and dialled her number. It rang once.

'DCI Lawrence,' Reid said. 'Your personal cell again. Are you trying to tell me something?'

'There are a lot of things I'd like to tell you. And the first of them is the get the hell off this case. Where are you now?'

'I'm approaching the west end of Hyde Park. Wanted to take another look at the site. I need to reconnect with the origin of this thing.'

'Well don't. You've caused enough trouble in the last hour to last us a year. What the hell were you thinking?'

'You've spoken to Holt at the Embassy? Has he confirmed Black Eagle?'

'No and no. I've had my ear bent here because you very nearly lost us vital US cooperation.'

'On Black Eagle.'

'No, not on your bloody Black Eagle. On al Sahm, on the vipers' nest of middle eastern political Islam. The *real* issues of the day.'

'The real issue is Black Eagle, and Holt knows about it. He was like a rabbit in the headlights as soon as I mentioned it. The man would make a crap poker player. I'm telling you, Harakat al Sahm might have been behind the bombing, but Black Eagle are behind them. The kid, Phillip Shaw, found the name on the Langley computers.'

'Stop, stop, stop! Have you any idea how crazy you sound? You're basing your theory of everything on the say-so of some kid who claims to have hacked the CIA? Reid, even if there's a shred of truth to it, you know damn well we can't go anywhere with intel like that.'

'I agree. That's why I went to see Holt. And it's why you need to bring him in. The CIA knows more about what happened yesterday than anyone. And they know what's coming next. They're the key to all of this.'

'Are you seriously suggesting we bring a senior diplomat in for questioning? Apart from the fact that it's legally impossible, we've got no evidence.'

'Then go and see him. Talk to him. You'll know I'm right.'

'I'm sorry, but it's just not enough. Unless you can bring the Shaw boy in for formal questioning, your part in this is over.'

'Shaw won't come, and it would be a big mistake to arrest him right now. He's feeding us useful information.'

'That's highly debatable.'

'What about Abulafia's father? Have you questioned him yet?'

'No. SIS are being evasive about his citizenship, and anyway, I seem to remember it was you who suggested we keep our distance. He's got no political affiliations, no legal problems. He doesn't even seem to be associated with any of the local mosques. We've questioned neighbours and the few that knew anything at all say that Ghada was a rare visitor. Seems they weren't close. We will talk to him, but unlike you we need to go through the right channels to do so.'

'You haven't even told him his daughter's dead?'

'Until we get forensics matches back, we don't know one hundred per cent that she is. She's involved in this somehow, but until we know for certain she was the bomber…'

'I'll go and talk to him.'

'No! You won't go anywhere near Abulafia or anyone else. Go home, Reid, now. Get some rest then call me tomorrow morning. If I can get it approved by any of the people you've gone out of your way to piss off in the last twenty-four hours, you might be useful processing evidence.'

'What evidence? You seem to be ignoring all the main leads.'

'We've got a whole department, plus MI5 liaison, gathering data and interviewing people. We're flooded with leads on ISIS returners and they've all got to be picked through. This was a sophisticated bomb, yes, but it was a lone, lucky strike.'

'Using military grade explosives?'

'Nothing ISIS don't have access to. And we'll find out soon enough how they got the stuff into the country. We've got a lead on a Turkish clothing exporter.'

'Well, you must have nearly solved it then.'

'I'm going to ignore that. Reid, go home. You need to get some perspective on this. Black Eagle is a blind alley, if it exists at all. Al Sahm were running a lone sleeper cell, simple as that. There's no evidence that there are going to any more attacks.'

'What about Mapleton?'

'It's secure. SHIELD Doppler fence on the perimeter, guards everywhere within the cordon.'

'CIA?'

'There's no US presence at the house. The PLO were insistent on that. It's just their guys, the Israelis and the PM's close protection. Met police and MI5 outside. So no Black Eagles swooping in through the darkness.'

'So you're still discounting a link between the move to Mapleton and the bombing.'

'We're discounting anything we don't have evidence for. Remember? It's how we do things. We cannot make a connection, nothing. And we're so snowed under investigating what we *do* know that we don't have time for flights of fancy. Now clock off before I really do fire you.'

The line went dead. She scanned the incoming call list to see if she had missed any other calls while the phone had been quarantined at the Embassy. There was nothing. Only Lawrence's.

She walked a few more steps and sat down on one of the benches overlooking the Serpentine. Hyde Park was back to normal again, almost. If not for the increased police presence it could just have been another hot summer afternoon in London. Japanese and American tourists wandered by the lake edge with bright shopping bags from the city's most iconic shops; a child rode past on a tricycle with his mother following closely with a pram; two girls in St Mary Abbots School uniform sat on the grass throwing their uneaten lunch to the geese. Kensington Road was open again and the traffic rumbled past behind her.

Would he really fire her this time? Had she really been so wrong?

Six months ago she had been wrong. CTC had been alerted to unusual trafficking activity by the Drugs Unit monitoring a known South Asian gang. Three million pounds-worth of heroin had been tracked from Afghanistan through Libya and into Southern Europe. It turned up in London but never made it to the streets. What had alerted the Drugs Unit to its possible terrorism connection was that this deal was vastly out of proportion with anything the South Asian gangs had been involved in before. It stank of arms funding.

Progress on tracking the money in Britain had been slow. The importers were careful and since their shipment had disappeared into the Met police's evidence lockers, they had gone to ground. For CTC it was also a fairly routine case and not one that demanded much attention.

For Leila it had been different. She felt – knew – it was a key to something big. Over the next three weeks she dug deeper and deeper into what little they knew. Everything pointed to an imam associated with a mosque in south London, but her CTC superiors refused to move until they had enough evidence to justify the storm of protest that treading on such delicate ground would bring.

Leila knew she had the evidence, but it was fragmentary, impossible to tie together into the kind of cohesive narrative her superiors demanded. It was a tip-off here, an untraceable transaction there, cell phones that came and went from traces, cars bought for cash in Yorkshire and found burned out in London. Something was in the pipeline and no one but her could see it.

Her mistake had not been in her intuition, but in her impatience. She had leaked what she knew to the press in the hope of ripping away the basis of any plan that was in the offing, and bringing more intel out of the shadows. The story had caused howls of indignation from the opposition back-benchers in the Commons and brought the secretive work of CTC more attention that Commander Thorne cared for.

There were street protests, accusations and recriminations. And, of course, her actions had been highly illegal.

The story had eventually led to five arrests. The cell had been blown, the ring-leader sent down for twenty-five years. Even Thorne admitted she had been right. His hands had been tied however, and she too had been sent down for a stretch of garden leave while the IPCC investigated.

Now, six months of suspension from duty later, the situations was subtly different. This time she was following solid evidence, however inconvenient its trail might be. There was a link; there *had to be* a link between the bombing, the death of Phillip's family and the move to Mapleton House. She just couldn't see it right now. It made no sense. If Phillip was right, why were the Americans trying to destroy the peace talks? And was it even remotely possible that they were running a Jihadist cell to do it?

A pigeon flew onto the arm of the bench beside her and sat looking expectantly at her. Leila's stomach grumbled for lack of anything but Danish pastries and coffee for the last twenty-four hours.

She suddenly felt bone-tired. Lawrence was right about one thing: she needed a break.

The pigeon flew down to the ground and started pecking at a cigarette butt. Leila watched him for a moment and realised that she couldn't even remember what she had done with her car.

She stood up and began to walk back towards Knightsbridge tube station.

30

Leila arrived back at her Victorian terrace in Upper Tooting at a few minutes to six.

She knew as soon as she opened the front door that something was wrong. There was no sign of forced entry to the door, no broken glass strewn across the kitchen floor at the end of the hallway. Just a feeling in the place: something was wrong. She drew her gun and slid along the hall wall towards the door to the front room.

She pushed the door open with her foot. The books had been pulled from the shelves, the paintings unhooked, the cushions from the chairs heaped in the middle of the floor.

She moved on, the gun trained on the door to the back room. It was the same. Every item had been moved. More books – including her treasured collection of dust-jacketed first editions – had been pulled off the shelves, the drawers of the bureau had been emptied and the phone-line ripped from the wall. The kitchen too had been ransacked. The back door stood open and she picked her way across the spilled cutlery and pans and closed it. She turned the key in the lock and retraced her steps to the foot of the stairs.

The entire ground floor had been searched. That was the word that described this mess: searched. Nothing obvious had been broken, nothing stolen. The Bose hi-fi and iPad were in the wrong place but intact; the Walker and Hall silver parakeet salts were still on the sideboard. Even the Picasso drawing that had been a present from her father had just been taken from the wall and leaned against the dining table.

It was not a burglary. In fact, as she walked through the debris, more annoyed than frightened or upset, she began to think it was not really even a search.

It was a warning.

There was no sound from above. She aimed the gun at the bathroom door at the top of the stairs and, keeping her shoulder to the wall, gradually crept up, one step at a time.

The bedrooms had not been touched and there was no sign of the intruder. She looked out through the net curtains over the front window. Three boys of about ten scooted past; an elderly woman shuffled along with her elderly Jack Russell; a suited business man checked the doors of his BMW and walked up the path of the house opposite. Another man, wearing a Turkish jubba and dark glasses, strode purposefully away towards Upper Tooting Road. Nothing out of the ordinary. But she knew they were out there. The intruder might have gone, but there would be others, and she was not going to disappoint them. This was exactly what she had been waiting for.

She changed quickly into a white skirt and black Damien Hirst skull t-shirt and ran back downstairs. She stuffed more clothes from the dryer into a supermarket carrier bag and put that, along with a baseball cap, into a small bright red backpack she used when hiking on the South Downs. Into a small handbag she tucked her gun, a wallet containing two hundred pounds in cash and her Oyster travel card. A spare tool-roll containing lock picks, an old monocular and a phone jammer went in on top. The only thing she carried in the skirt's flimsy pocket was her CTC warrant card.

She walked back along the main road towards Tooting Bec tube station. Rush hour was now in full swing, with dozens of people coming out of the station as she walked down to the platform. She was not the only person going in that direction, but she was one of the few. Anyone following would have to keep a good distance behind her to avoid being spotted. Going with the flow of people would have been far more difficult: a tail could walk within feet of her in a dense crowd and she would never know.

She walked quickly to the Northbound platform. The next train was heading up to Edgware, which suited her just fine. Already a plan was forming.

The rolling announcement screen gave her three minutes until the Edgware train arrived, so she made her way back to the ticket hall and found a payphone. She dialled 999 and the emergency operator answered the call after barely half a ring.

'Emergency, which service?' the operator said.

'There's a bomb near gate seven, Victoria bus station.'

'I'm connecting you to the police.'

'There's a bomb…'

The line switched and she hung up before the police phone was answered.

There was a rush of air from the tunnel and she pushed her way back to the platform. She caught sight of a man dressed in a black suit, dark glasses, loitering by the ticket machines.

She got on to a carriage in the middle of the train. Just as the doors began to close, Mr Black Suit ran past her carriage and squeezed through the doors of the next one along.

Leila pushed her way to the front of the carriage. Through the connecting doors she waved to a Transport Police officer. She banged on the partition glass and showed her warrant. The officer opened the door.

'I need to get to the back of the train,' she said.

'Is there a problem?'

'No, just a hunch. Nothing to be alarmed about. Just make sure no one else moves through the train.'

'I'll have the rear guard come back to accompany you.'

'Thanks.'

She walked quickly through the almost-full carriage towards the next pair of doors.

The train stopped for almost a minute at Balham, and Leila stood by the open door watching the platform. Mr Black was doubtless doing the same two carriages back, though she could not see him.

As soon as the doors closed, she began to move again. A second guard met her and escorted her towards the rear cab. She had about five minutes until they arrived at Stockwell, her next destination. She might be able to lose her tail there, but she doubted it. She was going to have to draw him into a trap to fully escape his attention.

The train pulled into Stockwell and she waited until the last moment to get off. She was almost opposite the exit to Platform 1, which would get her onto the Victoria Line train going on into the city. Mr Black was lost from sight as he pushed his way through the crowds behind her.

She saw him again as she got onto the waiting train. Again, he got in one carriage down from her. This train was far more crowded than the Tooting Bec one, and it was going to be difficult to put any distance between herself and her pursuer.

Not that it mattered much. Everything so far, from the distinctive t-shirt to the red backpack had been designed to make her easy to follow, to lull him into thinking she would always be within sight. But whether this man was trying to eliminate her from the investigation or use her to get to Phillip, it was now time to lose him.

Six minutes later the train stopped at Victoria and again Leila disembarked just as the doors started to close. This time Mr Black was already on the platform. She walked with the flow of commuters and tourists to the escalators.

On the main concourse Leila glanced over her shoulder. There was no sign of her pursuer, though she knew she had not lost him yet. He was holding back, waiting for her to move out into the open, away from the gaze of the twenty or more armed police in the station.

She stepped out of the station.

The most dangerous part of her journey was now beginning. It was time to disappear.

Five minutes after leaving Victoria rail station she came to the first of the crowds that were milling around outside the evacuated coach station. She pushed her way through to the uniformed officer at the cordon and flashed her warrant at him. He barely looked as she ducked under the tape and jogged towards the main entrance to the station.

At the door she looked back. Mr Black was now engaged in heated discussion with the policeman who had let her through. He was showing the officer something, but it was not convincing enough to get him through as quickly as she had. He would make it through eventually, but she intended to have vanished by the time he did.

She used her warrant again to gain access to the gate concourse. There were a dozen uniformed officers down towards Gate 7, plus bomb squad and a handful of her fellow CTC operatives. They had got here amazingly quickly. She almost felt guilty.

No one paid her any attention when she walked into the toilets by Gate 12.

She had only one chance to get this right. If she mistimed her exit from the toilet, if Mr Black got a clear sight of her, she would be trapped. It would be impossible to lose him twice.

The irony of what she was doing was not lost on her. She was changing her appearance to avoid detection, exactly as Ghada Abulafia had done before returning to the bomb beneath the Park Hotel.

Everyone had assumed that the bomber had changed to avoid being traced back to her point of origin. Leila now wondered whether in fact Abulafia, like her, had effected this transformation for an entirely different reason. Was she concerned about being followed by someone *before* the bombing and had disguised herself half way through her journey to throw him off her trail?

And if so, what did that mean? Did other members of the cell have good reason not to trust her?

Now dressed in a light-weight leather jacket, pale brown shirt, jeans and with her hair up beneath a New York Yankees baseball cap, Leila opened the door a crack. A line of uniformed officers were pacing slowly along the concourse. Mr Black was nowhere in sight. She hoped he had been held at the cordon and was waiting, watching for her. It was possible that he had called in backup and had the coach station ringed by spotters, all on the lookout for a woman wearing a black skull t-shirt, white skirt and a long loose plait of hair. Her red backpack was the real clincher: the thing that would have convinced Mr Black that she would be easy to spot in any crowd. That backpack was now in the bin in the Ladies', her previous identity rolled up on top of it. Close up, she was easy enough to recognise; from a distance, in a crowd, she was someone completely transformed.

She stepped out. Folding a copy of the Standard around her handbag and walked across the coach bays and out into Semley Place. From there, sure she was not being followed, she took back streets back to the main Victoria rail station.

She was confident that Mr Black had not picked up her trail again, but she knew he would have the very best technology available to back him up.

As she walked, she dismantled her phone. She also checked her pockets for cash. It would be unwise to use her

Oyster card for the next leg of her journey north. It might take Mr Black and his backers time to follow her journey using the data harvested from the card, but it would take them until the end of time to trace her if she used a single-journey ticket purchased for cash at one of the machines.

She purchased the most expensive six-zone single, thereby giving her pursuers no more specific a destination than somewhere in the two hundred and seventy stations that made up the London Underground system.

She rode the Circle Line to South Kensington, then changed to the Piccadilly Line that would take her far to the north of the city. With each passing stop the collective identity of the passengers in her carriage changed. By Arsenal almost no one wore a suit. White, middle class professionals had left behind the people of the northern estates; poor working people, black, white, South Asian, mostly middle aged.

From Turnpike Lane tube station it was a walk of a little over a mile to her final destination in Broadwater Farm. But she was not going to pick up Phillip Shaw. Far from returning to Northolt tower block to collect him and take him into protective custody, she was hoping that his minders would have room for one more refugee from the events of the last thirty-six hours.

She needed somewhere to hide out, to regroup, to figure out just who she was fighting here, before she moved in for the end game. Harakat al Sahm had not struck again, but they would, and it seemed they had the backing of one of the most powerful intelligence services in the world.

Day Three

31

Leila had woken in her car the previous day. Not a good start to any day, but, she thought now, preferable to this.

The tiny flat in Northolt was hot and airless. The heat had drawn the smell of stale tobacco and ganja from the wallpaper and brought the dusty odour of mould from the carpets. Her mouth felt like the inside of a vacuum cleaner bag and her hair was plastered to her face with drying sweat.

She stood up, carefully uncricking her back, and walked through to the empty kitchen. Bones had not bothered to check whether there was any food. It was six am, so there was little chance he was out getting her croissants and coffee. Still, he had at least kept her safe. Hopefully he would still be doing the same for Phillip Shaw.

She drank three glasses of water from a chipped half-pint glass then poured three more over her head. There were no towels, but looking out of the kitchen window at the harsh sunlight that was already burning the open spaces between the blocks, she figured her hair would be dry in minutes anyway.

Outside Turnpike Lane station she picked up a bagel and

an indifferent coffee then took the tube down to Ealing.

She heard Ibrahim Abulafia moving around in the flat for almost a minute before he opened the door a couple of inches.

'Mr Abulafia?' she said.

'I don't have time for visitors. I'm late for work.' He held the door open just a few inches.

'You need to make time,' Leila said. 'This won't take long.'

'Who are you?'

'My name is Leila Reid. I'm with the police.'

'I've already spoken to the police. And I'll tell you the same thing: I don't know anything. Some thugs. I've had plenty worse.'

'I'm sorry?'

'Last night, some skinheads shove me around a bit, call me some names. I can deal with them. I can't deal with you people coming out of the woodwork only when it's politically expedient for you to do so.'

'I'm…?'

'Yes, I can use words like 'expedient'. I haven't always been the man who sweeps up your rubbish in the bowels of the earth. I had another life once. Now, if you'll excuse me….'

'I think there's some misunderstanding, Mr Abulafia. If uniformed officers have spoken to you about last night, that's entirely coincidental. I'm here on a different matter. I just want to ask you a couple of questions, off the record, about Ghada.'

'Ghada's not here.' He tried to close the door. Leila did not put her foot in it, but instead pushed back with her hand.

'Can I just come in for a minute?' she said. 'There's something I need to tell you.'

'Then you can tell me here.'

'Your daughter's dead, Mr Abulafia.'

He did not reply at first. He just looked at her around the edge of the door. Then he released it and Leila gently pushed it open.

'She was killed in the bomb on Wednesday,' he said. It wasn't a question. He knew.

Leila nodded and when the old man turned and walked back into the flat, she followed, closing the front door silently behind her.

Abulafia stood looking out of the window when she joined him in his sparse sitting room.

'If you're still here,' he said, 'maybe she wasn't just another victim. You think she was involved somehow.' Again, not a question.

'How much do you know about what Ghada has been doing these last few years?' Leila said.

'Is this on the record now?' he said.

'Not if you don't want it to be. There's just some things I don't understand. Some things that don't fit. I'm hoping you'll be able to fill in the gaps.'

'You probably know as much as I do,' he said, still with his back to her, watching her reflection in the glass.

'Did Ghada ever discuss her political views with you?' Leila said.

'Political? No. We escaped from the West Bank when she was small. That was all behind us.'

'How did you get asylum in Britain?'

'I made a good case.'

'I'm sure you did. And I'm thinking it has something to do with why SIS is being so tight-lipped about you. Am I getting warm?'

'I'm sure you'll find out soon enough anyway, now that… ah, what does any of it matter now?'

'You were an informant.'

Abulafia nodded. 'MI6, SIS as you call them now, ran me for four years. I fed them information – dead drops mostly – and they paid me well enough. But they had me inside one of the most paranoid organisations in the world. People got suspicious.'

'Your cover was blown. They had to get you out.'

'Eventually. But not before my wife was murdered.' He studied her reflection in the glass for a moment. 'She was snatched from the street outside our house on the way to market. They tortured her for two days, so I'm told. She couldn't have told them a thing. She never knew. And when they'd finished with her they dumped her body at the Pool of Siloam like a sack of spoiled meat. I think it was a message. Isaiah 22:19 – 'I will thrust thee from thy post'. You know it?'

Leila shook her head. She was never much for bible quotes.

'It was a warning even my handlers couldn't ignore,' Abulafia said. 'The British arranged to send us to England before the truth had a chance to come out and other informants were compromised. They gave us new identities.'

'So you'd ensured Ghada was ripe for subversion from the cradle.'

'What I did, I did for the good of our people and we paid a high price for it. I can take only anonymous jobs now; Ghada could scarcely even do that.'

'So you did know she was into something?'

Ibrahim looked out of the window for a long moment. He took a cigarette from his shirt pocket and lit it.

'Ghada became secretive over the last few years,' he said. 'She would disappear for weeks, months on end. She said she was staying with friends, and sometimes she was. But there were other times it was as if she didn't exist at all. Her phone was dead, her emails went unread, nothing.'

'We have reason to believe she was out of the country,' Leila said. 'What I have difficulty with, is why.'

'I can't tell you what I don't know.'

'She never hinted at any involvement with extremist groups? No mention of radicalised beliefs, a hatred of Britain or the West?'

'Britain gave us shelter. Ghada loved her country and its people.'

He fell into reflective silence. Leila looked around the room.

'The photograph of the Dome of the Rock on your wall,' she said. 'What does that mean to you?'

'The Dome of the Rock?' He turned to the framed magazine picture above the TV. He pointed to the pale brown scrub land in the distance. 'The Mount of Olives, Temple Mount, the site of the City of David.'

'Jewish sites.'

'*Palestinian* sites, Miss Reid.'

'Sacred to the Jews. Ghada was Muslim.'

He laughed. 'Was she? Because she had brown skin, because she came from Palestine? No, Ghada was not Muslim. We are the people who fall through the cracks in your simplified view of the middle east. My family are old Palestinian Jews. I was an MI6 mole in Shin Bet, *Israeli* secret intelligence, not Fatah. And Ghada, my dear, was – *is* – Jewish.'

'I don't understand. She was working with an organisation called Harakat al Sahm; the Movement of the Arrow. Everything points to them being a radical Islamist group.'

'If you call a cat a dog, will it bark? You see what you want to see. Ghada loved this country, that's all I can tell you.'

'She wore a ring, didn't she? A key, folded round into a ring. The key's the symbol of return from exile for the Palestinians.'

'Miss Reid, religion isn't nationality. My neighbour here, Mr Abdul, he flies the Union flag, he sings God Save the Queen. He is British, and he is Muslim. Ghada and I are proud Palestinians, nationalists if you want to say that. Being Jewish does not mean we feel the pain of the situation any less acutely. Now, please…'

'You don't seem particularly upset that your daughter's dead, Mr Abulafia.'

'Is that a question?'

'No, just an observation.'

'We all mourn in our own way, Miss Reid.'

'Sure, but she was killed planting a bomb to murder innocent people. That must mean something to you.'

'All you have told me is that she was killed *by* the bomb, not that she planted it. I choose to believe my daughter died an innocent woman until you can show me proof of the other.'

'I'll get to the truth, I can assure you of that.'

'Or are you trying to frame her?'

'No, I'm not. I'd rather have no attribution at all than a wrong one.'

'Then you are unusual.'

'This whole scenario is unusual. I'm convinced there's something none of us is seeing, something else.'

'Another attack?'

'I'm sure of it.' She turned to go then stopped.

'Tell me one more thing, Mr Abulafia. Does the name Black Eagle mean anything to you?'

He shook his head. 'No.' There was no pause, no tell. If Black Eagle was real and Ghada had been a part of it, she had never confided in her father.

'OK. Thank you.'

'Miss Reid,' he said. 'If you are to stop whatever is coming next, change your direction. You must open your eyes and run at it head on. Don't stop until you see the truth.'

32

Raha Golzar had also started the day in very different circumstances to those she had grown accustomed to.

At eleven thirty the previous night she had been cuffed and shackled and processed out of Low Newton's custody. The Governor took her to a loading dock at the rear of the prison. Three vans waited, their doors open but with no drivers or guards in sight. Golzar was put into a cage in the middle van. All three vehicles were then secured and she heard voices outside. Fifteen minutes later all three moved off. All would take different routes to London and no one on board would have any idea whether they were carrying the real prisoner or not. Until they arrived at Holloway, the only person who knew where Golzar was would be the Governor of Low Newton. Any rescue was impossible.

At 4am she had been rearrested (or, more accurately, arrested properly for the first time) in the service bay of Holloway jail. The arresting officer cited Section 41 of the Terrorism Act but did not elaborate. All this meant was that she could be detained for up to twenty eight days without ever being told why. It was not a hopeful start to the day.

At a little after nine o'clock, she had been taken from her cell to a meeting room where Donald Aquila, the same sharp-suited man who had met her in the activities room of F Wing, was waiting.

She sat down opposite him and he took a thick sheaf of papers from a leather attache case.

'Please leave us alone,' he said to the guard hovering in the doorway. 'I have not been issued with written instructions that this is to be a Paragraph 9 interview and as such, as Miss Golzar's legal counsel, this conversation is subject to litigation privilege. Anything said in this room in this meeting will be inadmissible in any future legal proceedings.'

The guard did not move.

'That means fuck off, sonny,' Aquila said.

The guard consulted the two police officers outside the room then closed the door. It was locked behind him and Golzar and her lawyer were alone. A few seconds later the red light on the video camera went off.

'What was that?' Golzar said.

'Insurance. They know all that; I know all that. But if you do get caught up in the English courts, even under some obscure Terrorism Act charge, that little speech will slow them down a bit. They can only use anything said in here against you if they can prove Paragraph 9 was in place before I entered the room. They're probably running around like headless chickens right now trying to get a judge to sign off on the order. If and until they do, it's just us.'

He took out a micro digital recorder and placed it on the table between them.

'So why are you here?' Golzar said. 'I think I deserve the truth this time.'

'Yes, you do. I'm here to get you out.'

'Out of here?'

'Out of the country. Your friends have been trying to locate you since you disappeared from Jerusalem. We suspected you were alive, but beyond that, we could prove nothing. The British did a good job. Clever to hide you among the lunatics.'

'You're not working for British Secret Intelligence then.'

Aquila smiled. 'No, I'm not. You know who I work for.'

'Then why the elaborate ruse? Black Eagle had emergency extraction protocols back in Israel.'

'No one was sure who you were working for. Your mission was never sanctioned and you do have a history of defection, don't you? Black Eagle were watching you, but by the time they knew your true intentions, they were not the only people interested. Half a dozen governments wanted you out of there, and as usual it fell to the CIA to do the clean-up.'

'Who sold me out?'

'Hassan Hawadi.'

Golzar nodded.

'Your lover…' Aquila said.

'He was a mole. Paid by the CIA to work inside Fatah. He checked out fine.'

'Because he *was* working for the CIA, but he was also loyal to the cause of the PLO. He knew you'd set up a meeting with someone high up in Mossad and told his PLO handler. They couldn't act in West Jerusalem without causing a major international incident, but they could bring the Russian FIS in. And they did.'

'How ironic. You're telling me Russian secret service were ready to talk?'

'Oh yes. Moscow wanted you back. That's why the CIA had to take you out of play as quickly as possible.'

'So why didn't they just pick me up?'

'Because they had to keep their hands clean. They risked exposing Hawadi if they acted directly and he was still a valuable asset. British SIS were asked to arrange an apparent assassination and render you through Britain to the US. They got half of it right.'

'The bit where they shot me with a tranc dart.'

'They needed it to look convincing. The whole thing was staged.'

'So Hawadi never arranged the meeting at the Pinkhas Rosen apartment?'

'He did. His PLO paymasters asked him to lure you to the safe house. They would supply the FIS agent and you would be back in Moscow before anyone knew you were missing. Unfortunately for you, the CIA pay better and Hawadi follows the money. The meeting was brought forward twenty-four hours so they could get you out of Jerusalem – and out of play permanently as far as the Russians were concerned.

'They needed you in a public place, but not too public. No tourists, just a few locals. Hawadi had told them you always travelled by bus, so they knew you'd have to get off at Tsvi Krokh and walk fifty yards along an open street. You were shot by an SIS man in a sixth floor apartment in Holyland

Tower 1. It was witnessed and an ambulance picked up your corpse before anyone could get too close.'

'Then the British government dumped me in a psych ward in Durham. Not exactly a glorious end to the mission.'

'Unfortunately Britain no longer has a poodle government willing to do whatever Washington says.'

'So how did you find me?'

'Three months ago Richard Morgan made a deal to sell you back to the PLO.'

'As a condition of the peace talks.'

'Exactly. The whole success of the talks hinged on the deal. Hawadi had reported you dead, so when Richard Morgan told the PLO you were alive and well and could be made available, Abu Queria couldn't get to the negotiating table quick enough. They were being given a second run at you. Only this time it would be in the public gaze, so they'd have to settle for second prize: no deal with the Russians, just getting you into a position where there'd be no future deals with anyone. The West Bank Authority still has the death penalty on its books.'

'There's no UK trial then.'

'By rights you should be on a plane to Tel Aviv by this time tomorrow. You were to be taken back to Ramallah to face terrorism and treason charges. They would have made the charges stick, and there wasn't anyone coming to your defence.'

'Surely Mossad couldn't have allowed that? If it was widely known that I had arranged a meeting with them…'

'Mossad burned you the moment you were assassinated.

They believed you were dead and needed to make sure nothing led back to them. A dossier was prepared against you in case anything ever came out. You were, apparently, trying to smuggle weaponised biological agents into Israel and were resisting capture when you were shot. All of which is just true enough to make it plausible, and it suited their ongoing narrative perfectly. Iranian weapons expert trained in ex-Soviet Russia tries to bring biological material into Israel? You couldn't make it up!'

'I would never have exposed Black Eagle. You've got to know that.'

'Your very existence on the public stage would have been a disaster. If this had happened anywhere else it would have been forgotten in a matter of weeks, but in Israel? You'd have unleashed a firestorm of accusation and counter-accusation that would have made it almost impossible for us to continue. Anything that cast any light on the organisation and six decades of work, billions of dollars, our whole operation would have collapsed.'

'What now then? Black Eagle Executive have decided to rid themselves of an embarrassment?'

'If we were going to do that, it would have happened at Low Newton. No, you're worth far more alive than you are dead. Your mission is not officially over, just... repurposed.'

'You're putting me back in?'

'No. Executive need what's in your head. Raha, you possess knowledge and contacts that could change everything. Tensions between East and West are such that any negotiation is now impossible, but both sides know that without agreement, the world will slide towards a new, even more deadly, cold war. There are powerful elements in Washington and Moscow who are ready to deal. With what you know, Black Eagle could broker that deal and hold the balance of a new power. And where Russia goes, China will follow. What you set out to do fifteen months ago could be about to happen.'

'What I set out to do was get a better offer. As you said, Black Eagle never sanctioned the mission.'

'There *are* no better offers. We bring you back in, this time our old enemies come with you. The beginning of a new era.'

'If you can get me out of here.'

'You need to sit tight for a few more hours. In,' he glanced at his watch, 'eighteen hours you'll be out of here. In another twenty-four, you'll be back in Washington.'

'And then?'

'With your help, in six months Black Eagle will have control of the UN Security Council. After that, there will be no government on earth capable of writing their own script.'

33

Leila Reid reassembled her phone and scrolled through the incoming calls list. She found the number of DCI Lawrence's personal cell and prayed it would not drop her straight into voicemail. She wanted to keep the phone on for as little time as possible.

He answered after four rings.

'Hello?'

'Michael, it's Leila. Don't say anything. I think this phone is being tracked and I need to see you.'

'Reid, we got…'

'Please. Meet me at the first bookshop. Remember?'

'The…?'

'The *first bookshop*, one hour. Come alone and don't tell anyone you're meeting me. I found something.'

'Then bring it in.'

'I can't. Meet me.'

She ended the call and quickly flicked the SIM from the back of the phone. If anyone had been listening to her conversation, there was very little chance they would know what 'the first bookshop' was. Given the number of bookshops in central London it could keep them tied up for days. She just hoped Lawrence would remember.

On the day of her interview with CTC, Leila had had time to kill before going to Scotland Yard to meet DCI Lawrence and Commander Thorne. She wandered along the Thames, had a coffee and browsed the tables of books beneath Waterloo Bridge. She had inherited an interest in antique books from her father, and still indulged now and then if something particularly tasty came her way. This particular morning she chanced upon a first edition copy of T E Lawrence's Seven Pillars of Wisdom: a book she loved, the name of her prospective new boss and a first edition at a price she could afford. It was rather tatty, but it felt like an omen. It had been: she'd aced the interview.

As Lawrence walked her out to the front desk he commented on the book. A bibliophile himself, he was curious how she had bought even a tatty first edition for so little. She had told him that the Queen's Walk book market was the first bookshop she would try for anything. They'd been there together many times, though not for many months now.

She hoped he would still remember its significance.

For most of the hour she rode the underground, randomly changing trains until, five minutes before she hoped Lawrence would arrive, she emerged into the daylight at Waterloo station and made her way over the footbridge towards the South Bank. She stopped at the mid-point next to a group of Japanese tourists and scanned the riverside walkway through the monocular.

DCI Lawrence walked along the side of the Festival Hall three minutes later.

Leila moved as quickly as she could through the crowds and closed the gap to her boss just as he passed into the shadow of Waterloo Bridge.

'Buy me a coffee,' she said. 'And keep you head down. I don't know who's watching.'

In the café beneath the bridge they took a table just inside the door. A waiter was with them almost immediately.

'Two Americanos please,' Lawrence said.

'And could I plug my phone in?' Leila said. 'I just need to make a call and wouldn't you know it, battery's flat?'

'Sure. There's a socket just beside you.'

Leila unrolled her leather kit pouch inside her bag and took out the mobile signal jammer. She plugged it in and turned it on. As several startled drinkers looked around she leaned in close to her boss.

'Bring me up to speed,' she said.

'You were right about Ghada Abulafia. Forensics confirmed it from DNA on the passports and the safety deposit box.'

'Good, then I'm right about a lot more too.' She looked out of the café window. A man browsing the bookstalls met her gaze for an instant than looked away.

'Why all the cloak and dagger stuff?' Lawrence said. 'If you've got something, just bring it in. We shouldn't be talking about this here.'

'I can't bring it in. I found something, and it's big. Much bigger than we thought. Someone broke into my house then followed me half way across London. They know I know something. And Ibrahim Abulafia? He pointed me in a whole new direction. Michael, this isn't an Islamist plot. It's…'

'Leila, it *is* an Islamist plot. It's a sleeper cell activated for a single high-profile attack.'

'No…'

'Yes,' he said. 'Look. We've had a claim and it's backed up by very good circumstantial evidence. We've got enough to build a solid case.'

'For what?'

'For this being Harakat al Sahm working as a cell of IS, single attack, principally as a warning that they could strike wherever and whenever they wanted. Look.'

He took out his mobile phone and swiped through to a video. He placed it between them on the table.

A young man swathed in a keffiyeh scarf addressed the camera. Leila didn't need to read the subtitles despite the poor sound quality. The man spoke educated Arabic with a slight accent she recognised immediately. She herself had learned the language from speakers with exactly these inflections.

The man made all the usual claims: retribution for British interference in Kurdish Iraq, a threat of the unstoppable expansion of the Caliphate, kill the unbeliever… She stopped the video when the singing started.

'Bullshit,' she said.

'I'm sorry, but at this stage we've no reason not to believe it. We're directing all our resources to getting an identity on this guy and moving forwards from there.'

'You know where you'll find his identity? IMDB or Equity.

This guy's an actor. He's no more a terrorist than you are!'

DCI Lawrence shook his head and took a long draft of coffee.

'He's just reciting what he's saying,' Leila said. 'How long have you had this?'

'It first appeared about an hour and a half ago.'

'Who's seen it?'

'Apart from anyone with a computer? Tech are taking it apart as we speak.'

'Don't bother. Just get someone who understands Arabic to *listen* to it rather than reading the subtitles. This, for example: he refers to 'our beautiful martyr'. Listen.' She scanned back through the video until she found the section she wanted then played it. She repeated it with the sound turned up.

'It's hard to hear, but he says 'jameel'. Ghada was a woman: it should be 'jameel*ah*'.'

'Slip of the tongue.'

'Or whoever wrote his script doesn't know a damn thing about the bomber. We haven't released that information. Clean the sound up and I bet every reference is made in the masculine form. Plus, it makes no sense whatever that a Lebanese man would be speaking on behalf of Islamic State.'

'How do you know he's Lebanese?'

'Dialect. He learned formal Arabic at school, but he can't completely over-ride his natural dialect form. The glottal stops are a big clue. This is a fake. Even if it wasn't such a ham-fisted one, I already have evidence that this is not an Islamist plot at all.'

'And your alternative theory is…?'

'Black Eagle is real. You may be right that this was a specifically-activated sleeper cell, but it's a cell of a bigger organism than anything we've ever faced before. I don't know what Black Eagle is yet, but it *does* exist.'

'And you don't think it's an Islamist cell?'

'Micheal, Ghada Abulafia was Jewish.'

'Oh, brilliant. So we go public with your theory and we've pissed off another whole community. Just what we need.'

'I'm not saying she was acting as a Jew; I'm saying she was Jewish, which rather mitigates against this being an Islamist plot, don't you think?'

'To what end? There's never been an Israeli-inspired terrorist attack in the West. Ever. So why now?'

'The Peace Talks. There *is* a connection. Black Eagle…'

'Do not exist! And if they do, they're so far under the radar that they couldn't possibly function at this level.'

'Unless they had help.'

'From?'

'SIS, MI5, IDF, CIA would be my bet. Hell, Michael, even we're just a three-letter acronym. Who's to say someone at CTC isn't deliberately diverting attention from the real issue?'

'You're right, there is someone who's been trying to undermine this investigation, throw us off the scent.'

'Who?'

'You!'

'You don't believe a word I'm saying, do you?'

'You said you'd follow the evidence. I'm just doing the same. And so far the evidence points *away* from you and towards what we all expected right from the beginning.'

'How convenient.'

'Bring me something concrete – Phillip Shaw would be good – and we'll look into it. Otherwise, I can't help you. Now, is there anything else?'

'Has the second passport yielded anything?'

'It's a US issue. We can't get anything out of them. The Foreign Secretary's lodged a request with Homeland, but they're not exactly jumping at the chance to help. They've really had their noses put out of joint because the peace talks were set up on the 'wrong' side of the pond. And your stunt at the Embassy certainly hasn't helped.'

'At very least you have to increase security at Mapleton.'

'You still think there's a second attack coming?'

'I'm absolutely certain of it. If I'm wrong, it'll cost you some overtime. But if I'm right…'

'We can't get anyone else into the house. Each of the participants have brought their own people, and every name on the list has been thoroughly checked by the others. The whole process took months. We couldn't get the Queen herself into the house without the Palestinians and the Israelis raking through her family tree back to the dark ages.'

'But you can get more people outside.'

'We already have. There's Air Support doing regular fly-overs and increased perimeter patrols. There are check-points on all roads leading to Mapleton. Although I have to say, we have some of the most sophisticated security systems in place already. The SHIELD system has the entire perimeter locked down. If a stray deer tries to jump over the wall it would be a venison steak before its back legs hit the ground.'

'What's the schedule?'

'Details are classified. All I can tell you is that each party is being flown in on separate helicopters, all RAF, all checked and double-checked. They're meeting for a dinner tonight at seven and the talks get underway officially at ten tomorrow.'

'And they're all staying on-site tonight?'

'The PM is returning to Downing Street. Everyone else is staying put.'

'OK. You're certain there's no US participation inside or outside the house?'

'No. Which is a big problem for your theory. If the CIA are behind this, they must have help from either the Palestinians, which seems highly unlikely, or the Israelis, which granted is possible, but what's their end game? If the CIA and IDF want the talks to fail, then there are better ways of going about it than bombing London.'

'Maybe they were trying to shift the blame onto the PLO.'

'It's too intricate. Too risky. No, there's no evidence that the talks are in any way linked to the bomb, or at least not by the same people.'

'Richard Morgan agrees?'

'He won't hear of delaying or cancelling. He's spent years bringing this together. His efforts damn nearly got him assassinated five years ago when he was Shadow Foreign Secretary. He's got a lot riding on it.'

Leila sat for a moment looking our across the river.

'What if he's got more riding on it than just his reputation?' she said.

'Like what?'

'Ruth.'

'His daughter?'

'Yes. Has she been found yet?'

'There's not been any report that she's missing.'

'I told you that she needed to be looked into.'

'There have been no reports backing you up. The PM hasn't mentioned her.'

'So you've ignored it?'

'We haven't given it priority. It's not a CTC issue.'

'I think maybe it is. Look at what we know: Ruth Morgan was on her way to the Palace when the bomb went off. Her personal security left her unguarded, saying she was only a few seconds from safety and he had to get to the hotel. Then nothing.'

'Maybe there was nothing to report. She's fine.'

'No, listen: less than twenty-four hours later, the PM makes a unilateral decision to move the talks to a new location. Why? Maybe someone's encouraging him.'

'You think Ruth was kidnapped?'

'Yes. She rode in Hyde Park at the same time every Wednesday. The bomb would be perfect cover for a kidnap.'

'Listen to yourself! You're seriously saying that this Black Eagle would bomb a hotel, risk killing dozens of people, to cover one kidnap? There were plenty of opportunities to snatch her if they're that sophisticated.'

'I'm not saying that at all. The bomb was just that: a

terrorist attack. It's brought chaos to the streets and tied CTC and the rest of us up controlling the fallout. But it's not the *what* you need to be looking at: it's the *when*. It was timed to give them cover for the kidnap.'

'Then why was Abulafia there? If they were aiming the bomb to coincide with Ruth Morgan's schedule, why would they put someone back into the field and risk blowing their cover?'

'I don't know. But there will be an explanation, I'm certain of it, and it'll point back to Ruth's disappearance.'

'OK, then how do you account for the presence of Ruth's personal security Byers? How would they know he would not accompany her to the Palace before going to play the hero?'

'Because he was in on it.'

'Oh, come on!'

'No, listen. Byers facilitated the kidnap. It makes perfect sense. He was there to make sure she stuck to schedule and was in the right place at the right time. The kidnappers then have the talks moved to Mapleton while all the time CTC are chasing shadows and the rest of the Met are stretched to breaking point covering the riots.'

'Leila, you need to take a break. Your instincts on the ground are usually good, but there's no way we can tie all this together like that. It's absurd!'

'Then let me talk to Morgan. Five minutes and I'll know whether his daughter's safe.'

'There's no chance I'm letting you anywhere near the PM. Not today. We will look into Ruth's situation and act if we find anything.'

'It'll take too long. If you won't let me talk to Morgan, do it yourself. Ask him right out. You'll know if he's lying. And if Ruth has been taken and there's any connection at all with the talks, then shift all your efforts onto getting her back. They're planning to hit Mapleton House and they'll kill Ruth once they've done it. But if you can get her secured, Morgan might be persuaded to move the meeting back to London. We might still have time to stop this.'

'That's too many 'mights' and 'ifs', Leila. If I can talk to the PM I will. But on one condition.'

'What?'

'You back off. For your own sake and the sake of this investigation, back off. I don't want to see you again until this is over.'

'Last time was a mistake. I don't make the same mistake twice.'

'Last time was a royal fuck up, Leila. That's why I'm ordering you to stand down. You're too close to this, too…'

'Hysterical?'

'That's not my word, but there are those who would paint it that way, yes. You go in front of the IPCC twice for the same catastrophic lack of judgement, I can't bring you back. You're finished. So, as I say, back off. We can handle this.'

'Be careful who that 'we' is, Michael.'

'If there's a security services mole, it's not within CTC.'

'Just the same, be careful, because if I am right and you've ignored my intel…'

'Don't threaten me DS Reid. And from now on, stay away from the investigation.'

He drained the last of his coffee, left a pile of coins on the table and walked briskly out into the crowds. Leila watched him go then unplugged the jammer and headed back over the bridge. She needed to get to Broadwater Farm and find Phillip.

34

'Could you patch me through to Gavin Byers, Ruth Morgan's personal protection, please?'

'Please hold.'

Micheal Lawrence had called the PM's personal secretary as soon as he got back to Scotland Yard. There was no substance to Reid's theory, but there was a feeling. Ruth Morgan represented a gap in the investigation. Hopefully it was an irrelevant gap, but it was a gap.

'DCI Lawrence?' a voice said.

'Yes. Mr Byers?'

'Yep. How can I help you?'

'We're just following up a loose end from the bombing. You told one of our detectives you left Ruth near Kensington Palace, is that right?'

'Yes. No more than a hundred yards from the gates.'

'But you didn't actually see her arrive?'

'No, I went straight to the bomb site. I got a call, I don't know, three-ish from security at Windsor to say she'd just arrived with the royals by helicopter and that they'd keep an eye on her.'

'Good, that's fine. Have you been in contact with her since?'

'No. Rostered days off yesterday and today.'

'But you still answer your official phone?'

'I'm never completely off duty when it comes to Ruth Morgan. I can always use the overtime. Now, if there's nothing else, I'm fishing with my son, Sir. I would like to get back to it.'

'Certainly. Thank you for your help.'

Lawrence placed the phone back in its cradle thoughtfully. It could be the truth. He could be fishing with his son, but the fact that he answered his phone when off duty wasn't fully explained by his dedication to his employer. If there was something wrong with this picture, Byers would want to be the first to get his story into the mix. Delay an investigation, dampen suspicion.

And who was to say father and son were sitting in a sheltered spot by the Thames? By now he could be anywhere.

He dialled the internal number of SO14, the unit responsible for royal protection. He was put through to the officer in charge at Windsor Castle and immediately the already over-loaded investigation took a whole new dimension. Ruth Morgan had not been helicoptered in because she had never arrived at Kensington Palace. SO14 had already been in contact with the PM who had reassured them that his daughter was safely at Downing Street.

He picked up the phone again then immediately put it down. This was probably still just a misunderstanding. There had to be a logical explanation. He wouldn't take it up the line yet. Commander Thorne would dismiss anything Reid had said without good concrete evidence, and there wasn't any yet.

For the second time in two hours he logged out of the department and made his way towards Westminster. A few minutes walk, just check it out, look the PM in the eye when he asked… Or was he really trying to bypass protocol? Was there a doubt in his own mind about the security of his own department? Was he being infected with Reid's fantasies again?

As he walked he dialled the front desk at the Palace of Westminster. The PM was due in at 2pm when he would address the House. He was working at Downing Street on final preparations for the start of tomorrow's peace talks.

Lawrence arrived at Downing Street three minutes later. The door officer let him in without question and he was taken to the waiting room by Jane Marks, one the PM's most trusted aides.

'Sorry to arrive unannounced like this,' Lawrence said. 'I just need five minutes.'

'I'll see if he's available.'

Two minutes later Jane came back and took him through to the rear of the building. Richard Morgan met him on the stairs and led him up to the private flat on the top floor.

'If you want to speak to me up here, I take it you know why I've come?' Lawrence said.

'You people don't make unannounced visits, especially in the middle of a crisis. How did you find out?'

'Well, until you said that, I hadn't, not for sure. One of my officers had a hunch and something Gavin Byers said didn't add up. I wanted to hear what you had to say before I made it official.'

Richard dropped into the sofa and half-heartedly motioned for Lawrence to take the armchair opposite.

'This can't be official,' Richard said. 'They'll kill her. You know that, don't you? You've seen what they're capable of.'

'Who? Who are we dealing with here?'

'They didn't say. You probably know as much as I do, and that's not much.'

'Ransom?'

Richard shook his head.

'And no time-scale?'

'It's ongoing.'

'Was there anything that might get us any closer to knowing who they are?'

'The man I spoke to sounded English, home counties, Eton, but then the Shoe Bomber was born in Bromley, wasn't he? You get two lunatics killing a soldier in London and we no longer know who the hell the enemy is. It's everyone. Christ, they kidnapped my daughter in broad daylight! How can this be happening?'

'Planning. And that's what sets them apart from Richard Reid and Lee Rigby's killers. Harakat al Sahm, for want of a better name, are sophisticated. They are meticulous, well-funded, and highly organised. If you'll excuse my saying so, they've even got the Prime Minister dancing to their tune. SO14 tell me you confirmed that Ruth was safely here.'

'What should I have done? If I'd come to you, they'd have

killed her. If I'd told anyone, done anything, they'd have killed her. They made one very simple demand. It was so simple I would have been insane not to comply.'

'So moving the peace talks to Mapleton House was part of this.'

Richard nodded.

'It seemed so... I even convinced myself that the move was a good thing. Security's better at Mapleton, the atmosphere more conducive to a positive outcome. I just can't see what they're trying to achieve.'

'Nor can we, unfortunately. But they're going to a lot of trouble to achieve something.'

Richard hauled himself out of the chair and walked over to the drinks cabinet. He poured himself a whisky and took a sip.

'What have I done?' he said, still with his back to his guest.

'You've done what any father in your position would do. They backed you into a corner and gave you no time to think.'

'I honestly thought the move to Mapleton was the least worst option under the circumstances. This can't be a simple assassination ploy. The security is second-to-none.'

'And there'd be little to gain by assassinating all the delegates. And taking out only one side would reflect badly on the other. Any action would be political suicide. But Mapleton's the key: there's *something* we're not seeing.'

'If I could change it back, I would. But if I move the talks again, the Israelis will be suspicious of the Palestinians, and the Palestinians will be suspicious of the Israelis and they'll both be suspicious of us. We lose the best chance we've had in decades. And the bloody Americans'll love the whole spectacle! This is a mess. And the worst of it is, you're the only person who knows and you're up to your eyes in the shit-storm that erupted over London on Wednesday.'

'Which is exactly what they were banking on, Prime Minister. But they've lost that advantage now. In fact, as you imply yourself, this might even give us a massive advantage.'

'Meaning?' Richard turned to face Lawrence.

'Let's assume they're planning something at Mapleton. We don't know what, and right now it doesn't matter. You moved the talks, but so far they haven't released Ruth. Which means they may still need leverage for something. We find Ruth, they've lost it. Even now, they've lost the element of surprise.'

'You think you can find her?'

'In twenty-four hours? It'll be tough. But finding her is going to be a lot easier than trying to penetrate these people through what else we know of them. This is the first concrete lead we've got, and we really can use it.'

'What do you need me to do?'

'If Mapleton's under threat, the only weak point is from the air. Discretely get fighter jets on stand-by. A visible military presence on the ground wouldn't hurt either. Make it look like a routine back-up. Apart from that, do nothing that will arouse suspicion. Carry on as usual. Stick to your plans and leave us to worry about security. Don't do anything that will signal to them that we're closing in.'

Richard shook his head. 'I just don't know who the hell I can trust any more. Byers virtually handed her to them. He'd been with us for two years!'

'I'm sorry.'

'Maybe I was blind. Now all I can think is: is there anyone else? We've never seen anything this sophisticated on home soil before. Did they have inside help?'

'We don't know yet. This is a very complex investigation.'

'Complex? Not to me. It's really very simple. I want Ruth back. But tell me, DCI Lawrence: who can I trust? Who can *you* trust now?'

'You can trust me, Sir. And I've got someone on my side. Someone I should have trusted long ago.'

35

Leila arrived back at Broadwater Farm a little after one thirty. Bones's acolyte put her through the same rigorous and unnecessary security checks as the previous day and she was taken up to yet another flat in the Northolt block where Phillip was once again in front of his computer.

He nodded at Leila's hello but did not turn round. She leaned in the doorway and watched him for a couple of minutes.

'You got into the CIA computer, right?' she said.

'Not very far.'

'Far enough. Can you get into Homeland Security?'

'No.'

'No? Is that more difficult?'

'No.'

'No what? Phillip, could you be a bit more specific?'

'I haven't decrypted Black Eagle yet. I don't have time to get into Homeland Security.'

'I think that's where you're going to find Black Eagle.'

He stopped typing.

'We found a passport,' Leila went on. 'It belonged to

someone we believe was working for them.'

'Show me,' he said.

'I don't have it, but I do have the number.' She reached for a sheet of paper beside the keyboard.

'Tell me,' Phillip said. 'Don't write it down.'

'It's 311532421. We know the name, date of birth, all the personal stuff, and I've seen stamps for Washington, Tel Aviv, a few others. What I need is anything else you can link to it or her. Hotels, secure-entry buildings, car hire, foreign exchanges, gun shops, pharmacies, anything which might have used the passport number for ID. Maybe we can get some idea what she was doing.'

'Why aren't your people doing it?'

'They probably are, but as Bones said, they ask permission. I don't have time to play by the rules.'

'I'll look into it.'

'Come on,' Bones said quietly. He'd walked up behind her so quietly she hadn't even known he was there until he spoke. 'Let him do his thing,' he said.

Leila gave him twenty pounds to get them something to eat then took a shower in the flat's tiny bathroom. When she came out Bones was sitting at the kitchen table with two huge pizzas in front of him. She should have known he wouldn't leave Phillip alone with her: to get anything this fast he must have phoned out for it. He took a second slice and wandered off in the direction of the bedroom where Phillip was working.

Five minutes later he called Leila in.

'He says there's nothing,' Bones said. Philip had already

gone back to the files he had downloaded from the Black Eagle server.

'What's the problem?' she said. 'We know from the passport when she entered and left each location. There must be some trace that spins off from that.'

'There's nothing,' Phillip said. 'Not just a dead end, but nothing at all.'

'How is that possible? Aren't we all tracked all the time?'

'Are you sure the passport number was right?'

'Yes. I can remember a nine digit number.'

'Then it's all been erased. I can't even give you a name. I've looked at Homeland Security, US Immigration and two servers in the UK. No records. Do you want me to try… where's Tel Aviv?'

'No. No point. How hard would it be to erase every trace of someone like that?'

'If you know where all the records were, it's easy.'

'Easy for you?'

'I didn't erase them.'

'No, I know. But it could have been done by a hacker.'

'Yes, if they knew where to look.'

'So we're nowhere. Not much point reporting that back.'

'They already know.'

'Know what?'

'That the records had been erased, if that's what they were looking for. Wherever I looked, CTC had already been there.'

'They can't have been. We're liaising with the US Embassy, and they were supposed to be looking into it. Our people wouldn't have had access.'

'Someone's been there.'

'You're sure? Someone from within CTC?'

'Yes. I had to go through the logs on the Home Office server to find an alias to use and I saw the CTC identifier. I back-tracked and found the same one on all the other server logs.'

'Did you get a name?'

'No.'

'Do you know if this person did anything?'

'No. I can't tell what's happened to a file that isn't there.'

'Strange. It's probably not important.'

'I'm running background searches for any secondary data. There might be something. It's going to take a while.'

'Don't bother. It'll have been erased. As soon as the Embassy knew we were onto them, they'd have gone through everything to make sure. Thank you, Phillip.'

'Did that help?'

'It did. I think. We suspected that this woman had help from the inside in Washington – the fact that she had a US passport indicated as much. Now we know she did and we know whatever she was doing was not legit. Whoever her US handlers are, they needed her to disappear completely from their end. They assumed we wouldn't find this second passport, or at least, not so quickly. As soon as she was killed, they erased her US identity, leaving only what fragments we had of her time in England. And she was careful with that. She was the key. Without her, nothing makes any sense: it's all just bits of a puzzle that don't fit together.'

Bones appeared in the doorway.

'You know someone called Lawrence?' he said to Leila.

'He's my boss. Why?'

'Greg Stiles called. Lawrence is looking for you. Or more accurate, he's looking for him.' He nodded to Phillip.

'Nothing new there. Did he say what he wants?'

'Your phone's dead, and he's got a problem. Thinks maybe Phillip can help. Your call.'

'Lawrence is above board, and I think I know what his problem is.'

'What?'

'Ruth Morgan. He's finally figured out that something's wrong. My guess is he wants the kind of corner-cutting help only Phillip can manage. Phillip?'

'He'll trace the call. Your people are already doing things you don't know about.'

'Will he?' Bones said.

'Honestly? I don't know, but I do know he needs Phillip's cooperation, so I think he'll play it straight. We'll use one of your phones to make the call. As soon as we're done get one of your guys to take it out of the building, but leave it live. Even if they do run a trace, the closest anyone could get is Broadwater, and they know that much already. Phillip, this could be the key. Something's going on out there, and right now, you and DCI Lawrence are the only people I can trust with this.'

'OK,' Phillip said, still with his back to her.

Bones handed her the phone and she dialled Lawrence's personal cell.

36

'What convinced you?' Leila said.

'The PM himself,' Lawrence replied. 'Admitted everything, including that the talks have been moved as a result of the kidnappers' demands.'

'Does he have any idea why?'

'None whatever. But he's convinced they've made a serious miscalculation. Mapleton's perimeter is ringed by a SHIELD doppler fence and they're running Goshawk security within the building. There's no way in, and everyone working the site has been vetted by all the participating governments.'

'There's something you're missing.' She glanced at Phillip. He had opened another sub-screen and was typing rapidly. The phone was on speaker right next to the keyboard, but so far Phillip had ignored it.

'Air strike is the only weakness,' Lawrence said. 'The PM has authorised two Typhoons on standby throughout the talks.'

'OK, let's find Ruth then we can concentrate on what's really going on. Who else is working on this?'

'No one,' Lawrence said.

'You've got no one looking for the PM's daughter? Really?'

'Morgan insisted, and I'm inclined to agree, at least for now. These people have been one step ahead of us right from the start. They know what we're going to do even before we do. Like killing Jaafar right under our noses; like following you yesterday – how did they even know where you live?'

'So you agree that there may be a leak within CTC?'

'There's a leak somewhere. Until we know what it is, I can't risk bringing anyone else in. Even Commander Thorne has no idea about this. So that's where Phillip comes in. I've collated all the data from the time of the bomb – CCTV, phone mast records, ANPR, anything I could get hold of. I can give Phillip access to all the files. He'll have researchers' privileges, which will get the two of you a long way towards seeing if there's anything we've missed.'

'Apart from the fact that you've missed everything,' Leila said, 'researcher status isn't good enough. Give Phillip full access.'

'Can't be done. And before you even think of hacking past what I have given you, I've alerted the Hendon Data Centre that he'll be there. If he strays one inch off the path, and he'll be booted out. What he's got is going to have to be enough.'

'I'll need to run traces on any calls that look interesting,' Phillip said very quietly.

'That's fine,' Lawrence said. 'Just do it your way, not through the police computer. When this thing's over, there's going to be inquiries for years. I don't want anything illegal tracing back to me or my department.'

'Fine,' Leila said. 'Send over the access protocols to this phone.'

There was a pause of a couple of seconds and the text alert beeped. Leila switched to text and showed Phillip the screen. He barely glanced at it before he was opening up a socket in the Police National Computer. Seconds later he had traces running on phone numbers and two screens of CCTV footage rolling.

'He's on it,' Leila said. She left the room and returned to the kitchen.

'Michael,' she said, 'I need to know that however this pans out, Phillip's going to be looked after. He's got no family, he's not exactly worldly-wise and what we've got him doing could get him tried or extradited.'

'I'll make sure he's properly rewarded.'

'That's not what I mean. He needs immunity, maybe even witness protection. Promise me that or I'll pull him out right now.'

'Phillip will be protected. Hell, if he's as good as you think he is, he'll probably even be offered a job.'

'Thank you.' She sat down at the table and took a deep breath. 'Right, what's he's on now is going to get us somewhere, but we still need to know who we're dealing with. Have you got anything on the attribution?'

'Not much. You were right about the video. It led, eventually, to an American student in Chicago.'

'Lebanese?'

'Yes. He's not even a Muslim. He's been arrested, but it's not going anywhere. And Harakat al Sahm was a smokescreen. You might have been right about Black Eagle, but we're still no closer to knowing whether that's a codename for the operation or an established group.'

'Ask the Pentagon.'

'I'll suggest it!'

'Tell me, did you get anything from the passport? I mean the US one, the Mussan clone.'

'Five are working with Special Liaison over at the US Embassy. They've not reported anything yet.'

'No one at CTC's looked into it?'

'No. Someone seems to have pissed the Americans off and they're not being very forthcoming with access right now. If Five get anything, they'll tell us. Why?'

'No reason. Just wanted to know if any of our people were working on the identity.'

'They are, but you made sure it was all-but impossible to do it through official US channels. What are you going to do now?'

'I've got a few ideas.'

'Care to share them?'

'No, not really. Unless you can get me inside Mapleton.'

'Absolutely not. Commander Thorne would have to sign off on it before we even went to Five or the PM, and I can't see that happening, can you? Why do you need to be there?'

'All this effort just to get the talks moved to a place that no one can get into. Does that make any sense to you?'

'They miscalculated. They assumed a country residence couldn't be properly defended in the time we had to do it. Fortunately, Mapleton was always on the cards, so everything was in place. I agree that they were planning something else, but I can't see how they can execute it, especially if we can get Ruth out of the picture.'

'We will. The opening dinner's at seven tonight, right?'

'Yes.'

'Then that's when we'll see it. They'll strike at the first opportunity.'

'But the PM agrees that this can't be an internal assassination.'

'No. This isn't about assassination. I don't think it's even about the peace talks, not directly. Black Eagle wanted to make sure all the players were together in a place of their choosing, but that's not their end game.'

'What is then?'

'I don't know. That's why I need to be there.'

'Sorry, it's not going to happen. Work the kidnapping angle with Phillip. It's the best I can do.'

'The best you can do is give me a job that's illegal, assisting someone who doesn't even work for CTC? Thanks a lot, Michael.'

'I'll call you if anything comes up.'

He hung up.

She sat staring out of the window at Phillip's former home across the sun-baked open area between the buildings.

She had the beginnings of a plan, but there was one thing she needed to check out first. Lawrence too was convinced CTC was leaking information, and to have any chance of putting her plan into action, she needed to plug that leak once and for all.

She took one of the two remaining slices of cold pizza from the box and took a bite out of the congealed cheese. Bones walked into the kitchen just as she was beginning to wonder why she'd bothered.

'Would you be open to a little under cover work yourself?' she said.

'What you got in mind?'

'I need someone taken out of the picture. Someone from CTC.'

'Shit, you're calling in a hit on one of your own?' He sat down across the table from her.

'I don't want him dead,' she said. 'The inquiry that'll come once all this is over will take care of his long-term future. I just need him off the grid for tonight. There are things I need to do and I think he's watching me.'

From the back pocket of his jeans Bones produced a small tin and a Zippo lighter. In the tin were half a dozen pre-rolled joints, one of which he now lit and regarded Leila through the smoke.

'Who is he?' he said.

'Mark Ross. He's CTC's principal data analyst, does digital forensics, that kind of thing. Like Phillip, only legal.'

'And not as good.'

'And nowhere near as good.'

'What's he done?'

'I think he's the CTC leak. Black Eagle have known every move I've made, and he's the reason.'

'If you're asking me to take out a cop, you're going to have to do better than that.'

'He's not police. He's a civilian IT expert, the main link between Cyber Crime and CTC, and the only person capable of doing the sort of covert snooping Phillip's doing now. Phillip said someone else from CTC has been snooping around looking for our bomb suspect's background. My boss knows nothing about it, says the Americans are blocking our attempts to get at their data. Which means Ross is running his own parallel investigation, feeding intel back to Black Eagle. I think he also tried to frame me by leaking forensic photographs to the media. With him in the picture, the further we advance this thing, the more danger we're all in. That's why I need him out of the way tonight.'

'I guess he don't live nowhere like this.' Bones took another drag and let the smoke drift up out of his mouth. 'A hit's going to be tough in a nice white street.'

'I told you, this is not a hit. If you're not interested, tell me. I'm way past playing games.'

'Tell me where we can find him.'

'Out Greenwich way somewhere. I can get you the address if you can do something.'

'I know people.'

'I can't pay you much.' She took the roll of bank notes from her back pocket and flicked through them. 'Two hundred pounds. Obviously I can't put it through on expenses.'

'There's no charge,' Bones said.

'Really? Why would you want to help me? You've done more than you needed to already.'

'I heard you on the phone.' He snuffed out the joint. 'You

didn't need to do anything for Phillip either, but you make sure he's looked after, I'll make sure you're OK for tonight.'

Leila took the pile of notes and folded them.

'I didn't say I don't want it,' Bones said, placing his hand on hers. 'I said I don't need paying. Two ton's going to be used for supplies.'

'Do I want to know?'

'No. But your man'll be well out of the way for the next few days.'

'Unharmed.'

'Unharmed. We won't even see him.'

'Thank you. I'll get the address.'

37

Leila sat on the edge of the bed behind Phillip. He'd got her Mark Ross's home address from the police central server as if it had been on his own desktop. He assured her that no one, even Ross himself, would be able to tell.

'Phillip, there's one more thing I want to ask you, but this one could be almost impossible.'

'You want me to get you into Mapleton House.'

She laughed. 'Yes, that was what I had in mind.'

'I can't,' he said. 'I've already had a look. It's good; the overlaps make it almost unhackable.'

'Not a problem.' Actually a very *big* problem, but there was always going to be a point beyond which even Phillip could not go.

'This connection isn't fast enough to fool the SHIELD switching,' he said.

'It's OK. Like I said: not a problem.'

He continued to type. She couldn't see his face but she could tell he was smiling. It was in his voice. Bones sauntered into the room and sat on the windowsill. The sun through his dreadlocks gave him a curiously messianic look.

'What aren't you telling me?' she said.

'I said *I* can't get you in,' Phillip said. 'I didn't say you can't *get* in.

'What's the difference?'

'Can you get me full access to the Police National Computer?'

'I've got clearance. Why?'

'The central server that houses HOLMES should be fast enough to let me get inside SHIELD. I can send commands from here, but the hard work is beyond this machine or this connection. I need your log-in and password. I can move more freely if I'm there legitimately.'

'You can hack HOLMES to make it work for you? Really? Just like that?'

'An eight-year-old could do it. HOLMES is based on Windows, so basically it's crap. But the computer that runs it isn't. Nor are its connections.'

'This is the only way? Isn't it going to leave my fingerprints all over it?'

'It's the only way if you're in a hurry. If I can interrupt the SHIELD protocols as they switch, I could give you a few seconds of dead time.'

'Long enough to get in?'

'Let me take a look. What's your access?'

Leila took her wallet out of her back pocket and pulled out a small piece of card. On it were hundreds of random characters: only she knew which constituted her password for the highest level of the Met's central computer. She dictated her details and in seconds Phillip was inside the mainframe at the Hendon Data Centre. Full access this time; not just the researcher privileges granted by Lawrence.

After five minutes he turned to her.

'Got it. The programmer wasn't very good, but the software is. I'm holding a door open that will give me access to the system running the fence, but once I activate it we've got very little time before I'm discovered.'

'How long?'

'About ten seconds at seven or thirty-seven minutes past the hour. Maybe best to say five. I don't really know.'

'Well that really makes me feel better. Seven or thirty-seven minutes past the hour? I've got to choose?'

'I can only do it once. I use the PNC to send out an interrupt while the protocols are switching. It'll cause a glitch. The master machine at Mapleton will reconfigure, sending new protocols out to the three slaves. It's their weak-spot. I guess whoever designed it knew that only top-end proprietory machines would be fast enough to make the hack.' Phillip grinned at her. 'Good job you had one.'

'Are you sure about this?'

'Do you want me to explain it all?'

'Not really. Question is: will anyone know the system's been tampered with from outside?'

'I won't have been. The down command will appear to have come from within SHIELD itself. Even if anyone looks at the screen at that exact moment, they can't do anything until the reconfigure has completed, and by then I'll be out. All they'll see is a glitch that the computer sorted out itself. They happen all the time. The operators don't look for them;

they only look for the results of them, and in this case, there won't be any.'

'And that's when I move…'

'You've got five seconds before the system resets. No way back in through the same door, and I can't see another one.'

'OK.' Leila adjusted her watch to the time on the screen.

'Five seconds,' she said.

'Five seconds, max. But you'll need to figure out where the doppler fence is. I can't tell you that from here.'

'Can't SHIELD tell you?'

'It could, but if I get out of the system that's running the alarms now I probably won't be able to get back in. I can tell you where the fence is, or I can turn it off. Your choice.'

'Turn it off. I'll figure the rest out.'

'That ain't gonna work, you know?' Bones said.

'I trust Phillip. Even if there isn't much hope, it's the only hope I've got.'

'Then you're screwed. I know something about breaking into posh people's houses, and I bet they're nothing compared to this place. You can get into the grounds, but how you gonna get into the house? Your man said everyone on the security roster's been background checked for weeks.'

'Damn it.'

'Just get on the roster,' Phillip said.

'I can't, there's no time. And technically I've been kicked off the investigation anyway.'

'Then I'll get you on it. Are the police running the operation?'

'No. MI5 are in charge on the ground. Uniformed officers

and some CTC are working it, but we're not in charge.'

'Any police in the house?'

'I don't know. I don't think so, but as long as they've got the right clearance, it's perfectly possible.'

'I'll get you on the roster and log your biometrics with the internal security system.'

'I don't have any biometric data on me.'

'I do. I had a look at you in the central database. Your current dental records, showing the recent loss of your upper-16 molar, are lodged with Myson Partners in Highgate, you have a tattoo of a blue butterfly on your upper left thigh, you…'

'OK, enough. That's just visual ID, anyway. The biometrics are…'

'Computerised. Of course. I downloaded those too.'

'Bloody hell, Phillip, I'm so glad you're on our side. Yes, OK, log me in, but do it after you've opened SHIELD. I don't want to show up on any last-minute checks.'

'I'll open a port. Don't talk to anyone for two minutes after you're into the grounds.'

He returned to his screen and Bones stood up.

'If Phillip can get you on the roster,' he said, 'why not do it five minutes earlier so you won't have to risk going over the fence?'

'Wouldn't work,' Leila said. 'Inside and outside are isolated from each other, for security. Standard procedure. It means no one outside the perimeter knows who's working inside. No chance of corruption or extortion, unless you can bribe the Home Secretary. Plus, gate security is being run by the

Met, so if I show up there, with or without being on Phillip's roster, I am, as you so poetically put it, screwed.'

Bones nodded. 'Is there anything else you need?' he said. Leila thought for a moment.

'Mark Ross is taken care of?' she said.

'You won't be seeing him for a while. But he's still got all his teeth.'

'Good. I will need an untraceable phone and a car,' she said. 'Something mid-range, anonymous but credible.'

'What happened to yours?'

'Fuck knows. I left it somewhere. It'll be in the police lock-up by now.'

'We got a Beemer,' Bones said, 'six-year-old 3-series.'

'Pimped?'

'No. Tinted windows, small reg plates, all legal.'

'No good. There'll be road-blocks. No traffic police would believe a fellow officer would drive something even that modded. Especially the windows.'

'Then you're on the bus.'

'Come on, there must be something else. At a push I could even drive a stolen car in there. No one's going to report a vehicle missing on a night like this.'

'You giving us permission to jack a car for you?'

'I'm saying this is important. Greater good and all that. If I can't get a car, I can't get to Mapleton. If I can't get there, I can't stop whatever's about to happen.'

'Give me five minutes.'

Bones left the flat and double-locked the door behind him. Phillip continued to type in silence, the soft click of the keys interrupted for a few seconds now and then as he read incoming messages on the screen.

'You sure you want to do this?' Leila said quietly.

Still with his back to her, Phillip said, 'I've got nothing else to do. I can't go home. My family is dead. Steven says I'll be safe here; they'll look after me.'

'Steven?'

'You call him Scaz Bones. His name is Steven.'

'We can take you into protective custody. There are things we can do to help you.'

'There are things I can do to help you. But I have to be here.'

'OK, when this is over, I'll make sure you're looked after. And we will get whoever hurt your mum and sister.'

Phillip stopped typing for a moment. 'Did he hurt them?' he said.

'No, I think they were killed very quickly. They didn't suffer. It was a figure of speech.'

Phillip nodded without much conviction.

The locks in the front door clicked. Bones walked into the bedroom a few seconds later and held a phone and a key out to Leila.

'Phone's pre-paid. Never been used. Car's under Martlesham; dark red Mazda 3. Bucket of shit, but it'll get you in and out unnoticed.'

'Bucket of shit,' Phillip whispered. His shoulders hitched a little as if he was laughing, then his attention was once more absorbed by what he was doing.

'I take it you didn't steal it.' Leila waved the key in the air.

'Friend of a friend. It's not red flagged on the ANPR Database so your friends won't notice it. All legal. But you break it, you buy us another one.'

'It'll come back just fine. Thanks.' She glanced at her watch. 'It's a little after six thirty now. I should be at Mapleton in about an hour and a half, allowing for roadblocks and finding a suitable place to cross the fence. Let's aim to get the fence off at 8.37.'

'How will I know you're there?' Phillip said.

'Send a blank text message,' Bones said. 'Just a full stop. The fence will be off at the next switch after we get your message.' He took the phone back and added his own number to the directory. 'You get picked up, you lose the phone. Nothing traces back to me. You get stopped in the car, we'll swear it was stolen this afternoon. Phillip can falsify the crime report log. Got it?'

'Fine. All I ask is you get the fence turned off. Then you're out of this.'

38

There were police vehicle checks at three and two miles out from Mapleton House. There had been a high-profile presence on the motorway bridges and A-road laybys too. At the three mile checkpoint Leila was waved through. By two miles out security was tighter. She was flagged down and came to a stop behind an elderly couple in a Nissan Micra.

It had taken her almost an hour and a half to drive from Phillip's hide-out at Broadwater Farm due south to Mapleton. Already the streets were busy and she had been forced to take numerous detours around gangs of people – youths mostly, but plenty of older people who should have known better too – out waiting for the balloon to go up and the night's festivities to start.

The traffic officer waved her forwards as the Micra continued its slow and halting journey up the narrow lane.

Before he could speak, Leila showed her ID.

'You expecting trouble?' the officer said.

'No. Just relieving a colleague. Gone down with food poisoning. Can I get straight in through the front gates?'

'You not been briefed?'

'Of course, but I was told to confirm with outer perimeter security before I got there.'

He looked at her for a long moment.

'You can drive through the concrete chicanes, but stop at least twenty metres from the main gate. They've got some high-tech invisible fence up there, runs right along the front wall, but it's twitchy. Keep your distance until they've checked you out.'

'Will do, thanks.'

He waved her through and turned his attention to the rusting Ford Transit that had come to a stop behind her. She watched in the rear-view mirror until she had crested a low hill and the van was lost from sight. With luck that should keep the road behind her blocked for at least ten minutes, and keep the traffic officer busy long enough that he forgot all about her. She could do without him deciding to check her story with base.

She drove past the turn-off that led up to the house and continued along an avenue of poplars that marked the edge of the estate. It was eight seventeen, still fully light, and with the car window down she could hear the Air Support Unit helicopter somewhere over to the south of the house. She needed to lose the car and make her way across the three hundred yards of no-man's-land between the lane and the secure perimeter of Mapleton on foot.

She pulled the car off the road beneath an ancient oak tree. It would be obvious to anyone driving past, but she thought it was unlikely that security would be doing regular sweeps of the outer lanes. Any locals who saw the car would think it was just someone out walking the dog. Most importantly, the car was not visible from the air. If it was spotted by ASU it would bring a lot of unwanted attention to this side of the estate.

A hundred yards back towards the main drive a hedge cut up towards the house. As she walked, she sent Phillip a single full-stop text message indicating that she was ready. She had eighteen minutes to get to the fence. If she wasn't in place then, it would only be because she had been discovered and arrested. If she was there, she just hoped Phillip was as good as he said he was.

On one side of the hedge was a field of ripening wheat; on the other a field of cows. Leila took off her leather jacket and scrambled through the hawthorn hedge and the ditch beyond. With the jacket rolled up against her chest, she began to make her way through the rustling ears of wheat. They provided very little cover against being seen from ground level, but should ASU make a pass overhead, she hoped her pale shirt would blend in enough not to be spotted easily. As it was still light, they would not yet be using thermal imaging against which there was very little defence.

Ahead was a five-foot dry-stone wall topped with barbed wire. Beyond, some two hundred yards away, was the house. Since she had not tripped the SHIELD alarms yet, this wall must be the boundary.

She checked her watch. Six minutes until the switch.

She crouched by the foot of the wall and waited.

The minutes went by agonisingly slowly. If Phillip had been wrong, if there was another layer of security that he knew nothing about, she was a sitting duck. There could be snipers outside the perimeter, external patrols, sniffer dogs. She could do nothing but wait and watch the seconds tick by.

At eight thirty-seven precisely she took a deep breath. Counted: *one… two…* threw her jacket over the line of barbed wire, scrambled onto a protruding stone, committed…*three.* She dived over, hooked her jacket free and rolled into the long grass at the foot of the wall.

No alarms sounded, no screaming sirens or running feet.

She counted ten seconds and glanced up towards the woods. All was quiet. Two uniformed officers were chatting in the distance. As they parted, she ran the fifteen yards to a huge beech tree and again crouched, scanning the ground ahead. An MI5 man crunched along the gravel path a fifty yards away.

She'd been inside the perimeter for forty seconds now. It could be over a minute before Phillip would have her on the roster, but she couldn't stay here.

When the MI5 man was out of sight, she stood up and began to walk towards the house. She knew she would have been spotted after no more than a twenty paces but no one paid her any attention. Even the ASU helicopter was now up at a thousand feet, making slow passes down-wind of the building so as not to disturb the dining guests.

Nothing was out of the ordinary. Nothing was wrong with this picture of English peace and quiet.

But something was coming. She knew it was coming.

39

What Leila didn't know was that Black Eagle were already inside the perimeter too.

They had been for over a week.

Four hundred yards from the main building, the Mapleton ice house lay abandoned and forgotten. Daniel Peretz had walked right over the top of it as he wandered through the woods. He'd seen no trace of it, but it was still there, a huge conical structure lined with brick and buried beneath the ornamental woodland through which British security agents now patrolled. In its heyday it had been an unseen architectural marvel. Like a giant forty foot-wide laboratory flask, it contained two hundred tons of lake ice packed with snow. This was taken to the house along a deep tunnel that ran beneath the gardens as it was needed. From its creation in 1772 to its final abandonment with the coming of artificial refrigeration in 1922, two men had been employed doing nothing else but stocking, maintaining and carrying ice. Other than the odd tree root that poked through the double skin of brick, it had been maintenance free and had served its purpose perfectly.

In 1923 the small hut that stood at the top of the entrance shaft had been demolished, and the entrance to the conical workings of the ice house had been covered over. Decades of leaf-fall and the snaking roots of grass and trees had entirely buried the small flat area where for years two men took their lunch at the top of the shaft. The 1945 map of the grounds marked its position only vaguely, and a 1968 National Trust survey map failed to show it at all. Even in the 1960s it was assumed that the structure would long since have collapsed without regular maintenance so no one bothered to try to find it. It would have been pointless anyway: as Peretz had confirmed, the other end of the tunnel had collapsed and been walled up decades ago.

Six months before the Peace Talks had been moved to Mapleton House an elderly gentleman with a walking stick and a springer spaniel had ambled through the woods at the edge of the estate. Where trees had fallen and not been cleared, thickets of bramble had grown up. A badger set pocked the ground near the outer edge, and years of neglect had rendered the ground difficult to navigate. There were no footpaths through here, and other than occasional security patrols, no one had been in here in years.

In his pocket was a GPS device. He threw a ball for his dog and wandered this way and that through the trees, tapping his stick, probing the ground for more then half an hour. Eventually the tip of his stick met resistance at the edge of a thick tangle of blackberries and ferns. If he had not been told roughly where to look he could have stumbled about for hours.

He called the dog back to him and as he crouched to stroke the animal he dug his fingers into the frosty ground. Brick: several bricks arranged in a uniform pattern.

He pressed a button on the GPS and continued to walk after his dog. Mapleton security spotted him and told him to clear off. He bowed his head apologetically and made his way down the main drive and back to his car half a mile away.

A week before the peace talks, that same gentleman, now an athletic thirty-three without the heavy disguise, led a group of ten men back to the spot marked on his GPS. They came on a moonless summer night, pitch black, and stole across the fields in total silence, keeping below ridge lines and skirting hedges so that they would be undetectable from any of the inhabited buildings in the area.

This time there was no grounds security because the only thing alive at Mapleton was a conference of NGO AIDS agencies, and they were not really anyone's first choice of target. The conference ended that night.

He had lowered them one at a time through the shaft into the ice house's conical body, then had sealed them in. They would live and work down there for a week in appalling conditions. And only then would their true mission start. Few, if any, of them would get out alive.

For five days they took shifts digging through the blockage and shoring up the tunnel, forming a widely-space chain to pass plastic buckets back and forth along the ever-lengthing passage. Back in the ice house the earth and brick was carefully stacked and their equipment constantly moved as the floor rose upwards. The tunnel was ventilated by a hand-pumped air compressor feeding a long pipe that snaked its way to the working face. It kept them alive, just. The effective oxygen percentage made it the equivalent of doing hard manual labour at the summit of Kilimanjaro. Fit though these men were, progress was slow. They also had to maintain total silence. Mapleton House, usually used as an exclusive conference venue, had been cleared three days into their dig. It had always been a back-up venue for the peace talks, and as such had to be security-checked whether it was to be used or not.

They had broken through to the wall at the end of the narrow passageway at almost exactly the time the Hyde Park bomb had exploded. It had then been a matter of rebuilding a bank rubble and brick thickly and solidly enough that should anyone take the trouble to unseal the wall in the cellar, the tunnel would still appear to be blocked. Only the most thorough investigation would indicate that the collapse was now only four feet thick.

The blockage had been removed and the wall dismantled quickly and silently in the hour and a half that it took Leila to drive to Mapleton. The heavy shelves beyond the wall, cleared of their loads of copper and glass when Peretz visited the room the previous day, moved easily.

While Leila waited for Phillip to get her into the house, ten Black Eagle men waited in the darkness of the cellar.

40

'Stop! Turn around slowly, keep your hands where I can see them.'

Leila had made it half way across the closely-mown lawn that led to the front of the house when the MI5 officer spoke. He approached from the cover of the shrubbery with a SIG P229 trained on her.

'Who are you?' he said.

'DS Reid, Counter-Terrorism Command.'

'Open your jacket.'

'I've got a gun in a shoulder holster,' she said. 'My ID is in my back pocket.'

'Hold that side open so I can see the weapon and slowly get your card.'

Leila turned slightly so that her holster was clearly visible, then reached round to the back pocket of her jeans. She took her warrant out and opened it.

The MI5 man read the number into a microphone attached to his cuff and listened. His face gave nothing away.

He moved so fast that Leila was unaware that he was coming for her until he grabbed her arm and span her around. He kicked the backs of her knees and an instant later she was face down on the grass with the agent pinning her down. He unclipped her weapon and threw it some distance across the lawn. She felt the cold barrel of his own gun pressed into her neck.

'Who are you?' he said.

'DS Reid, Counter-Terrorism. Can you let me breathe?'

'You're not on the roster. Put your hands behind your back.'

'You're kneeling on my fucking arm!'

He took her free arm and pulled it round behind her. Shifting his weight slightly, he did the same with the other one. He held her wrists together and snapped plasti-cuffs around them. He performed the entire operation in seconds and without his gun ever leaving her neck.

'Get up, slowly,' he said as he took his weight off her. Leila got to her feet.

'How did you get in here?' he said.

'I'm part of grounds security! Check the roster again!'

'You're not listed.'

'You read the number wrong. It ends four-five. You said five-four.' She knew he hadn't; she just had to sow enough doubt to get him to check it again. If Phillip had failed to get her onto the roster by now, she was in trouble. If it had just taken him a little longer than he had anticipated, she might get away with it.

The agent picked up her ID and read the number back to control. He frowned.

'You got me this time?' Leila said.

'Yes. I apologise DS Reid. You understand we can't be too careful.' He holstered his weapon and snipped the cuffs off. He was even good enough to retrieve her gun and hand it back.

'Reassuring to know you're that vigilant,' Leila said.

'I've not seen you here before,' he said. 'You weren't at the morning briefing.'

'I was drafted in at the last minute. I'm going up to the house,' Leila said. 'Anything I should know?'

'All quiet. This place is secure. Again, apologies for the mix-up. Have a good evening.'

She headed for the house before he could think of anything else.

Flanking the drive that led to the road was a pair of Foxhound armoured personnel carriers. They were arranged artistically, but there was no doubt as to their underlying message: don't mess with Mapleton House. Armed guards stood beside the vehicles. Two men were positioned behind the parapet of the house's roof, pointing their assault rifles out along the drive. It would be impossible for anyone to get near the building through the main gates without being spotted.

She walked quickly along the side of the house and up the newer driveway that led to the service entrance at the back of the building. There was a slight dip in the middle of the path and rainwater from the previous night's storms, sheltered by the deep shadow of the house, still glistened in its hollow. She absently thought a sewer must have collapsed underneath here, then the thought was gone.

She took a few more steps the stopped, turned around and walked back to the puddle in the drive.

Sewers.

'Shit,' she whispered. 'They're coming in underground!'

She ran.

At the back of the house, between the main building and the old stable block were several vans. Two had brought police in, another two were with the official caterers. A fifth, with blacked-out windows, bristled with antenna and a thick cable snaked from it to the double door to the house.

Two uniformed police officers stood by the door, each holding a standard MP5 carbine across his chest.

'Evening,' one said.

'Hi. DS Leila Reid, CTC. I need to get into the house, now.'

'No one goes in or out. Sorry.'

'I've got clearance. Check you records.'

'No one goes in or out.'

'Look. I don't have time to debate this with you. Check your records, then get out of my way.'

'Fine.' He radioed for assistance and a few seconds later the back door of the blacked-out van opened.

'DS Reid, this way please,' a man in civilian clothes said.

She stepped up into the van and the officer motioned for her to sit. The van was packed with surveillance equipment. Eight high definition screens showed CCTV feeds from various points around the house; other screens streamed data from infra-red and tremble sensors, audio monitors and, of course, the SHIELD perimeter system.

'Look into the camera, DS Reid,' the officer said. She leaned forwards and stared into the light, hoping that Phillip had managed to hack into whatever was driving this system.

'OK, you're good to go,' the man said. 'Wish they'd bother to tell us about these last-minute changes. So why's CTC going inside?'

'Just a precaution. Best to mix things up a bit, keep the element of surprise. You've not seen or heard anything out of the ordinary?'

'Nothing. Minor blip on the fence system a few minutes ago, but base think it was just a switching error. There's no way anyone could have got in in such a short down-time.'

'And you're certain there's no other way in?'

'There's some concern about air security, but we've got jets on stand-by. Advantage of this place is that it's on the edge of one of the busiest airspaces on the planet. Every inch of the sky is monitored.'

'Good. Thank you.'

This time the officers at the door let her pass. She stepped into a small internal guard-room where she was once again invited to look into the searching eye of a retinal scanner.

An internal door clicked open automatically, and Leila stepped into the cool gloom of Mapleton House. She checked her watch.

Eight fifty-seven. The delegates were at dinner.

And they were sitting ducks.

41

Ten men emerged into the little white room at the end of Mapleton House's cellar.

Each carried a small rucksack containing a vacuum-sealed change of clothes and the weapons necessary for the operation. They quickly changed into clean black jeans and black t-shirt over ultra-lightweight liquid armour vests. C-4 charges, detonators and ammunition magazines were already loaded into custom-made webbing.

Seven of them carried Jericho polymer pistols with sixteen shot magazines. Three, including their leader, Eben Kriel, carried small CZW9 sub machine guns. Although little more effective than the pistols, they were impressive to look at. They also made a hell of a lot of noise, and that could be just as effective as raw fire power in close quarter battle. They did not carry a great deal of ammunition as most of the necessary disabling of security would be performed using their Entourage automatic knives. Ninety per cent of their training was in hand-to-hand combat. Guns were only for when things went bad.

Each was also equipped with a tiny two-way earpiece,

loaded with five grams of high explosive. These could be remotely detonated or, in the event of live capture, would be activated manually, killing the agent and making any kind of facial or dental recognition impossible. Black Eagle Executive routinely falsified the DNA records of all field-operatives at the time of recruitment.

The final piece of equipment each carried was a simple black balaclava. No armour, no protection. Just anonymity and intimidation.

They knew the layout of Mapleton House as well as they knew their own homes. Gaining access to the ground floor would be impossible through the cellar and kitchens, so they shinned up the narrow shaft of the dumb waiter one at a time and fanned out into the building to their pre-arranged positions. The gang would be greatly out-numbered, but they had surprise on their side.

The grandfather clock in the main entrance hall chimed nine. Kriel checked his watch. The clock was thirty seconds fast.

He moved out of the cover of the servants' corridor and stood with two of his men outside the wide oak door to the dining room. He attached a thirty gram shaped C-4 charge to the door lock and stepped back.

At precisely nine o'clock he detonated the charge. A six inch hole appeared in the door. He turned the lock and kicked it open, stepping into the room with his men close behind. So far there had been no shots fired anywhere in the house, but that would change very quickly now that the door had been blown.

One of his men ran across to the main door into the hall and jammed the locking mechanism. Fists pounded on the wood. The agents outside would be through in seconds.

'Come with us, now,' Kriel ordered the assembled guests. There were nine of them; The three Prime Ministers – Richard Morgan, Aaron David and Abu Queria – plus two close aides for each. Six men and three women in total. For a moment no one moved.

'*Now*,' he repeated.

'What is this?' Richard Morgan said.

'This is your peace conference. So we need to move you to the conference room, right now. Go!' He hauled Aaron David to his feet and shoved him towards the door at the back of the room.

The main door from the reception hall burst open. Kriel let off a short burst of fire from his sub-machine gun and the two security officers fell back. He covered the door while his men herded the delegates through into the servants' corridor.

A hand appeared and tossed in a flash-bang grenade. Kriel got a single shot off before the hand withdrew. Flash-bangs are designed to disorientate hostiles and give rescue forces the upper hand for the few crucial seconds necessary to change the balance of power. This time it didn't work. All Black Eagle field operatives were trained to ignore these grenades the hard way: Kriel had, on numerous occasions, spent an hour at a time locked in a darkened hangar with his fellow operatives lobbing grenades at him randomly. They don't hurt, and once the subconscious mind understands this, they lose most of their usefulness. Kriel ran, head down, for the exit door even as the MI5 men outside were steadying themselves for an assault.

By the time he was in the corridor the last of the delegates was being pushed into the conference room. He dashed the few yards along the corridor and in behind them. His second-in-command was already at the door into the main hall, securing it with the twelve-point hardened steel locking bolts designed to keep anyone from breaking into the room. No one had considered that one day those who were being kept out might be exactly the people they most wanted inside.

Kriel locked the door to the servants' corridor. This too had been designed to be impenetrable.

Less than ninety seconds after blowing the first door, the nine delegates and three hostage-takers were sealed in the conference room; a room designed to be impervious to everything from radio signals to rocket propelled grenades.

'Sit,' Kriel said. A volley of semi-automatic fire echoed around the building above them.

'You're trapped in here,' Morgan said. 'There's no way out. Let these people go now and we can do a deal.'

'Sit down.' The others sat around the conference table. Morgan did not move. Kriel raised his hand to push him to the table but Morgan grabbed his wrist.

'I need to look into the eyes of the bastard who did this,' he said. 'See what kind of man you really are.'

'I'm just like you, Prime Minister. I'm doing my job.'

'My job doesn't involve the deaths of innocents.' The tip of the submachine gun was lightly pressing against his chin and he let go of Kriel's wrist. 'You know my government won't negotiate with you. You've got nowhere to go.'

'Sit down, Mr Morgan. We have no intention of negotiating with your government. Your part in this is over.'

'What is this? What do you want?' Abu Queria said.

'You will shortly make a phone call, Prime Minister Queria. If our demands are met, you will all be released unharmed. If not, everyone in this room will die.'

Kriel took an iPad Mini from his rucksack and plugged it into one of the ports on the desk. In this steel- and lead-lined room, radio communication was impossible. The land-line phones would work, but he needed a method of communicating with his own men on the outside, and the computer could send encrypted spoken commands directly to each of them as well as audio and visuals to whoever was monitoring the line. By now, that would be half the UK security services.

His first message was to ensure that the computer link was not severed.

'Any interruption on this line,' he said, addressing the iPad's camera, 'will be met with the immediate execution of all the hostages. This will be our main means of communication.'

There was no response, but he'd been heard.

While Kriel checked in with his men on the outside, his two fellow-operatives unpacked equipment. Each carried several narrow plastic strips about eighteen inches long, with a small black bump in the centre. These were looped around the necks of each of the hostages and secured with zip ties at the back. One then took a small device out of his webbing and walked to the front of the room. He placed it on the floor, flicked a switch and rested his left foot on it.

'You are wearing rings of det-cord,' he said. 'The trigger in under my foot. If pressure is released, either through a rescue attempt or through resistance on the part of any one of you, the cords with detonate. You will be decapitated immediately.'

Kriel established that three of his men were dead. The remaining four had disabled nine of the in-house security officers and had begun to sweep the building. He triggered the tiny PX charges in the downed operatives' earpieces and a series of dull explosions could be heard from distant parts of the house.

There was a heavy thump on the main door.

Kriel propped the iPad up, angling the camera towards an empty chair at the head of the table.

'You,' he said, addressing one of Queria's aides, 'sit there.' He motioned the woman to take the empty seat.

He stood behind her and spoke to the camera.

'I am aware that you are trying to rescue your hostages, and we would expect nothing less. However, know that no one will be alive should you manage to breach the room's security perimeter.'

There was another bang on the door. It sounded as if something heavy – probably one of the marble statues that stood in the entrance hall – was being used as a battering ram.

'I need you to clear all your operatives from the building. I have men patrolling the corridors and they will kill anyone they find. The hostages will be released when we have finished here, so any attempt at rescue will only be bad for you.'

Again something heavy smashed against the door. It barely moved under the impact.

'Back your men away from the room,' Kriel said, still addressing the camera. He raised his sub-machine gun just above the woman's head and pointed it at her. 'Clear the building, now.'

There was another bang on the door.

Kriel squeezed the trigger and a single bullet passed through the woman's head and slammed into the table in front of her. She wavered for a moment then fell face-down onto the wood.

'Clear the building.'

42

Leila stepped into the stone corridor beyond the guard room just as the deep boom of the first C-4 charge shook the walls. Someone shouted; feet pounded along the corridor above.

She backed up and addressed the two guards.

'Call in an emergency,' she said, 'but don't let anyone else into the building.' There was a crackle of automatic gunfire. 'Did you hear me?'

'Yes. What the hell's going on?'

'I don't know. I'm going in. Log me out of the system: make it look like I left.'

'What…?'

'Get me off the internal logs! If they don't know I'm in the building, they won't be looking. And keep everyone else out until we know what we've got here. Move!'

She shut the door and ran along the still-deserted corridor to the kitchens.

Inside, six of the caterers were still working. They had obviously not heard a thing over the noise of the washers and the radio.

'You need to leave, right now,' she said. 'Go to the back

door. Quickly!' She flashed her ID at them and began to push them out into the corridor.

Single shots, from two different types of handgun. The caterers began to run. Over the next ninety seconds there was sporadic gunfire and three percussive thumps as small high-explosive charges detonated.

There was then a single, muffled shot from the front of the building.

Checking the corridors were clear and that there was no one on the stairs, she ran up to the top floor. For now any hostiles in the building would be engaged with security. She had a brief window to find a base to plan her next move.

The top floor was deserted. All the doors were open. These small ex-servants' rooms had been converted to administrative use. Some were little more than store-cupboards; the larger ones were offices. Leila chose one with a window that overlooked the front drive and slipped in.

She did not dare risk closing the door. A large partners' desk stood at ninety degrees to the door and would provide her with good cover. She crawled under it and dialled Lawrence's private cell. It rang for what seemed an eternity before he picked up.

'Hello? Who's this?'

'Reid,' she whispered.

'Who?'

There was a series of small explosions on the floors below her – four in quick succession, small, high-explosive charges.

'It's Leila Reid,' she whispered. 'Listen. I don't have long. I'm inside Mapleton House.'

'You're what?'

'You wouldn't get me in, so I did it myself. This was always going to be the target.'

'Leila, hold the line, I'm going through to the briefing room. They need to hear this.'

'No! Not until I know what's going on.'

'You have no idea?'

'No. There were shots when I arrived then all hell broke loose. I'm on the top floor.'

'The delegates and six of their aides are being held in the conference room. One has been killed. Our people have been neutralised or forced out of the building. Three minutes ago we lost the feed from the Goshawk system, so we're completely blind.'

'Black Eagle?'

'It's as good a name as any. We still have no idea who they really are.'

'Do we know what they want?'

'Not yet. Five are handling the negotiations. I'll tell them we've got someone on the inside.'

'Don't do that. Not yet. Whoever's behind this must be getting help from somewhere. Until we know who, I don't intend to trust my life to anyone but you.'

'OK. Look, I have to get back to the briefing. I'll call you on this number in a few minutes with whatever we've got.'

'Let it ring. I'll have to put it on silent and it might take me a while to get to it.'

'Be careful.'

Leila ended the call without answering.

Outside, the helicopters swept their searchlights over the building. Additional support would be on the way, but it would be at least an hour before an SAS rescue team would be on site. By then, this would probably be over. Leila was on her own.

Footsteps approached along the corridor, soft and muted by the thick carpet. Through a gap between the desk and the wall she could see a little of the corridor outside. The sound came closer.

She had no more than a half-second view of the man who walked past. He was dressed entirely in black with a balaclava covering his face. His arms were bare, muscular, and in his right hand he carried a small pistol. Then he was gone. He hadn't even glanced into the room.

So the gang were confident that they had eliminated all the security agents. They were making routine patrols, but were not expecting to find anyone. It was probably no more than a ploy to confuse whoever was outside trying to figure out what was going on. The best anyone out there would have was thermal-imaging now that the Goshawk system with its infra-red and tremble sensors was down. They had lost their eyes and ears inside the building, and figures appearing and disappearing as they passed close to windows would not tell them much.

The phone buzzed softly. It was Lawrence, again using his personal cell. She held her hand over it and listened. There was no sound outside the room so she risked answering.

'What have you got?' she said.

'One of the agents, a Mossad man called Peretz, managed

to get a call out. You've got just four operatives patrolling the main house. Two MI5 agents have been killed, all the others captured or expelled. He thinks as many as three of theirs are down. The hostages are being guarded by three heavily armed hostiles with a video feed to the outside controlled by them. The hostages have been booby-trapped with explosives on a dead-man's switch. The conference room, of course, is impenetrable.'

'Do we have their demands yet?'

'No. But whatever it is, there's no way Morgan's going to sanction it. He moved the talks because he thought he could out-manoeuvre them. He was wrong, but the government policy still holds. No concessions to terrorists.'

'We'll see,' Leila said. 'They'll already have planned for that.'

'And what are you planning? We've got reinforcements on the way. Special Forces are being scrambled.'

'They'll have planned for that too. What do we know about Peretz?'

'SIS confirm he's Mossad. Exemplary record. They think he might be ex-IDF Special Forces.'

'Shit! They let a Kidon agent in there?'

'There's nothing on file, but even if he is Kidon he's there for security, not an assassination job.'

'You believe that?'

'He was vetted by all the parties. And he's feeding intel out to us. He's working for us right now.'

'OK. I need to find him. Maybe there's something we can do from the inside.'

Before Lawrence could give her an order she would ignore anyway, she ended the call.

Her odds were good. Four Black Eagle agents loose in the building, plus Peretz. No one else. In a house this size, it should be easy enough to avoid detection. Her biggest problem now was finding Peretz. He was alone, he was outnumbered, and he had no idea she was here.

She moved out into the corridor and, hugging the wall, slipped back towards the rear of the house. She looked over the rail at the narrow servants' stairs below. On her way up, the stairs had been unguarded. This time she was not so lucky. A shadow crossed the wall two floors down and she withdrew. Far below her a voice said something she did not catch. It was a one-way conversation, probably through the gang's intercom. Although she did not hear the words, the accent was unmistakable. This guy was English.

The shadow moved off. She took a step down, keeping her weight as close to the wall as possible and constantly scanning the stairwell below.

It took almost a minute of carefully testing each step before committing, then easing her weight slowly down for her to reach the first floor. She moved back into the main corridor to assess her position.

This floor, above the two huge rooms used for conferences and dining, was divided into large meeting rooms. As she expected, each door stood open and all the curtains were closed.

A figure moved at the far end of the corridor. For a moment she saw him in profile. No balaclava. Could this be

Peretz? He moved off and Leila was about to follow when she heard voices from below.

She crept to the top of the wide sweeping staircase that led to the main reception hall. The stair-rails were open and offered almost no cover so it was impossible to see who was below her, but she heard them. The two men spoke quietly; not to each other but to a third person on the end of their comms.

Suddenly, unexpectedly, they began to move away. Leila shrank back against an ancient sword chest and listened. They were no longer speaking. Soft, muted footsteps moved across the stone hall below and then were gone. She had to move, now. She had just moments to make the decision: continue to search for Peretz up here, or take this opportunity to get down to the ground floor. She decided to go down. Peretz would most likely be moving to get as close to the centre of the action as possible too.

She glanced behind her, but she didn't see him. Only when she stood up did she feel the sudden tug. A man clasped his hand around her mouth and hauled her backwards into a darkened room.

43

Prime Minister Queria stood up to cover the head of his murdered interior minister. Blood snaked from the aide's single head wound and pooled at the edge of the table. Kriel turned the gun on him and motioned for him to sit down.

'An unworthy death, even by your cheap standards,' Morgan said.

'We do what we need to do,' Kriel said. 'You, of all people, should be familiar with the concept.'

'So what now? More bombs? More death? I suppose you're going to kill us all, am I right? That's why you went ot so much trouble to get us here. Well, get on with it. See how far that furthers your perverted aims.'

'Prime Minister, you are embarrassing your guests. Please…'

'Who are you?' Aaron David said. 'Take off your masks and face us like men!'

'Who we are is of no importance. We need just one thing from you, then we will melt back into your background.'

'So what is it that you want?' Morgan said.

Kriel held up a finder to the assembled delegates and listened to a voice in his ear. He tapped the screen of the iPad and read for a moment. Neither of the other men moved from their positions or even looked at the hostages.

'Answer me one thing then,' Morgan said. 'Answer us *all* one thing. Why the bomb? Why tourists, maybe even some of your own countrymen? You had leverage without it.'

'You are weak, Prime Minister. Our 'leverage' might have been enough to persuade you to comply, but not those around you. It was necessary to make your people think the bogeyman they had spent so long dreaming up had finally come to pay them a visit. When you have been in the haunted house for an hour, the slightest creak is enough to send you scurrying for cover. The bomb was our creak. And your people did exactly what we thought they'd do, leaving the way open for us to do what we had to do.'

'So you were behind the riots too.'

'We populated the internet with calls to arms, but we were not responsible for the anger that led to battle. Your predecessor managed that very effectively on his own. When people are fed a diet of stupidity, what will you reap but destruction? Hitler, Pol Pot, Stalin: they all made a virtue of it. You people are surprised when it happens.'

'So you've made your point! What now? We admit to the public that we lied to them? You bring down three governments? Then what? You think your people can fill the vacuum?'

'No. You misunderstand. This is about a much longer game. Prime Minister Queria,' Kriel said, turning to the

Palestinian leader, 'you will make a call to your head of internal security. There is a change of plan regarding the transportation of a prisoner from the UK to The Palestinian Territories.'

'What are you talking about?' Queria said.

'Prime Minister Morgan's plan to release Raha Golzar into your care. We need to change the pick-up.'

'It's too late,' Morgan said. 'She's already left.'

'No, Mr Morgan, she has not. For reasons of security she is to be transferred from Holloway at eleven o'clock tonight. Since your predecessor granted diplomatic status to the Palestinian Authority in London, she will be taken by diplomatic car to Heathrow where she will be held awaiting a private charter. She will technically leave Britain as soon as she enters the car, and we believe that would be a mistake.'

He turned back to Abu Queria and placed the iPad in front of him. 'You will instruct your Mission's head of security to meet one of our people at Holloway. He will hand over the release papers and return to central London. Your part in this will then be over. I do not expect the order to be questioned. I am connecting you now. Read this, and only this. Any deviation and many more people will die.'

'I will read nothing! Do you think we are not *all* prepared to die? Our peace is bigger than any one person.'

'Not to everyone.' He indicated his second-in-command to move behind Aaron David. 'A dead Israeli Prime Minister because of one act of arrogance on your part would not play well in Tel Aviv.' He nodded and a pistol was pressed to the back of David's head.

'Don't read anything, Abu!' David said.

'Prime Minister David,' Kriel said. 'Abu Queria has your life in his hands. If you die here because he chose not to defend you, what do you think will happen? Do you really want the finger of blame pointed at the highest ranks of the PLO? Any uneasy peace you now enjoy would fail, and you understand the implications of a new Intifada.'

'He's right,' Queria said. 'It would mean all-out war. None of us can afford to open our territories up to the people who would come to finish what this one act would start.'

'Don't do it,' David repeated. He turned to meet the eyes of his opposite number and the pistol was pressed harder into the back of his head. 'Do you not think that the effects of giving these people what they want might be even worse?'

'I would prefer to deal with the possibility of a conflict we can manage over the certainty of one we can not.'

'Read it,' Morgan said. 'We are here for a purpose higher than that of our enemies. We will move forwards whatever the outcome of tonight.'

'Very well,' Queria said, turning to Kriel. 'We will play your games, for now.'

'We thought you'd see it that way.' He tapped an icon on the iPad's screen. A phone rang and when it was answered, Abu Queria began to speak.

44

'Easy,' the man said. 'I'm going to let you go but I've got a gun on you, so don't make any sudden moves.' Israeli, Tel Aviv accent, mid thirties, calm and extremely well trained.

The grip around Leila's mouth loosened and she wriggled free. She heard a key click in the lock behind her.

She turned to face him. 'You Peretz?' she whispered.

He was tall – six-one at least – slim but broad shouldered, with the even, balanced stance of a military man. In his left hand he held a snort-nosed pistol.

'I said, are you Peretz?'

He nodded slightly. 'And you are?'

'DS Leila Reid, Counter-Terrorism.'

'You're not on the internal roster.'

'I am, or I wouldn't be in here.'

'Maybe. How did you know I was alive?'

'I got a message from base. They filled me in on the situation here. And that situation means you should stop treating me like the enemy. We're the best chance these people have of surviving until the outside world figures out what the hell to do about it.'

'What do you know of who's behind this?' Peretz said.

'A lot more than they think we do. They're a US-based group that goes by the name Black Eagle, but so far we have no idea what their objective is. They leveraged the move to Mapleton by kidnapping Prime Minister Morgan's daughter during the bombing in Hyde park two days ago.'

'Has she been found?'

'No, but two people I trust are on the case. If anyone can find her, they can. We're very close. We've got all the pieces, we just can't figure out the picture yet.'

'You think they're planning more than just destroying the peace talks?'

'Don't you? They've got the place booby-trapped. They're heavily armed and we've got no agents other than us inside the building. But they're just sitting there. They have a bigger aim – something that only holding hostages from all three parties could achieve.'

'So they sent you in as a one-man… sorry, one-woman, army?'

'I'm not exactly here on official business. Let's say I'm trying to save more than just the hostages.'

Peretz spoke again, this time a little more loudly.

'Did you get all that?' he said.

'Wha…?'

Peretz held his hand up to her and cocked his head slightly. He was listening to a voice in his ear that Leila could not hear.

'No,' Peretz said, 'we kill her. She's told us what she knows.'

He listened again.

Leila had fallen right into their trap. The Black Eagle agents patrolling the corridors of the house had captured or neutralised every one of the friendly agents guarding the building... but somehow Peretz had managed to evade them? He'd done that because they already knew he was there. He was their inside man. Reporting back to CTC had been the perfect bluff to ensure that anyone else in the house would seek him out as an ally.

'I'm not bringing her down,' he said. 'She's done enough damage.' He raised the gun and pointed it at the middle of her forehead, the tip of the barrel less than two inches away.

'On your knees,' he said, clicking his earpiece off.

'Fuck you. If you want to shoot me, you're going to do it eye to eye.'

She took a step backwards and Peretz followed. In the mirror between the windows opposite her she could see the two of them as if watching the scene on a TV screen. She took another step and so did he.

She reached the door. There was nowhere else to go.

'Go on then,' she said. 'What are you waiting for?'

Peretz took a breath. She saw his finger tighten on the trigger.

An instant before he fired, she snapped her arms up and knocked his hand aside, at the same time sliding a little way down the wall and bracing herself. The bullet slammed into the wall an inch above her head.

In the moment between the first shot and Peretz taking aim again, she pistoned her right foot out. It was a perfect hit. With her back against the door and with a distance of two feet in which to accelerate, her heel made contact with Peretz's knee with maximum force.

The Israeli reeled sideways and Leila reached again for the door. The knob turned uselessly and the key was not in the lock. Running was not an option.

As Peretz righted himself she charged forwards, bent at the waist, head down. Her right shoulder hit him square in the gut and she kept pushing. With a broken knee, there was little he could do as she used her momentum against him. The gun clicked inches from her head as he struggled to clear a jam.

In seconds they were across the room. She just hoped the upper floors had also been fitted with toughened glass or they would both be in trouble.

At the last moment she gave an extra shove and Peretz's back hit the curtained window. It barely moved, but he did. He doubled over, his head hitting the small of her back and the gun spilling from his hand. Leila straightened and brought her knee round against his ear. His head jerked sideways and he fell to his knees, scrabbling for the gun a few feet away.

Without thinking Leila span on her heels and kicked him squarely in the jaw. He went down, sprawled and inert.

What now? She had had only one ally in the building, and he had been no ally at all. She had no retreat, no way back out of the building. But it seemed the leader had told Peretz not to kill her. She might still have some value to them alive.

There was only one play here.

She rolled Peretz onto his side and took the door key and his earpiece. She found the mute switch, clicked it off and put it in her own ear. The wire snaked back into Peretz's jacket collar so she crouched to ensure she didn't break the connection.

'Looks like your man's not going to be killing me after all,' she said.

There was a pause, a click and a voice spoke.

'So what now, Detective?'

'I'm going to do what I came here to do: stop you.'

'You think you're just going to be allowed to walk out of here and carry on your crusade?'

'Not at all. I'm on my way down to the conference room…'

'No!' The voice was muffled, distant, but she recognised Prime Minister Morgan instantly.

'If you can all hear me,' Leila said, 'this will be over very soon. The security forces have the building surrounded and we're very close to bringing down the people who are behind this.'

'You'd better come down then,' the voice in her ear said.

'Keep your men back. You give me safe passage to the conference room, you've got yourself another hostage. Agreed?'

'Come and find out, Detective Reid.'

Although she had little idea of the internal layout of Mapleton house, there was no doubt where the conference room was. Immediately outside the room's double doors was a broken marble statue and a lot of dust and rubble. The door itself was barely dented. Beside the statue were two large pools of blood. Droplets arced up the left wall. The assassin had killed his prey with a single deadly swipe of a blade across the throat. They were saving ammunition.

At the far end of the corridor a man dressed in black t-shirt and jeans stood with a pistol pressed to his chest. He watched her but did not move.

The door opened as soon as she knocked. She stepped in and it was locked behind her.

'Leila Reid,' a voice said. In the relatively bright light of the conference room, she was momentarily unable to see who had spoken. She never did discover his name, but Eben Kriel's voice would haunt her for the rest of her life. Any South African accent would be forever linked with the horror into which she had just stepped.

Aaron David and his two aides sat with their backs to her; Richard Morgan's group sat at the head of the table; opposite her was Abu Queria and one of his party. At the end of the table a woman lay face down in a pool of blood that spread out over the polished surface and dripped onto the cream carpet. One Black Eagle agent stood against the main door, another beneath a large LCD screen on the front wall. His foot rested on a black box. The man who had spoken was on the far side of the room.

'Congratulations, Detective Reid,' Kriel said. 'You evaded us at every turn. For two days you slipped through our net. Clever to use a bomb hoax to outrun the man we sent to find you. You even pretended to leave tonight, though we had already seen your biometrics logged into the entry system.'

'Well if I'm what you wanted, let these people go.'

'All in good time.' He stepped up to the table and tapped

a few lines into the iPad. Leila drew breath to speak but he held his hand up to her. He read the reply on the screen and turned back to her.

'You have caused us a great deal of trouble,' he said. 'Now you are going to do something for us. Balance your account, so to speak.'

'I'm doing nothing for you. Your time's running out.'

'You mean Ruth Morgan? No, Miss Reid, that was perhaps your one mistake.' He turned to Richard and said, 'this agent of the state, an employee of your security forces has just killed your daughter, Prime Minister.'

Morgan made a sound that was barely human. His shoulders dropped and he visibly crumpled. All the others seated around him looked down.

'If she's dead, I had nothing to do with it,' Leila said. 'You were going to kill her anyway.'

'That is possible, yes, but when you began looking into the background of our operation, she became a dangerous distraction. She was shot five minutes ago. Her body will be found quickly and can be given a proper send-off. We ensured she would look well in an open casket.'

'And you still think I'm going to do something for you?' Leila said.

'You are about to take a drive back to London.'

'Me?'

'Yes. Not quite as we planned, but as soon as we saw you enter the building we knew we had found the perfect person for the job. In a few minutes you will drive to London to collect a prisoner from Holloway jail. You will then take her to an address you will be given and, if you do as you are told, you will go home and all this will be over. These people will be released and should they wish to continue their charade of making peace in the middle east, they are welcome to do so.'

'Oh really? I'm going to London? You've got nothing left. I knew I might not make it out of here alive, and I'm fine with that. Ruth's dead and you've already applied your maximum pressure to the delegates. You've nowhere left to go.'

'I think you'll do it without any coercion at all, Miss Reid.'

'And why the hell would I do that?'

'Because you have to know. You've risked everything to solve this puzzle. You've almost certainly made any legal process impossible, you've probably lost your job, alienated the only people who ever stood by you. And for what? Glory? Money? No. *Ego*. You *have* to solve it; you *have* to find the final piece. You will do exactly what we ask, because your ego will make it impossible for you to do anything else. Black Eagle is already more important to you than the air you breathe. And in that, you and I are exactly the same.'

'We're nothing alike.'

'We'll see. Maybe when this is over, you'll understand.'

The iPad on the desk pinged softly. Kriel glanced down and Leila did too. A single word had appeared in a window at the top of the screen: PROCEED.

45

When she had entered the conference room, Leila had expected many things. What she had not expected was that she would be leaving, alive and well, less than half an hour later. She still had her gun and phone, and the keys to one of the official agency cars parked outside.

Outside, the powerful lights of two ASU helicopters were trained on the front and back entrances to the house. Shafts of blue light flashed through the trees from unseen vehicles beyond the apparently useless SHIELD at the garden's edge. Leila clicked the electronic key and scanned the parked cars. A black BMW 525 winked at her.

It was a little after eleven o'clock. The night was hot and overcast, without the promise of a storm to clear the air. She made a quick detour to the red Mazda parked along the lane. She retrieved the small bag containing her tool roll and dropped it into the passenger footwell of the MI5 car. With Scaz Bones's phone wedged into the cradle on the dash she turned around and headed out towards the main road. She dialled Lawrence's direct line. He answered it after one ring.

'Leila, where are you?'

'Just leaving Mapleton House. I'm their nominated driver.'

'For Raha Golzar?'

'If that's who's in Holloway jail, yes. First, I need you to clear the roads heading north. I'm in a government registered 525, alpha-charlie-one-five golf-lima-papa. I don't have time for roadblocks. How are we doing at you end?'

'Leila, have you heard about Ruth Morgan?'

'Yes. He told me she'd been executed because Phillip got too close.'

'Phillip didn't get anywhere. There was no mobile phone, no digital records. He drew a complete blank.'

So she *had* been responsible for Ruth's execution. Black Eagle had no idea about Phillip's involvement until she herself told Peretz. After that, they couldn't risk Ruth being found before this was all over.

'Leila?'

'Yes, I'm here.'

'What can you tell us of the situation inside the conference room?'

'I can tell you Peretz isn't working for us, he made that very clear. Of the three men in the conference room, I've got nothing. No names, masks, couldn't tell you anything. The leader's South African, my guess would be Special Forces, but you know that already.'

'Peretz told us they'd booby-trapped the room.'

'They've got C-4 necklaces on each of the delegates. There's a wireless connection to a dead-man's switch on the floor under the foot of the second man. They're all armed, but they're casual about it. The delegates are way past any kind of resistance, if they had any to begin with. Communication is via an iPad plugged into the Mapleton LAN. He's communicating with other agents within the building and at least one person on the outside.'

'They're using proprietary encryption for most of it. We can't even get into the network let alone hear what they're saying.'

'Have you tried Phillip?'

'We're handling it from here.'

'Mark Ross?'

'Ross? No. That's a whole other story.'

'Tell me.'

'He was arrested just after seven o'clock. Anonymous tip-off alerted Major Crime to a whole other life Ross was leading right under our noses. Sixteen rocks of crack cocaine was found in his flat, along with a gun that links back to a gangland shooting two years ago.'

'That's too bad,' Leila said. Bones and his friends in Greenwich had done a good job. 'Michael, I know you need to keep things tight, but don't write Phillip off because he couldn't find Ruth. He's the only reason we've got *this* far.'

'I'll keep it in mind. What can you tell us about the bombs?'

'Half-inch thick strips of plastic C-4, small detonator at the front.'

'How are they attached?'

'The loops are closed with plastic cable ties at the back. They're on tight enough that there's no way they could be removed in a hurry. Hold on a moment.'

She had been waved through the one- and two-mile checkpoints and by the time she reached the three-mile cordon she didn't even bother to slow. She flashed her lights half a mile from the cluster of flashing blue lights and floored the accelerator. She was doing over seventy when she whistled past the assembled armed guards on the outer limit of Mapleton Security.

Still planning for yesterday, she thought.

'OK,' she went on, 'fill me in on what I'm driving into here.'

'Everything's in place at Holloway. There's also CTC officers closing in on the prison.'

'All I need is an outrider, marked car, to clear the road of traffic. They'll be watching.'

'OK. CTC will follow discretely. I'm going to patch Sir Malcolm Stevens into the call. He can fill you in on what Five have got on Golzar.'

There was a few seconds of silence then Stevens spoke.

'DS Reid?'

'Sir Malcolm. What do we know about the prisoner?'

'Officially not much. She's an ex-Iranian, ex-Russian, now-US citizen. According to her limited file she was killed in an assassination in West Jerusalem in April last year.'

'Mossad?'

'Fatah, officially. She had links to a double agent by the name of Hassan Hawadi. He set her up.'

'No shit! So what really happened?'

'She was picked up by SIS agents working with the CIA. Rendition was arranged via RAF Lyneham to Joint Base

Andrews in Maryland. But Richard Morgan had planned the whole thing: he needed her here as his ace card in the peace deal. She's been kept at Low Newton as a maximum security mental patient since she arrived.'

'But she's not mental.'

'Far from it. We just don't have a Guantanamo Bay here. Low Newton was the next best thing. It was the perfect cover – hiding in plain sight. Her story was so unbelievable that no one was going to think she was anything other than a paranoid schizophrenic. Someone high up in the government created a whole back story to keep her away from prying eyes, and of course the CIA had to deny they knew anything about her.'

'And now she's being handed over to the Palestinians.'

'Right. No one outside of the PM's immediate circle and a handful of people in the security services knew about it.'

'Someone knew she was at Low Newton,' Leila said. 'Do we know why she's so important?'

'We don't know very much about her at all. SIS have opened their files to us, or at least some of them. She first appeared on the security radar when she defected to the US in 1998.'

'From Iran?'

'From Russia. She has a doctorate in biochemistry and epidemiology from Tehran University, and she furthered her speciality at Biopreparat in Kazakhstan.'

'Bioweapons.'

'Exactly. From there she joined the Russian military station at Omutninsk, then in 1998 the US Defence Threat

Reduction Agency. She's *the* world authority on weaponised hemorrhagic fevers and she's got a contact book that would be the envy of any world leader on earth.'

'Are you thinking she was in Jerusalem to sell bioweapons technology to the Israelis?'

'Probably not. That kind of weapon has no place in close-quarter conflicts. SIS think it more likely she was in Israel flexing her muscles. If she made just enough noise in just the right places, Iranian intelligence would know she was operational again: they'd pay attention. That would wake up the Russians. Obviously the CIA had to take her down.'

'But Morgan saw her as a lever to get the PLO to the negotiating table.'

'Not just the PLO. The Israelis weren't that thrilled that she was still alive either. The fact that she'd decided to advertise her services in Jerusalem was acutely embarrassing.'

'That still doesn't answer why she's so important to Black Eagle. There's no evidence they did anything about her death, so why go so far to release her now they know she's alive?'

'Obviously they couldn't risk her going on trial, especially not somewhere as sensitive as Ramallah,' Stevens said.

'This is still overkill. They could have just had her assassinated. Properly this time.'

'As I said, she's got quite a contacts book. Since the end of the Cold War there's always been a threat of a truly global black-ops organisation appearing. With Golzar in the picture, that could be what we're facing.'

'So they're not afraid she'll bring governments down: they want her to bring them together.'

'It's a very real possibility.'

'What do you want me to do with her?'

'Leila, I'm not going to lie to you,' Lawrence said. 'This is very high risk. These people have shown their willingness to kill anyone, anywhere, to get her. You'll be walking right into their firing line, and until we've secured the hostages we'll have no choice but to let this run. The problem is, what you know puts you at especially high risk.'

'I agree. But that's not going to change. Right now, I'm the only person with any chance of being able to stop Golzar slipping out of our grasp once and for all. If Black Eagle are going to kill me, I'd rather it be for national security than just to clean up loose ends when I'm out buying milk.'

'Good. We hoped you'd see it that way. Pick her up. But until the hostages are released, we won't be able to give you any close back-up.'

'I'm to be given further instruction when I get to Holloway. You just want me to go along with it?'

'Yes. All we can do it try to follow.'

'There's very little chance I'll be allowed to keep the phone live once I'm with her.'

'We know. You're in one of Five's cars, aren't you?'

'Yes. It's a black 525.'

'Check the drop-down panel in front of the passenger seat,' Stevens said.

Leila leaned across and fiddled with the catch, revealing a large opening where the standard car had its glove box.

'What am I looking for?'

'Micro ear-piece. It'll be in a white plastic container.'

'Yes, got it.' She opened the box and pulled out a tiny earpiece. 'There's a watch too.'

'That's the transmitter. Got a serial number on it?'

'No, nothing.'

'We tell them not to do it, but they remove them anyway. OK. Put the earpiece in and wear the watch. We'll see if we can get the unlock for that unit from the car registration. We've got people in place close enough to Holloway that we'll be able to relay some comms to you. Good luck.'

'Thank you.' She pushed the device into her ear and slipped the watch onto her wrist. It looked ridiculous, so she stuffed it into her jeans pocket.

'Make it obvious you've got your phone when you reach Golzar,' Lawrence said.

'I know how to do my job. I'll keep it on as long as I can. If you can't get anything from Five, we're just going to have to let this play out.'

'We'll find you. The intel you've supplied already has got us much closer to Black Eagle than we've ever been before.'

'With respect, you didn't even know they existed.'

'No, but thanks to you, we do now.'

'I have an idea, if I can put it to you.'

'You can speak freely.'

'First, get Phillip into the Mapleton LAN to try to disarm the necklaces. Trust him.'

'You think he can do it without being noticed?'

'I think he can do anything he sets his mind to, but we don't have much time. As soon as Golzar is safe they'll move, so if the bombs are not neutralised by then, they're just going to be able to walk out of there and away.'

'Then that's the way it's going to have to be. We've lost one of the delegates already. We can not afford to lose anyone else. If either Queria or David don't make it out, it's a guaranteed war in Israel. With ISIS all around them and Iran back in from the cold, it's a war that would be impossible to contain.'

'But we can't afford to let Black Eagle fly either. Golzar is important – important enough to stage this whole operation just to get her out. If they go, we lose. This might be the only chance we'll ever get to bring them down, to find out who the hell was really behind the Hyde Park bomb.'

'I can't see any way we can do both. If we stop Black Eagle, we lose the hostages; if we save the hostages, we lose Black Eagle. Phillip might come through, but it's asking a hell of a lot of someone who doesn't even work for us.'

'Have you got anywhere with the link to this earpiece yet?'

The background sound of the office cut out and the phone went silent. Leila looked down but the connection had not dropped. She was about to take the phone from the cradle when the line clicked.

'They're still working on it,' Lawrence said. 'Why?'

'I think there's a way we can save the hostages and not lose track of Black Eagle. But it would be better if you can hear what's going on.'

'Go on…'

'I go with Golzar. Black Eagle are going to want at least one hostage to ensure secure passage anyway.'

'Only as far as being able to get out of the country.'

'I can persuade them of my value as an ongoing bargaining chip. I get on the plane with them.'

'We have no idea where they're intending to go. It's not going to be a big commercial airport; we can't get agents into position to protect you.'

'Then we let it run, see where it leads. If you've got comms to me, even one-way, you'll get a good idea of where we're going.'

'And if we can't get a link, you're completely exposed. No, Leila, I can't allow a course of action that would almost certainly result in your death. Personally or professionally. We've got a little time to find an alternative.'

'You don't have any time and you don't have any alternative. Without live intelligence on the ground, you'll lose her, and you'll be back to a botched assassination and rendition. At *best* the whole thing starts again.'

'No. I'm not going to sanction a suicide mission.'

'Then all the deaths, all the carnage of the last two days will have been for nothing.'

'DS Reid,' Lawrence said, 'I am ordering you to stand down as soon as the hostages are released. I will expect you back here for a full debrief.'

'I'll check in when I've got Golzar,' she said and hung up.

46

A little before twelve thirty Leila drove along the wall outside
Holloway Jail, scanning the pavement. The streets were quiet.
No one flagged her down so she turned in to the short
service road that led to the prison's main reception. The lights
were on inside but there was no sign of anyone waiting for
her. She pulled into a disabled parking bay just short of the
barrier and killed the engine. A guard in the gatehouse looked
out at her, so she pressed her CTC ID to the car window and
shook her head. The guard sat down and went back to his
book.

A few people walked past along the main road in the next
couple of minutes, but there was very little activity on the
street.

Only now did it occur to her that no arrangement had
been made for the rendezvous. Kriel could have no idea how
long it would take her to drive across the city. He'd given her
no number to call when she arrived. And it didn't seem likely
that Golzar would just be allowed to walk out of the jail and
wait on the side of the road.

'Shit,' she hissed. She started the car and threw it into

reverse. Had this all been a ruse to get her away from Mapleton and tied up on a wild goose chase?

She turned right onto the main road to retrace her route along the long blank wall of the prison. Technically this was a one-way street, and not the way she was going. She jinked across the pavement outside a used car garage and rejoined the road in the right direction. She drove the full length of the block then came to a stop in the bus lane.

What now? Wait? Go back to Mapleton?

Suddenly the rear door opened and the car sank a little as someone got in behind her.

'Don't turn around,' a voice said. A man, mid-Atlantic accent. Probably fake: an American disguising his place of origin.

'Where is she?' Leila said.

'Close.'

'So what the hell's this? Checking I came alone?'

'We know you came alone. We've been watching you since you left Mapleton. You think you chose this car at random?' He shifted slightly in the seat. 'Pass me your gun.'

'My…'

'Pass me your gun. I know you still have it. You'll get it back when this is all over. By then you'll realise shooting me is not an option, but right now I could do without you being distracted by planning something stupid.'

Leila reached into her shoulder holster and passed the Glock back to her passenger.

'And the phone.'

Reluctantly she handed Bones's mobile over.

'Where's Golzar?' she said.

'Drive.'

'Not until you tell me where we're going.'

'Drive. You'll know where we're going when you need to know.'

Leila pulled out into the road heading back towards London.

'Who are you?' Leila said.

'I'm Raha Golzar's legal representative. Donald Aquila, if you want to call me something. Turn right here.'

Lawrence didn't speak in her earpiece. He might be listening, or he might not have managed to trace the transmitter's frequency. For now she would have to assume she was on her own.

She drove north east. For ten minutes Aquila was silent.

'Where are we going?' Leila said. They were within a couple of miles of Phillip's location in Broadwater Farm and for a moment she thought she was going to have to drive right to him.

'Have you somewhere you'd rather be?' Aquila said.

'No. I just want to know this isn't a waste of my time.'

'Keep going and you'll find out. Or you can get out here if you prefer.'

'You know I can't do that.'

They drove on north for another fifteen minutes in silence. She felt Aquila move in his seat behind her then he spoke very close to her ear.

'Pull into the car park on the left here,' he said.

Leila drove into a near-deserted car park with a

McDonalds isolated like an island in the middle. A few cars were parked around the edges, outside dark and shuttered superstores.

'Stop beside the Lexus over there, driver's door to driver's door.'

Leila reversed in beside a black GS. Aquila pressed the key remote and the indicators flashed.

'Now get in, nice and easy.'

She opened her own door and quickly moved across into the driver's seat of the Lexus, dragging her small bag behind her as Aquila rounded the back of the car. It sat low on its skinny tires and the seat had been set back for a much bigger driver. Beneath the smell of pine air freshener was a faint scent of medicinal alcohol and basic soap. It was there and then it was gone. Aquila slipped into the seat behind her.

'Where is she?' Leila said.

'I told you, she's close. Now get moving. Back to the main road then north again.'

She started the car and reversed out. The fuel gauge showed little under a hundred miles remaining. They wouldn't be going far. Time was running out. Three miles north of here was a small airport mainly used for freight and pleasure flights, but capable of handling a private jet. It would take them no more than ten minutes to reach it. That had to be their destination. If Phillip didn't come through with the disarm codes by the time they arrived there was nothing she could do to stop Golzar leaving.

'Since you've got both the guns,' she said, slowing the car slightly, 'I think you can tell me one thing before you kill me.'

'What's that?'

'Who the hell was Ghada Abulafia, your bomber? Wherever I've looked, she doesn't add up. I can't get the final picture, and I need it.'

Aquila looked at her in the car's central mirror. 'You really don't know? They never told you?'

'Who?'

'Abulafia was one of yours, SIS.'

'Bullshit.'

'Many of our field operatives are recruited from the ranks of secret intelligence organisations: CIA, SIS, Polish AW, SASS in South Africa, Mossad… you get the idea?'

'I don't believe it. If SIS knew who she was, why didn't they tell us?'

'And admit they'd been infiltrated? If Abulafia was one of us, who else might come under suspicion?'

'That's why we could find no trace of her. She had a US passport from you, and at least one more from British Intelligence.'

'Ghada was a chameleon. Jewish, Palestinian, British… she could slip between warring factions invisibly, arousing no suspicion at all. Except that in the end, she did. What set her apart was that we never really turned her. She was a spy, so to speak. We'd been watching her closely for months, and this operation was the perfect opportunity to flush out her real allegiances. She was involved at the top level in planning the bombing, though not what came after it. She knew that with a timer-operated device, any of our people would be well away from the building in the final few seconds, so she would be free to go back to it. And she did: she tried to stop it. As you saw, she failed. The bomb was detonated manually from the roof of the building opposite.'

'You sacrificed one agent to free another…'

'No. And if you let your speed drop any further, I'll put a bullet in the back of your head.'

Leila glanced in the mirror; Aquila checked his watch. She raised the speed to thirty.

'We disposed of a rogue agent to get another out of what could have become a very public spectacle,' he said. 'If Golzar had gone on trial in the Palestinian Territories, barely a government in the western world would have escaped unscathed.'

'And Harakat al Sahm? Was that just a flag of convenience? A fiction to keep us busy?'

'Of course. You wanted Islamist terrorists, so we gave you Islamist terrorists. There's no 'cell' in any sense that you would understand. Our sleepers are everywhere: in governments, the military, secret service… Take a left here and stop outside the last hangar.'

She turned onto the deserted road that ran along the perimeter of the small commercial airport as she had expected. She came to a stop outside an open hangar. Inside was a Gulfstream G150, the baby of the range. With a seating capacity of eight, it would be a squeeze to get the remaining Black Eagle agents in alongside Golzar and her lawyer. But with a range of three thousand nautical miles, Golzar's new home could be in Moscow, Dubai or Tel Aviv, or Washington with a following wind.

She killed the engine.

There was still no word from Lawrence.

47

While Leila was driving along the airport road twenty miles to the north, Michael Lawrence sat at his desk in Scotland Yard with the computer open in front of him. He watched the unfolding events at Mapleton on a series of feeds being relayed to CTC. Outside his office, Commander Thorne was overseeing the live operation. Maximised on Lawrence's screen was the feed from Kriel's iPad on the desk in the conference room.

The iPad camera swung round the room. All the delegates wore their det-cord necklaces. The image steadied on the man at the head of the table whose foot rested on the trigger. He stooped, picked it up and held it with his thumb over the switch.

'We're coming out,' Kriel said. 'If anyone shoots, if anyone moves within fifty feet of us, the bombs will be triggered.' The camera went dark and the feed switched to a head-cam view from an MI5 officer outside the room.

Lawrence turned the mute off on his phone line to Phillip, ten miles away in the Waterboys' safe house in Broadwater.

'Phillip? Have you found the code?'

'A couple more minutes.'

'They're leaving. Right now.'

No response.

'Phillip, if they get on that helicopter, we'll lose them.'

'Then let me work.'

Ten minutes earlier a military helicopter had landed on the front lawn of Mapleton House. It was not the expected SAS squadron, who were still twenty minutes out. It was an ex-Army Lynx and no one in CTC or the security forces knew anything about it until it had appeared on radar fifteen minutes earlier. The pilot had not responded to calls and had maintained a flight-path low over towns and main roads. Air Traffic Control had had no choice but to let it come in. And as long as the delegates were necklaced with bombs, there would be nothing anyone could do to stop it leaving either. If Phillip came through too late with the disarm, if the helicopter was already back out over a populated area, they would be powerless to bring it down.

'Phillip? Talk to me,' he said when the silence became unbearable. 'Anything?'

'It can't be done,' Phillip said.

'What? There's no disarm code?'

'There is one, but I can't crack it. They're using…'

'I'm not interested in what they're using. Just give me a way to stop the bombs before that chopper takes off!' He muted the phone but kept it to his ear.

A CTC constable knocked and entered the room with a sat-phone and sheet of paper in his hand. Lawrence scanned the message and pressed the phone to his other ear. For a moment he heard nothing. The note said the communications to Leila had been activated, but he could not hear the sound of a car. Either she wasn't driving, or the MI5 wire had been discovered when the comms went live, and she might no longer be alive. Then, faintly, he heard a police siren in the background.

'Leila,' he said. 'We've got a link you. We can hear you. If you can hear me, cough three times.'

There was a long pause and three coughs crackled in his ear.

He looked back at the screen. The seven surviving Black Eagle operatives were emerging from the main door of the house. The spotlights of the two ASU helicopters were trained on their progress. Their own dark green chopper was waiting on the front lawn, its rotors at take-off speed.

'Black Eagle are exiting the building,' he said. 'We've not got the hostages yet.' Leila did not make any reply.

'Got it!' Lawrence jumped at the sound of Phillip's voice from the desk phone. He clicked the mute off.

'You can do it?'

'Sort of.'

'OK, I'm patching you through to the Command Room: they all need to hear this.' He looked Commander Thorne through the glass partition. Both men nodded and Phillip's call was relayed to the speakers next door.

'Go ahead,' Lawrence said.

'I can bypass the wireless connection,' Phillip said. 'There's a back-up system that will switch the detonators to a count down in the event of any interruption to the power.'

'How long?'

'Don't know. If I had to guess, I'd say less than three seconds but more than one.'

'Is that based on anything?'

'Yes, a guess. It won't be less than a second because sometimes there are minor blips in the power and they wouldn't want a false interrupt…'

'But it might be long enough to get the necklaces off?'

'It depends how quickly you work.'

'OK. Hold the line. Be ready to move as soon as we've got bomb squad ready. Confirm: Leila told us they're held in place with platic cable ties. They're not wired. We can just cut them off.'

Commander Thorne relayed the message to Mapleton as Lawrence ran from his office to the Command Room. They all watched as a group of army bomb disposal engineers entered the conference room and took up positions behind each of the delegates. Four heavy containment vessels were wheeled into shot.

'Phillip?' Lawrence said.

'Ready.'

'Count us down.'

'You're clear to go on one: three, two, *one*….'

Instantly, bomb officers began to work, snipping the cable ties and pulling the det cord away from the necks of the hostages. Everyone in the Command Room held their breath.

In moments all nine of the necklaces had been cut free and dropped into the containment bins. Just as the squad commander pulled one of the delegates to her feet, the first of the explosions rocked the room. The camera feed was momentarily lost and when it restarted ghostly figures ran through a fog of smoke and dust. One of the bins had not been closed fully before the detonators finished their countdown. There was no sound now, but everyone watching the screens could image the screams of panic.

The smoke began to clear. Chairs lay scattered across the floor and the shutters beside the windows were in tatters. Two of the delegates lay on the floor and paramedics were picking their way through the debris to get to them.

On the next screen, the head-cam of the same MI5 officer who had detained Leila when she had first entered the grounds showed the Black Eagle helicopter beginning to take off.

'We're clear!' Commander Thorne said. 'Don't let the helicopter go. Lethal force.'

At the bottom of the image, the MI5 man's gun came into view. Other agents were moving in on the chopper. A shot was fired; the screen cracked, but the helicopter was already ten feet off the ground and rising fast.

'Bring it down!' Thorne said.

There was a crackle on the line and a voice came through.

'CTC, this is Prime Minister Morgan.'

'You're breaking up,' Thorne said. 'Is everyone clear in there?'

'We're all alive. Don't let them leave. Are the Typhoons in the air?'

'Yes, two miles out.'

'Then use them.'

'Are you giving permission for air-to-air engagement?'

'Yes.'

'Confirm. Lethal force?'

'Shoot these bastards down!'

Commander Thorne opened a channel to the RAF commander in charge of the operation. He relayed the Prime Minster's orders and instructed ASU and ground personnel to evacuate the area.

Outside Mapleton, the helicopter had been holed by small-arms fire, but was still climbing. At two hundred feet it banked towards the woods at the edge of the grounds.

Seconds later the first of the typhoon jets screamed overhead, flying east. The chopper too turned east and dipped its nose to gain speed. In ninety seconds it would be out over densely populated towns and it would be easy for the pilot to find a corridor along which it would be impossible to shoot them down.

The second jet buzzed the chopper just as the first made a tight turn half a mile out.

They were waiting for the helicopter to pass over the woods and the field beyond.

There was a bright flare as the first jet unleashed its sidewinder air-to-air missile. The Typhoon climber vertically, white clouds spilling from its wings and glistening in moon light.

The sidewinder wriggled in the air as its radar system made its final lock-on. The chopper, five hundred yards in front of it, dipped and the missile followed.

The people gathered in the Command Room in central

London did not get a good view of the impact. They didn't need to. The missile slammed into the back of the helicopter and tore through it in a ball of flame. The rotor blades sheared off and a shower of glass and metal fragments rained down into the woods.

Lawrence left the room.

Back in his own office he spoke quietly into the sat-phone.

'Leila?' he said.

There was a long pause before she spoke.

'Here.'

'Black Eagle are down. No survivors. All hostages rescued.'

'They're all OK?'

'Yes. Agents are on their way to your location now.'

'No! Keep them back.'

'But it's over.'

Lawrence heard a click on the line. The click of a gun being cocked.

'Michael,' Leila said. 'I've got to go.'

48

Leila pulled the earpiece out and looked at Aquila in the rear-view mirror. The tip of his pistol was barely six inches from her head. For several seconds she met his gaze in silence. The car rocked slightly. She glanced at the jet in the hangar: lights off, engines at rest. The wind sock at the end of the runway hung limp and low cloud blanketed the sky to the thin band of dawn light on the horizon.

'It's over,' she said. 'Your friends won't be joining us after all.'

'So I heard. Clever to use a concealed earpiece then hand over your phone with such reluctance.' He removed his own earpiece and put it in his pocket. 'I should have been more thorough. Give it to me.'

Leila handed it back and took the watch from her pocket.

'Golzar can't escape,' she said. 'CTC and MI5 have been shadowing us since I arrived.'

'Golzar has already gone.'

'What?'

'She was removed an hour before you got to Holloway.'

'Then why all this charade?'

'You. You were already too close to discovering the truth when you went to Mapleton. We couldn't let you continue.'

'So why not just kill me?'

'Killing you wouldn't have killed your ideas. Your people trust you; they rely on you. Your death would only have confirmed your theories, but we saw that we could use their trust to run enough interference to complete our mission. A mission which you so nearly destroyed.'

'All this was just to keep me out of the way?'

'Golzar was taken out by road, a long way from here. A new identity is being prepared and she will leave when it is convenient for us to take her back to Washington.'

Aquila clicked the door open and Leila did the same. They both stepped out onto the tarmac. Leila glanced at the car. She took in the details of the vehicle for the first time and realised that maybe this was not really over at all.

'So what now?' she said.

'Join us.' He dropped the MI5 earpiece and watch and stood on them.

'What?' Leila laughed. 'Join you? Was this some kind of insane recruitment?'

'Think about it. You can't beat us. You can't even find us. But you can be one of us. We could use talents like yours.'

'Go to hell! I'd rather you shot me now.'

'No one's getting shot. Walk away, DS Reid. It was a fair fight. You almost won.' He slid into the driver's seat and handed Leila her gun and phone. 'Goodbye.'

'You can't escape. The airfield's surrounded.'

'I will drive right through your cordons. This is a

diplomatic car. Prime Minister Queria's men handed it over along with Golzar.'

'You think that'll stop you being prosecuted for kidnap, murder, terrorism?'

'Where's the evidence? Everyone in the helicopter is dead. You've got a story but no one to corroborate it. Without the smoking gun, everything you have is circumstantial.'

'Peretz is still alive.'

'Peretz too has diplomatic cover. Under the circumstances, do you really think your Prime Minister would want an international incident with the Israelis over a matter that would still be impossible to prove? I think his futile quest for peace will keep him too busy for that.'

'Then that just leaves you,' Leila said. She raised the gun.

'And I'm just a lawyer. My only contact has been with Raha Golzar. She is a US citizen who has been held for fifteen months without trial in a mental facility, without consular representation, without any recourse to the law whatever. My role was nothing more than to give her that representation. She escaped. What's more, she escaped as a result of a secret deal done between your Prime Minister and the unrecognised government of the West Bank. Even the UN wouldn't dare get involved. It's over, Miss Reid.'

Aquila started the car. Leila waited, her finger curled around the Glock's trigger. The car was low on fuel, and yet it sat low on those skinny tyres… It had moved when Aquila raised his gun to her head, but there was not the slightest breeze. And then there had been that smell of hospitals hanging just beneath the pine-fresh odour of a valetted car.

I told you, she's close… Aquila had said.

The Lexus pulled away slowly. It did have diplomatic plates; she couldn't shoot the driver.

But she could shoot the passenger.

As the car began to speed up, Leila levelled her weapon and squeezed the trigger. A single shot pierced the back of the car just below the boot catch. Aquila stopped and slammed the car into reverse. She shot again; the boot sprang open. The car swung round into a j-turn and as it was side on to her, she loosed the remaining bullets from the gun.

Aquila floored the accelerator and drove right at her. For a long moment she stared at him through the windscreen. She smiled.

Just feet from impact, Aquila turned away and screeched around in a tight arc. He drove away with the engine screaming, an arm hanging over the lip of the Lexus's boot.

She had got eight bullets right on target. The back end of the car was riddled with holes.

She walked a few feet and crouched on the dark tarmac. She dialled Lawrence's number.

'Leila?' he said.

'She was in the boot.'

'You found her?' Lawrence said.

'She was in the boot, Michael. It's why we waited here so long: Black Eagle were joining us from Mapleton, then they'd fly out. The jet's waiting; Golzar was in the car all the time.'

'And?'

'She's dead.'

'Then we won, Leila.'

'We haven't won anything! We don't know any more about Black Eagle than we did three days ago. Who's to say that's really even their name? Everything they've done, every action has been covered from all angles. We've got nothing!'

'We'll find them. We know what we're looking for now, and Golzar's death will slow their spread into new territories, let us catch up.'

'These people have cells throughout the western world. They're everywhere…'

'Stay there, Leila. I've got a car on the way to pick you up.'

'No. Don't come.'

'Leila…?

She stared out across the runway.

'What are you planning?' he said. 'Don't do this… We consolidate what we've got, and then… then we move on.'

'Three days ago you asked me to take a look and see if I felt anything,' she said. 'I don't. I can't do this, not your way. All this, and we've solved nothing… I'm done. *We're* done.'

'Stay there…'

'Look after Phillip, Michael.' She ended the call and dropped the phone onto the runway.

The first rays of sun were just turning the eastern sky red as she walked across the wet grass and away.

Also by Alan Porter

GM

Ethics and technology at war in the jungles of West Africa.

Run

Take a terrifying journey to the edge of madness...

Available as paperback or ebook.

For details of these and other books by Alan Porter

visit **alancporter.com**

12719942R00188

Printed in Great Britain
by Amazon.co.uk, Ltd.,
Marston Gate.